The
River's
Memory

Sandra Gail
Lambert

Twisted Road Publications LLC
Tallahassee, Florida

SOMERSET CO. LIBRARY
BRIDGEWATER, N.J. 08807

Twisted Road Publications LLC

Excerpts from this novel have appeared in the the following publicatons:

A version of "Half-Boy" – *Big Fiction No. 4, Summer/Fall 2013*, Heather Jacobs, editor. Knickerbocker Prize, 2nd Place, Lauren Groff, Judge.

A version of "In a Chamber of My Heart" – *Saints + Sinners: New Fiction from the Festival 2013*, Paul Willis and Amie Evans eds. Bold Stroke Books, May 2013. Winner of 2013 Saints and Sinners Short Fiction Contest, Judge—Felice Picano.

Copyright © 2014 by Sandra Gail Lambert
All rights reserved
ISBN: 978-1-940189-00-0
Library of Congress Control Number: 2013957248
Cover image by Peter Carolin

Printed in the United State of America

This is a work of fiction. Any resemblance to real events or persons, living or dead, is entirely coincidental

www.twistedroadpublications.com

Acknowledgements

The generosity of strangers—that's what any writer who does research knows about. My generous strangers include the staff of the Silver River Museum, the Marion County History Museum, the Matheson Museum, and the libraries of Alachua County and the University of Florida. I also have to thank the people who make Ocali Country Days such a grand celebration of the area's diverse history. And whoever it was who put those oral histories of Ocala online—you should write your own book.

I'm also lucky enough to live in a community of friends, a lot of them lesbians, some not, some writers, some not, who have supported me in all the ways there are to support a person. So to those who bring me birthday presents of ink cartridges and reams of paper or just straight out give me money for writers residencies, to the dog sitters and apple pie bakers, to the writers who squeal with me at each small success, to the ones who drag me out of the house to have fun, to those who edit draft after draft of manuscript after manuscript—thank you, all of you, for the unrelenting belief in my work, in me. And to the monthly Lesbian Readers Group and Potluck, thank you for the twenty-six years of listening.

Much of this novel was written propped up in various beds at a variety of writing retreats. The bed in the back of my wheelchair-lift van was parked at the Everglades National Park as well as the Silver Springs, Collier-Seminole, Little Talbot Island, Kissimmee and Paynes Prairie Preserves and the Ochlockonee and Myakka Rivers State Parks. I'd recline into my pillows with the van's back doors thrown open and write for days while bobolinks scurried past or turkeys scratched around the tires. I procrastinated by watching cinnamon ferns unfurl and alligators lounge in the mud. Thank you to all the rangers, volunteers, and activists who love and protect these natural places. The beds at the Corporation of Yaddo and the Atlantic Center for the Arts came with food and a long tradition of support, and saying thank you to them will never be enough. My bed at home, under live oaks and palms, is my, well, I was going to say bedrock, and perhaps I just will.

Finally, Joan Leggitt, editor extraordinaire, had this dream of starting an independent literary press. And here we are. I'm so proud to be part of Twisted Road Publication's debut year.

SGL, 2014

The
River's
Memory

Wisdom is
sweeter than honey,
brings more joy
than wine,
illumines
more that the sun,
is more precious
than jewels,
She causes
the ears to hear
and the heart to comprehend.

I love her
like a mother
and she embraces me
as her own child.
I will follow
her footprints
and she will not cast me away.

Makeda, Queen of Sheba (ca. 1000 B.C.E.)

Women in Praise of the Sacred: 43 Centuries of Spiritual Poetry by Women, edited by Jane Hirshfield.

"Her full nature, like that river of which Cyrus broke the strength, spent itself in channels which had no great name on the earth. But the effect of her being on those around her was incalculably diffusive: for the growing good of the world is partly dependent on unhistoric acts; and that things are not so ill with you and me as they might have been, is half owing to the number who lived faithfully a hidden life, and rest in unvisited tombs."

Middlemarch by George Eliot

Contents

The water may have been rain two weeks or a thousand years ago. It trickled into the dirt, settled around roots, pooled over clay, soaked through pores in the rock, and entered a maze of underground rivers where no weather exists, no wind, no light. After long separation from the growth and decay of living things, it rises to the surface and becomes the river.

From My Chest, Dragonfly Wings
1528

My fingers press into clay. I balance at the edge of my mind. The excitement rises and wants to spill into bright colors and glare. It whispers out of my bones and demands that I continue. It says that I will not fail, that I know enough, everything.

I stop and stare into the morning. The routine chores of waking will sometimes quiet my mind and keep the edges of things more certain. Children race past the women pounding acorn meat and circle the fire keeper as he spreads last night's coals under the stacks of drying pots. He will heat the fire with pine. The tall pines that sway over the meadows of a thousand flowers give the hottest fire, and after the summer storms, I'll send people to cut the hearts out of downed trees. Across the work yard, my bed companion washes the sleep from her daughter's eyes. "Little Cat," the children call and she escapes her mother to run with them. My clay workers come close and ask about the day's plan. I stare. I stare, and try to answer, but the space around me goes the watery white of the summer sky. My workers ripple in the wet air. I look down at the bowl between my thighs. Nothing else is important. My fingers stretch over it.

A line of sparks trails each movement of my hands. The work of muscles under tattoos flattens the light running along my arms and throws it into a second, flickering skin. My vision narrows and stretches, and I'm a child again, hiding inside a cypress tree that lays over a length of river bank, hollow, ready for the fire and chisel that will make it into a canoe for my aunt. Only now, in the circle of light at the end, instead of an arm holding a wolf jaw steady, ready to cut, I see clay form into coils. The coils rise out of cupped palms, and fingers on my far away hands wind them along the rim of the bowl. I lick the pad of my thumb to spread wetness on the walls and taste marsh and the grit of dead sponges. The thumb smoothes the edges. The structure is disguised.

I know this clay. I gathered it from our river. I can stretch it higher. I want light to shine through the bowl as if it were our spring water kicked through with sand. The bowl moves my hands. It pushes palms apart and spreads fingers. It widens inside to fit the shape of my fist.

"Teacher, may I help you?"

This boy from the southern coast, the best of all my workers, the most clever with design, wants to take my pot. I ignore him. The light is all glint and flash like the first sun after a storm, and it shields me from the others. I feel the clay rise under my hands. Voices crowd around me.

"She's stretching it too thin."

"Go get her companion."

The salt-watered accent of the boy whispers in my ear. "Teacher, look, the pot is finished. Let me take it to dry."

I can bring the sides higher. I know it. Anything I do now will hold in the fire. The voice in my bones shouts it to me. I smell the sweat of too many people. Feet surround me. They want to take my pot, but I wrap my legs around it. The feet move away, and I hear my companion's voice, just hers, behind me. She throws words through the air with a strength that is harsh and unfamiliar.

"You, take this skin and wet it in the river. Bring it back. Hurry. The rest of you—move away."

I've kept her with me longer than any of the others. I found her in my aunt's town. She passed me as I went to fetch my aunt's new cape from the hide tanner. I watched the way she held her daughter's hand and matched her stride to the toddler's unsteadiness. Her patience attracted me. I am deer clan. She is panther. I could have compelled, but I gave her a choice, and she came with me to this small river with its headwaters that rush out from sunken caves.

The warm orange of her body heats my back as arms reach around my ribs. I push her hands lower until the heat between my thighs is as bright as holly berries. My desire softens the clay. I let go of her to reach for the pot, and her arms rise over my belly and tighten at my waist.

"Forgive me," she says, and lifts us to our feet. The pot is taken.

I can get it back. I am not young anymore like they are, but I'm strong—stronger than anyone. I turn in her arms. The light swirls around me, hiding her, hiding them. I fling my still closed fist forward. It hits with a soft give before it smacks bone. The arms release and I'm free. Other hands reach. One grips my girdle, but I twist it away.

Now, we're all here in the dance of the light. The boy from the south moves to my side, and his gold wrist band glistens and reaches toward me. I can see inside him, see the hot yellow wind filled with salt and sand. In front, in collusion, to distract, my companion calls for me in a softened voice. She carries within her the complicated shadows of my aunt's pole-protected town where wide, tamed roads spread ambition.

The boy comes too close. When he appeared this winter, travel worn, in my work yard, I knew him for a potter from the corded strength in his arms. He said he traced back the trading path of one of my burial pots until he found us. I mustn't let him get hold of me. They both dart into the watery rainbow of color between us, and I back away. Like the chatter of a spring flock, I hear the rest of my people. Their voices scatter over the yard.

"Child, take your brothers and race to the river. Then stay and look for clams. Do it now."

"Move the fishing cages."

"Get that ax out of her way."

They're too late. I grab the ax and let the shell blade wave in front of me. I spread my arms and sway one way before I sprint the other. I am unreachable.

"Don't trap her against the fire. She'll step on the bowls."

My heels warm in the spent embers of last night's curing fires. They hit clay. I hear pots breaking, my work, their work, and I laugh until the colors around me shake. I will destroy every one. Only this last piece matters. Everything before is inferior. I turn and jump, ax raised, and linger in the air. Time stops. I control it. I flick my eyes in a signal for it to resume, and I drop, stiffening my feet for the best impact, swinging the ax down.

The only warning comes in the rush of yellow just before the full length of the boy falls against me. His leap over the fire throws us to the ground. The ax spins out of my hand, and we roll in the earth until I'm pinned. His body covers mine.

"Release her." I relax at the sound of my companion's voice. She will stop this. The boy rolls off of me, but before I can escape, a wet hide slaps over my body. It covers my face. It chills my skin. There is no air. There is no light

"Did you save it?" I'm inside, lying on my sleeping platform, and the smudge fire under it tastes of sumac and snake root. Am I speaking out loud? How long has this incapacity lasted? I try to wave the smoke away, and my wrists twist against the scratch of the palmetto cords tied around them.

"Release me." No one answers, and I close my eyes against the bite of the smoke.

The scent of tobacco and old man comes close and something presses against my forehead. I open my eyes to the tattooed, too-close face of my aunt's healer. Why is he here? Years ago, I killed his brother. He doesn't know this. But he must wonder. My aunt required it as the price for me to return to this small river where my mother paused in her travels to squat and scream and give birth to me. During the heat of every year, she brought me back to swim in the cool waters that calmed my mind. One death, a quick one, and I earned my river as a place to work outside of my aunt's schemes and plots and hunger for trade.

The raccoon tail attached to the healer's topknot flops over my cheek. His tube has flared ends and one side cups into the space over my eyes. His lips suck on the other. He makes the noises I remember from when my cousin, my aunt's only child, had an arrow in the stomach—another fight with the northern people for a trade route across their river. My aunt broke with rage when her son died, and that healer, this one's brother, knew to leave in the night. But I waited for him just beyond the town's gates.

I wait for the final marshy wheeze. I wait for the quick pulling away of the tube. I made the tube. The fire cracked three of them before I got the shape right. I didn't understand then how heat is held and released. I wait until he drops the piece of charcoal out of his mouth and shows off the illness removed through my forehead. He gathers the arrows placed around my platform and wraps them carefully in deer hide until only the white crane feathered ends still show. Before he leaves, in the light from the opening, I see him shake the arrows and pull his lips back in triumph. I try to move, and my hips ache where we hit the ground. The ability to feel pain indicates the return of my mind. Maybe he did help. I speak again.

"Did you save it?'

My companion sits beside me. Today she has a stalk of red-lipped flowers wrapped in her hair. The panther clan people often have these faces that show every emotion. I used to like that. She unties me.

"Yes. The pot is on the drying stand." I hear a thickness in her voice and a gentle amusement. I remember hitting her nose. She pats my hand. I pull it away and reach without looking to touch the old statue, the one from before memory, that I keep tucked into the wall. My fingers feel along the curves and lifts of the pattern, and I know the ancient potter lived here, at this same spring, with its upwelling from deep under the ground. Sometimes, touching it, I can sense older yearnings and a time before clay and fire met. If my pot is still drying, not too much of my time has passed.

"Get this smoke out of here." My voice is bitter from more than the smoke. My companion hears this and stands away from me.

At my eye level the folds of her smock wrap around each thigh, and one of her hands rubs along a hip. Desire lingers inside me, but I never want them after. Their eyes change. She saw me without power, she helped me, and now she thinks she owns some part of me. My work compels respect. I will not have it given to me the way people give it to the old and sick. My last time of helplessness was before I met her, just before. How did she know to wrap me like my aunt's servants used to? My companion kneels to hook the entrance flap open, and the daylight makes the smoke glow around her. She stares away from me, into the distance outside the palmetto walls. I won't send her back to the town. The others like her, as they don't me. She is useful to my work.

"Arrange a meal for the healer. Pulling the evil out of me must make a man hungry. And then send him back with his choice of the pipes just out of the fire and instructions to give respectful thanks to my aunt."

"Your aunt."

"You're right. Send a gift for her as well—the pot with the deer on the lid. The woman never likes anyone to forget our esteemed clan. Arrange for that. You now speak for me. You have my authority. And you may move into the spring house with the child." There, now she knows her new position, everything. Nothing more will have to be said. But she doesn't leave. She turns back toward me. "And check the slurry ponds, right now. Tell them to add less sand. I'll want clean clay."

"Your aunt." The emphasis in her voice makes me pause.

In the silence between us, I hear the flutes and I know what it means. My aunt has arrived on her litter, surrounded by porters, and with that old priest at her side. She better not have brought her hounds. Last time, they broke pots. The music continues in a weary rise and fall.

"How long has she been waiting? Did she see? When she arrived, was I still . . .?"

"No. And she's just finishing the first offering of snails."

"Give her fish heated with pickerel seeds. She likes that."

My companion ducks through the entrance.

"Wait." She crouches back down to face me, and hope rises in her eyes. I turn my head from it before I speak. "Did my aunt give a reason for this visit?"

"No, your aunt does not speak to me. And I have been here, caring for you."

She speaks to me as if I were a child. And she is lying about something. It shows in a shadow under her voice. Or perhaps my aunt scares her. The old woman makes people feel as if they never do enough. It's a trick of power. What does my aunt want with me? I told her to give me more time. I must prepare myself. I look up and my companion, no, not my companion, is still here.

"Do what I have said."

Instead of leaving, she walks to my platform and leans into my neck. I breathe the sassafras oil she rubs into her hair.

"Shall I remove my blankets and clothes now?"

I hate this part when the colors have faded, but I can still feel everything from everyone. Her emotions exhaust me.

"Do it later. Go please my aunt."

On the way out she taps a sharpened fingernail just once on the deer antlers over the door, and I feel the resentment of a lesser clan. I hope she can make this change.

The smoke has cleared, and I see the boy from the south standing by the hearth, watching everything. If I choose him as my next companion, he'll know what to expect. I consider him. His people don't have tattoos, and, no matter how the other men tease about sharp bits of straw sticking everywhere, he's never traded his grass loin cloth for our leather ones. I motion him to me. He offers a gourd of water, freshly cold from the mouth of the spring. A lingering of yellow shakes around him. It should shake. He attacked me. My aunt would have his arm broken.

"How many did I hurt?"

"Three bowls, all of them mine. Not the biggest loss."

I like that he didn't think I asked about people. And I like his willingness to risk punishment to save the pots. I don't like the disrespect in his false humility. He and I both know that his work will soon rival mine. I give the gourd back to him and let our hands touch. The red stripes of my tattoos press against his bracelet of black beads. They reflect light in a way I don't understand. Two unevenly crossed pieces of gold hang from them and tickle the inside of my wrist. I feel no attraction. Are the young finally too young for me? Did desire leave with my bleeding? Some would think this a good thing. His gold necklace swings past my eyes as he leans closer. It is etched with more crosses. He has said it came from the sea.

"Leave."

He sets the gourd by my side before he goes. I splash water over my neck and under my arms, but objects still streak with brightness. That healer puts strange herbs in his smoke. I finger through my hair until it swings loose around my waist. I reach into the ancient pot and pull out the stick of bone my mother gave me. She told me that it came from one of the giant animals that lived before time. After storms strong enough to throw trees into the river, when roots pull up through the earth, old things come to the surface. We find knuckles of spine bigger than two fists together and winged back bones as wide as arms can reach. On my mother's bone, in slanted light, I can see the work of human hands in the faint, carved line of a creature with tusks.

I use it to tie my hair into a knot on the back of my head, just below where a man would wear it. Hawk feathers stuck into my hair, as many strings of beads and shells as I can find, the copper disk my aunt gave me between my breasts, an arrangement of moss over my femininity, and I'm ready. I stop at the entrance. I rub the snake coil design on the copper bright and grimace into the reflection. Go, it says. I move the flap away and step into the sunlight. My new authority strides across the work yard with her hands pointing right and left.

"Why isn't this all cleaned away? You, stop kicking that ball around and go check the slurry ponds. And don't put in too much sand. Move faster or you'll spend a season in a guard hut at the edge of a corn field." Her voice stings through the humid air. She's adjusting.

The overhead sun spikes light into my eyes. The world blurs. My aunt will have to wait longer. I need the river. I ignore everyone but notice everything—the smell of half-cured fish from the racks, the woman who jumps her weight onto the pestle and grinds corn more quickly as I come near. Beyond the hedge of holly trees, down the slow drop of land, the air cools. I pass a bay tree all in white bloom. I look away before the petal shine can fill my mind, but the sweet of them follows me. The earth softens and I step through the humped roots of cypress trees. Purple and red stalks of water plants brush against my legs. Black butterflies gleam blue as they scatter, circle, and fly close to the shine of my necklaces. Dragonflies with gold-netted wings hover over their patches of water territory. Ones with shimmering green bodies perch on guard posts of broken stalks and watch with eyes that bulge beyond their heads. At water's edge, the children rush away from my aunt's canoes and pretend to dig clams in the mud. They don't look up as I walk through them and farther into the water.

I let my fingers linger on the woodwork as I pass the canoes, but the designs depend too much on depth for me to use on a pot. I push them aside and hiss as the cold rises along my legs. This water is clear like air. My legs, my feet, my toes look no different except for the soft, wide way light bounces against them. At the drop, I dive. I swim through deepening shades of blue to the spring's mouth and, for a moment, I am past the teeth of rocks, past where light can reach, and in the source of our river. The water beats against me, rushing out of the earth. I stop swimming and rise. Around me, braids of water inside water twist to the surface in long strands. I pass ledges of pitted rock where long fish shelter in the dark. My mother and I would roast them in their own skins until just a touch of knife split them open. The pressure of the water lifts me to the surface and beyond. Flashing like a mullet, I flop to my back. My arms stay solid when I lift them into the air. The colors around me remain within their boundaries. I swim to shore and sit beside a bush wrapped around with leather flower vine. The blooms hang like upside down pots and the edges curl back on themselves and flip forward again. The design for a next bowl fills my mind.

Still dripping, I walk to the curing fires. Yesterday's pots, the ones I didn't break, rest alongside the ashes. The heat cracked only two, but another has the dark stain of an uneven fire. This must not happen with today's pot. It pulls at me. It needs the roughening that will strengthen it. After, I will burnish the sides until they shine like the wings of a dark ibis. This pot wants a long, hot fire of oak mixed with the inner core of pine wood. It wants me. The sound of flutes pulls me away. I snap the water out of my feathers and stick them deeper into my hair. I'm dry enough to greet my aunt.

My clay workers stand as I near.

"A simple bowl for each of my aunt's people, this pipe for the healer, any of these jugs for the priest—how can that old man still be alive—and does my aunt already have her bowl?" She did, but I add a plate with otters along the rim. My mother loved otters, and it will not hurt to remind my aunt of her affection for her dead sister. They follow as I lead the way.

And now we see each other. She sits as straight as she ever
has, her eyes clear, but age shows in skin too thin to cover streams
of blue blood and the tight outline of bones. She plays the hand
clap game with my companion's daughter. Once I watched a
marsh bird chick, still all fluff and chirps, at the mercy of an owl.
As I wait for my aunt to acknowledge me, a hand curves over
her shoulder from behind. Slim fingers press into the hollow
under her collar bone. I raise my eyes until they reach the face of
a young man with a nose the shape of an eagle's beak. It hangs
over plump lips that pout in my direction. I don't know him. My
aunt looks up, and they both smile the same smile at me. It feels
bad. I snap at the child.

"Girl, go to your mother and help her." Instead of leaving, the
child looks to my aunt for permission. She whispers something
to the child that makes them both laugh and only after does the
girl jump down from the litter and run past me.

I motion my workers forward with the gifts and put hand to
forehead in the ritual greeting.

"My Mother's Sister, welcome."

"Your mind." Her words accuse me. Any lack of control
repels her. Even so, she helped my mother learn how to contain
me.

"A brief episode and gone now. I apologize for inconveniencing
you. And my thanks for the help of your man." I nod at the
healer standing beside her.

"Stop. We all know of your disrespect for him and his kind. I
have brought corn." Her men pull three baskets forward.

"Thank you, Aunt." I motion to have the baskets put in the
granary. Two of my people move toward them.

"What about the prayers?" The man's voice resembles his
fingers—thin and agile.

I don't answer him. I won't until my aunt acknowledges his
existence.

"Sister's Daughter, this priest comes to me in friendship from the North. And he has asked a question. Have you lived too long away from me? Have you forgotten the rituals?

"Of course not. Perhaps, Aunt, you would honor us."

My aunt rises and steps down to the earth. She shakes off the hands offered in help. She walks to my side. Age has stolen inches from her, but she is still as tall as I am. I present an arm, and she grabs it and pretends to lean. Her sharpened nails stop just before piercing my skin. She whispers.

"Do not shame me. I grow old, you still refuse to take my place, and the priests gain power. Some of them want to separate their authority from mine. If you want to keep this refuge, you will do everything I'm about to tell you. I will not lose position. I will do what I have to. Now, I know you don't remember the prayers. Just echo me."

She loosens her hold on me, but I wrap my hand around hers and squeeze until her nails break my skin. I almost touch her ear with my lips.

"Do not threaten me. My pottery, this refuge as you call it, gives you power in the trade routes. What other type of power is there?"

My aunt places her other hand over mine and rubs along my knuckles. As far as those watching can tell, we cling to each other in affection.

"Conflict brings power, my dear niece. In the south, they shout news of invaders from across the ocean, and everywhere the war chiefs want an audience. They say the time has come for them to lead."

My aunt begins the chant, and we release each other. As she speaks, the words come back to me, and I also pray to the sun for abundance and fertile rains and tassels streaming golden in the wind.

After the corn rests in the shed, after we say the prayers again, my aunt returns to the center of her people.

"Niece, you may let your people go back to their work. We need their labors."

My aunt puts on the head covering of painted egret plumes. I sit in front of her, alone. The prayers still circle in my head as I try to reason through my aunt's last, shrill words. Fear traveled her body, and my mind saw it as the color of the smear that can spread over the water on hot days, killing fish and stinking the air. The priest comes to stand beside her. He's like all the young priests. They assert their authority in too many plumes and beads and bright ear bobs. This one looks like a green heron in mating season with its feathers all outlined in yellow.

"Niece, you spend too much time on your experiments and most of them fail. And you waste your workers by taking them on far walks for clay and wood. We have plenty of both here on this river."

How does she know about my work?

"You will organize your people to make more plates and simple bowls—the ones pressed with corn cobs. Continue with the lidded pitchers. They are quick to form, and their usefulness makes them valuable in trade."

My aunt has never held fresh clay in her palms. Someone here, someone close to my work, belongs to my aunt and sends word. I do not move or answer. I bring each of my people to mind. The food gatherers don't know enough about the pots, the clay workers don't know enough about trade, but that boy from the south goes everywhere, asking questions of everything. But I know him. He wants only to surpass himself with every new pot.

"Hear this." My aunt uses the words that forbid discussion. "We have come to an agreement with the old man and his sons from the north. They will own all commerce beyond their river. In return, we will supply their traders with our pots. I've promised them six porters worth by the last heat of summer."

I find myself standing, arms raised, before she finishes. Who is this "we" she claims for herself? I will not take orders about my work. I will not give up my trading routes for the ceremonial pieces, the ones that travel farther than any single person ever has. My mind loosens from itself, and, again, light and feelings blend. My aunt's brown bloom of anger leaps and her porters become the dull orange of violence-at-the-ready. The musicians fall to the back, disappear. Part of me watches and knows the danger of this coming, too public, confrontation. Still, I cannot control myself. But as my mouth opens, I notice the priest. He smiles. Around him float eager wisps of ambition the colors of a cedar-heated fire. Curiosity diverts my anger. He wants this. He wants me to enrage my aunt. He does not move or speak, but his light trembles with anticipation.

I will myself to sitting. I will myself silent. I imagine my next pot. If I add more ground rock and mix the sandhill and marsh clays, I might accomplish the shape I see in my head. I turn the pot in my mind the way I wish I could when I build it. I hear my aunt speak.

"Niece, do you understand?"

"My Mother's Sister, I must ask a favor. My mind is unsettled, and I need to spend time in private. May we resume our discussion tomorrow?"

"This is not a discussion. But yes, until tomorrow."

As I leave the meeting, I stumble over my companion's daughter. She holds what looks like a new doll. I grab her shoulder.

"Where did you get that?"

"From the Aunt." The girl tucks the doll deep into her armpit and stands sideways to me. "It lives with me now."

I get on one knee in front of her and try out a smile. I loosen my grip.

"Child." I slow my breath to soften my voice. "Little Cat. Your doll is pretty. How do you know my aunt?"

"I think we used to stay with her. When I was little. There were dogs."

Understanding drops me down on both knees. The child stops talking. I look up, and her mother stands behind her. The bruise has spread under both eyes. I remember our first meeting again and how my aunt sent me on the errand to that particular tanner. All the pieces of my life since rearrange themselves into a new story, and my body dissolves into a rush of feelings, all the feelings. I rise. She cradles her daughter's head into her waist and settles her legs wider, defiant. She knows that she and the child are safe with my aunt here. Still, I let her watch as I recover and remove all emotion from my face. I stare until her hands shake, and she pulls her daughter closer. I do not touch her. I have to retreat until I'm recovered. Then I will break both her arms.

I step around her as if she didn't exist and walk into the work yard. Everyone works without speaking. I look down the line of hunched backs, and only the young man from the south turns to greet me. His ambition is plain and uncomplicated and a relief.

"You, come with me to gather clay. The rest of you, help him prepare. I'll wait at the river."

I float on my back, my hair coming loose from its pin and wrapping around my spread arms, until I hear him on the path. He has the empty baskets over each shoulder, a food satchel looped underneath one of them, my travel kit hangs from a wrist, and a water gourd bounces against the hip opposite his knife. I take the travel kit from him, tie it around my waist, and lead the way to the narrow path that follows the edge of the river.

The excitement stays in my mind, and its energy jerks at my muscles. I sprint along the trail to release it. The boy can catch up. The trail curves to and away from the river. In the shade of trees, flies attack my forehead and mosquitoes swarm where my muscles have pumped blood close to the skin. The path finds a way through cypress trees bigger than what they use for war canoes. They block sound. I slow and turn in place. No one can see me. I raise my hands and spin in the tree-scattered light until I hear the boy's gear jostling through the palmettos.

I take one of the baskets from him. It weights me to the earth with its bulk and the smell of male sweat and plant that rubs off the dried grasses. The boy pants along behind me. He offers water. I drink and run ahead. He catches up and stops us for food. I run again and watch the river, the way the banks form, the colors of the mud and water, until I find a side creek cutting up out of the earth. Now, I let myself tire, not just in strength, but in my mind as well. The boy comes up beside me, and we stand at the edge of the river while waves of coolness blow off the water. They dry our sweat and scatter the insects.

The sun hits low on the far bank. Below us, ibis dig orange beaks into the mud between a thicket of the white poison bush. Its domed blooms have a repeated pattern that excites and eases me at the same time. And my aunt wants me to slap a corn cob on my pots and call it a design. The sun thins into shadows. I turn to the boy.

"We still have time. Take off your gear and let yourself down to the water."

He drops into the mud. I pass him the baskets before using his shoulders and the hanging roots to lower myself beside him. I feel along the bank, reach, and plunge my hand into the circle made by two cypress roots.

"Look for pure clay with no layers of rot or mold. Feel for softness, like rabbit fur." I push his hand in beside mine. "This clay, I can make our lightest pots from it. Here, you try. Dig past the roots and find clear spaces."

We take turns and the baskets fill. I forget my aunt and the tangled secrets of her council house. I forget the betrayal of my companion. Even the new pot loosens its grip on my mind in the pleasure of good clay. The boy boosts me into the hole we've made, and I scoop clay out past me for him to drop into a basket. He complains that my toes tickle his neck so I throw clay on his head. The boy laughs. He becomes careless and pulls too hard on a root. A section of the bank releases, I fall against him, and we stumble into the water, slip and roll in mud. He laughs even more. He doesn't see our food satchel, filled with dried fish, float into the current.

I should have noticed that he brought it to the water's edge. People from away don't know what to be careful about. Out near the food, the skin of the water flattens. Something swims near the surface. I ignore the thick heat of the evening air to make up a different story than what I know is real. In my desperate pretending, I see a grey giant, the gentle ones that come up our river only on the coldest of winter days. They live in water but taste more animal than fish. They eat only plants.

But they never arrive in the summer. I grab for the boy to pull us both onto the land, but before I can stop him, he has seen the satchel and belly flops into the river and reaches. A surge moves toward him, against the current, as his fingers close one by one over the trailing strap. A swirl of water lifts the leather into the air. A shout dries inside my mouth. The boy turns to look at me, his hand still wrapped in the strap. Behind him, the satchel pulls under the water and takes the boy with it. I throw myself over his feet. A wave breaks into the air and scatters in all directions. Within it, I see a scaled head. Yellow teeth lift and drop, and I hear the crack of the boy's shoulder leaving its home. I grab a foot, set my feet into the bottom, and pull.

I'm screaming now. "Let go, let go." I can still see the way the strap is wrapped around his hand. But I hope. And I pull. His body lifts back above the surface. He gasps for air just before a force rolls it to one side and the other, up and down. My feet scrabble into the sand, but still slide farther into the water. The boy's loose arm flails into the air. He's trying to reach his knife. He fails. I make a choice. I let go, unsheathe my own knife, and leap. I press it into his hand and fall back. Now nothing holds him against the pull into deeper water. I see him take a large breath before he disappears, and I hold my own breath with his. The water recomposes itself. A dragonfly with red smoke in the black of its wings hovers over the site and flicks away. A kingfisher screeches from bank to bank. My lungs complain. My eyes won't blink. My body forces a breath, and as I gasp, the water lifts. He swims toward me using only one arm. I wade out and pull him to shore. He sobs with pain as I brace our feet into the small cave we've made digging clay and throw us both up and over onto the bank.

"Stupid coast person. We keep food away from the shore. We don't splash in the shallows at dusk. Didn't someone tell you about the alligators?"

He pants and sweats in pain. One arm falls in a wrong angle from his body. Blood leaks around his ear.

"I thought you people were teasing me." His voice shivers.

"Like you do with those tales of fish that strike and kill without warning? Or the white boat bigger than a hundred canoes and taller than a summer storm cloud?"

"Those are real."

I'm not sure I believe him, but that's not what's important. His shoulder needs repair. An arm might have broken. I pull off my girdle and wrap his arm to his body. He clenches his teeth against the pain and drops to the ground, not quite unconscious. I have to go get the clay. We need to get back. I can carry one basket and support him along the trail. I'll send people for the other one.

Or maybe I should leave with both the baskets. I consider this. He could rest. My aunt's healer can come get him. He can survive through a night on his own. I look at him. He's shivering. The night is warm, but still, I'll make a fire before I go. I'll leave water at his side. I keep planning how to leave him even while my hands make the preparations for both of us to spend the night by the river. I clear a place for a fire to keep away wolves and panthers and night-biting insects. I find dried palmetto fronds and gather dead oak branches from close by. I reach for my knife to shave curls of wood and remember that the river has it. He moans and tries to stop me as I lean over to take his knife. It reminds me about the baskets still down by the river.

I'm not gone long, but he's paler and a bruise swells over his ear. I set the new clay down beside me. It's necessary sometimes to take care of people. I slap him.

"Wake up. You have to talk to me." Even I know to not let him sleep.

"I didn't think you encouraged us to talk."

I put off his impertinence to the head problem. He's right though. I can't think of anything I want to hear him say. But this is the easiest way to keep him awake.

"Tell me about your people-eating fish."

"They have a thousand teeth and are bigger than a canoe." He starts to show me how long with his hands, and the pain makes his mind fade again.

"What else do you have in that water of yours?"

"We have turtles rounder than your largest bowl. And birds with red pouches at their throats big enough to hold a baby. And I've seen one of the white ships. A storm wind pushed it to our shore and killed it. We found cloth softer than a sea breeze. And we found dead men with hair thick on their faces and shirts as hard as rocks. I took this necklace from one of them."

His people have a reputation for good stories, but I'm not going to argue with a boy whose face has faded to the color of river-bottom rocks. He shifts his head carefully and watches as I spin the firestarter. He returns his head to center and speaks into the air.

"You tell me a story. Why aren't you your aunt's second and heir?"

"Because I'm a potter."

His eyes close. I prod him with my toes and he startles. Which hurts him.

"You have to stay awake. Tell me about your journey here. How did you avoid capture?"

"You can't be a potter forever. What about then? Will you take your aunt's place? What will happen when she dies?"

The embers catch. I blow gently. He's asking questions beyond his place, and he implied that I'm almost too old to work. A head injury doesn't explain this. I stare at him. His eyes stay shut. The bruise has dropped into the skin below his neck. The night is sticky hot, but he's shivering again. I pull moss off branches and add it to the fire. It smokes the mosquitoes away. I push at the boy and he whimpers.

"Listen. I'll tell you the secret of my mixtures." His eyes open, not all the way, but enough.

"You think I'm dying." He whispers, but I hear the resignation.

"No. But yes, I don't think you'll remember. Now, you're good with designs, but limited because you don't know enough about clay. The way you've been spying on everything, you should know more than you do."

I grin in a way that causes him to lose the rest of the blood from his face. His eyes widen to all black. His spying is a compliment to my talent, not a betrayal, but I won't tell him that. I can find a use for his fear. Perhaps, sometimes, I resemble my aunt.

"Did you think I didn't know? I've had ones like you before—young people who think they can surpass me if they just knew my secrets. You haven't found much, have you? Except hard work and repetition." I grin and pat his knee. His legs twitch as if he wants to scramble away, but looks relieved in a way I don't understand. I'm not as good at this as my aunt.

He stays awake as I tell him how to wait for a drought and how the clays should squeeze through your grip. How each one needs a different mix. How each mix both allows and limits shape and design, and finally, about fires.

"Hotter. And for longer. And control the heat in a steady way. You have it right when the delicate pieces have strength and sound echoes when you strike them." I have become talkative. It happens sometimes. But I remember to shove my foot into his ribs to keep him alert. I add scraps of cedar to the fire, and it flares the smell of sweet wood around us. As the night settles, stars crowd into the sky.

"I've never understood how the sky can become this bright with stars and yet it doesn't help me see, but the moon will. The moon even throws shadows. Do your priests understand these things?" I tap my foot against him, and he shakes his head.

"You weren't lying about the men on the ships, were you? Do you think any have survived?" I have to push twice before he answers.

"The people from the west say yes."

"Your necklace is fine work. They will want my pots. We can trade with them, and it will satisfy my aunt for awhile longer. I have the pot, my final pot, in my mind. My aunt has always known that I would return to her. I just want time, a little more time.

"You will take her place?" I haven't touched him, but he speaks anyway. Perhaps, he's getting better.

"Sometimes the river stays high year after year. Then you have to dive for the clay. That clay has to dry longer before you form it."

I add more wood to the fire. The moon rises over the trees and shines into our campsite. I catch the boy awake, staring at me. Wolves sound in the distance. I take clay from the basket and coil it in my palms before I make the shape of a wolf and her cub, heads lifted. I roll more clay and think of my mother. My hands open, and an otter holds a minnow to her mouth. The boy sleeps. Through the night, I form the other shapes of my home—turtle, frog, beaver, fish, and owl—until morning spreads over the river and blurs the black reflection of stars.

My hands shake from the night's work. I have not eaten or taken water or rested. In the new light, I see that the boy hasn't moved. I press a finger to his belly and he doesn't flinch. I press harder, and his legs and penis shift. He lives. I put the water to his lips. He manages a long gulp. The excitement of my mind whispers in my ear. It hugs so close that the morning dew feels like its tongue on my neck. It wants me. I want it. It tells me this boy will burden me, that only the clay has meaning.

He struggles to sit with one arm useless and swollen. He might not heal enough to work again. I take my own long gulps of the cold water, and my mind settles. This boy has never betrayed me. I'll get him a staff to lean on, and he can follow the best he can. I walk into the trees to search for downed branches. Farther from the river, the night lingers in shadows. That's where the colors always begin—in the shadows. The purples have started. They reach out of the deep places in the leaves. Voices float to me on waves of colored air. We are no longer alone.

"Has she left you to die? I'm not surprised. That one is like her aunt."

I recognize the priest's voice even with the polite smoothness stripped away.

"No, the clay is still here. She'll be back." The healer gasps out his words in what sounds like excitement or frenzy.

Is this real? Are they both here? I move with no sound, closer. The boy fears them. I can feel it in the air.

"Did she tell you anything?" The priest oils his voice again, the way he did with my aunt.

"She will take her aunt's place. I found out for you. Now, you have to let me go home." The boy sounds like a little child begging.

I'm on my knees in the undergrowth at the edge of our campsite. I push my face into a mat of thorned vines until I can see through them. The healer is not here. The priest stands behind the boy and has a hand on his hurt shoulder. I can see both their faces. The priest smiles and squeezes the shoulder. The boy gasps.

"Are you sure?"

"Yes, she said they have both always known it. She just wants more time with her pots. You could let her stay with them. She's going to teach me about clay. She saved me." The boy babbles in pain. "Just a little more time. I'll learn about the clay, and then I'll go home to my father and the ocean where I can stretch my eyes into a long distance. Away from this closeness of trees everywhere. You promised. You said."

The priest looks down at the boy. He pulls a knife from his belt.

"My son, you have not thought this through." His voice seems kind and, for the first time, genuine.

I see the widening of the boy's eyes as he understands. He reaches for his missing knife as the priest leans over him like a hunter over a wounded deer. Strength fills me. Thorns scratch at my neck and arms as I race into the open. The priest cuts the boy's throat, and blood leaps. It shines too bright. It stops me and I stare at the priest. He smiles at me and beyond me.

"Do it now." His voice is exultant.

An arrow flies into my thigh. I wrap my hand below the fletching of white feathers. I hold my breath and pull the arrow until I see the blue shine of the point. The arrow drops to the ground and red heat pours down my leg. The priest nods into the brush beside me, and an arrow cuts into my ribs. It turns me, and I see the healer, bow raised. My strength leaves me. I hurt. The river blows the sweet green scent of the morning over my face like a dream. I reach toward it until I'm at the edge of the bank. The priest rushes to me, grabs, and his fingers wrap around my necklaces to twist me toward him. He holds me suspended backwards over the edge and reaches again for his knife. His breath spreads sour heat over my face. I hear the leather tear before he does and smile as the beads scatter around us. I leave him with the copper disk hanging from his hand.

The tumble into the water is a slow float through air until the cold slaps against me and I sink. They will shoot me like a fish if I swim. I claw into the overhang of the bank and squirm feet first, ignoring pain, kicking the space wider, into the hole left from our clay harvest. The earth wraps close and damp around me. I can feel the weight of the priest and the healer. They stand above me, at the edge, and wait for my body to rise. My mind reaches

for answers, reasons. The old man must have always known that
I killed his brother. I shift, and the arrow in my side breaks and
falls out of the cave. I suck in pain and listen.

"Do you see her? I need the arrow."

"It doesn't matter. You have your revenge as I promised. And
now the old woman has no heir. She will ally with my people
and give her men to our battles. This must happen. The invaders
come closer with every report from the scouts."

"It does matter. If they see the white crane feathers, they will
know the arrows are mine, that I killed her."

The old man has also not thought clearly enough. The priest
will kill him. I understand this even before I feel the scuffle of
feet above me and hear the shouts. He will die, and my aunt
will look no further for my attacker. Sand and pebbles of clay
shake loose and scatter over my back, and the low morning light
coming into my cave flickers as a body falls past the opening. I
look out over the river. The old man flails in the water. He sees
me. He says nothing. I understand vengeance, so I hold his eyes
in witness until he sinks below the water.

I hear the priest move back and forth. He throws my girdle
out into the river. I understand more now. It must not look as
if I cared for the boy. He prepares the scene for whoever comes
to find me. Like his rituals, it will be open to many answers.
That's what I would do, what I've done. I wait for him to leave.
The hard shells of beetles clack and snap around the roots above
me, and I smell the rot of crab tunnels with each quiet, careful
breath. The sun rises beyond the cave's opening. Around me,
only a grey light remains. The world above becomes silent. He
has left.

It does not matter. My blood soaks into the earth. I will never
leave this place. I turn onto my back and scrape clay from the
walls around me. It falls on my stomach. The space behind my

eyes fills with the purple, pink, yellow, red of flowers that bloom along the river. Controlling my mind has no further purpose. I let the colors pour out of me, over me, and bathe the clay. My hands coil and shape. I understand the past of this clay. How small animals died and their bodies softened the earth. I see the future as the priest does—the men from the sea, their metals, the size of their boats. He is right to prepare for war. But, still, I see into a world where we, all of us, north or south of the big river, will die, and my hands stop moving from the grief of it. The pot crumbles in my palm.

I need wetter clay. I pull earth, liquid with blood, up from under my body. I mix it into the next layers, and soon a bowl balances on my belly. I shake. My breath comes only in gasp after gasp, and the bowl topples.

I reach for it, and as my fingers sink into the clay, I see a woman. Her hand smoothes the wing of a heron made of shined copper and streaked through with rock the color of a storm cloud. The heron's neck curves like the bones of a spine and stretches as high as a child riding on her mother's shoulders. She hesitates, uncertain of her power. My mind spills into hers and fills us both with my brightness and the jagged image of her next creation. My body lies under her hands. My bones shout to her. From my chest, dragonfly wings spread out longer than the breadth of my arms. The veined patterns of their netting hold the air, and I lift through the clay to the surface. I see with eyes of metal as clear as captured water. Light shines through and back and over anyone who comes near. My vision breaks into a thousand images and she, the woman, fades. I am inside the earth again.

I press the bowl to my chest. Only purples and deep blues have stayed in my mind. The clay and sand and roots press around me and muffle sound and light. Finally, in my head, there is quiet.

The current spins him around a bend and pushes him to the surface. The healer splashes toward the far shore and trips and pants through the cypress knees and into the walled safety of their trunks. He runs and never stops except to find the herbs that give strength and stop sleep and hunger. He runs west until he finds a marshy river and then a settlement's cornfield. The plants lie ruined across the dirt, their roots dripping soil and their tops stripped. There is no bored or sleeping boy in the guard hut. He slows but keeps going past trampled vines of squash and gourds. He has to have food.

The land becomes a clearing and he hears moaning from the first shelter he comes to. He kneels and pulls back the skin. The light enters on a long wedge and, wherever it falls along a face, arms jerk and flop to cover the eyes.

The healer spends the rest of his life being who he wishes he had always been, who he had been before his brother died, before revenge diminished him. He pours ladles steaming with witch hazel over body after body to soothe the rashes that start behind ears and spread all the way down to ankles. He smoothes the sap of butterfly bush over the chests of the coughing ones. He can do nothing for the women who deliver their children too soon. He prays and then screams anger to the sun when infant after infant dies in a stew of vomit and diarrhea.

He thinks the old woman of the group has lost her mind to the heat that glows through her when, in frantic whispers, she tells of men furred like animals, too many to count, who rode on top of beasts. But the still healthy say she is right. And they say that the hair dangled off their faces like moss and some of their chests shone like the sun. Weapons bounced off of them. One

of the invaders had a hairless face and skin the color and shine
of an otter. The still healthy wail as they tell how their wives
and brothers and children were corralled by slathering dogs and
taken away. But then the still healthy look around them and
stop crying. They leave to hunt for deer, trap fish, dig for the
roots of water plants—anything to replace the food taken by
the monsters that had arrived at the full moon. It is the next
full moon when the healer feels the itching behind his own ears.
He coughs to death, living a few days in a twilight where he
confesses to his crime over and over. The survivors bury him in
their own mounds. They scatter red ochre over his body and set a
fire that smolders with laurel leaves as they cover him with earth.

The river carves a shallow path toward a distant sea, distant continents. From a quiet splash of paddle to the vibration of engines, change is brought up the river. Alligators sink under the water. Turtles overlapped on a fallen trunk, shell lipping shell, scatter. Bear, panthers, and wolves learn what it is to be prey, to be hunted, to startle like deer at the unfamiliar.

Cracked Beads
1858

They hung him.

The townspeople heard the scream when the slave catcher grabbed the back of the tailor's neck and yanked him onto his toes. The sheriff's mustache rose dripping from a tankard of beer. A dropped sack of flour spread white dust over the back of a wagon. In the blacksmith's shop a hammer paused mid-swing, and a silk purse slid into the pocketed fold of a whore's wide skirt. The town ran into the street.

The tailor had stopped screaming. In that pause when his lungs were spent, before he breathed again, all the fear of his whole life pulled out of his bones and left him in a sort of ecstasy. With his next breath, he took the gun. He had never held one before. It fired and flung his hand sideways. The man who had come for him, the one his people called a soul catcher, attacked.

A knee dropped hard into his back, and his face slammed into the dirt of the street until the gun fell out of his hand.

After, even the man with his warrant, who wanted his reward, couldn't stop the child's father. The man picked up the gun that had killed his daughter. The stains on his clothes smelled of fresh blood and old venison. His other daughter pressed her body along his leg, her head into his thigh, and twisted her fist into the heavy cotton of his pants. He held the gun loose but pointed at its owner until the slave catcher realized his danger. When the gun flipped handle first toward him, he understood the terms of the exchange and lifted the weight of his body off the tailor. He moved to the side.

The father gentled his daughter's hand loose from its grip. He dug his fingers into the tailor's hair and dragged him to the tree near the courthouse as if he were a deer carcass, something already dead. The child limped along beside them. The crowd followed like a flock of birds. Only the whore had regrets. She had almost enough money for her dress shop. The tailor would have worked for cheap and not dared say anything when women came to her pregnant and wanting more than their waistlines let out.

Under the tree, waiting, the tailor remembered his mother as a blur of sweat and love and hard-angled arms. He remembered the textile factory. He remembered breathless, terrified sex on piles of raw muslin behind machines that threw clouds of cotton lint into the air. He and his owner's son shared only their body pleasure and fear of discovery. When the son arranged for his escape to the wilderness of Florida, the tailor had no illusions. He knew his lover only wished to put desire out of reach. And he knew the word lover for an illusion, but the tailor liked to roll it around in his mouth and imagine.

He knew of this day's inevitability despite the protection of forged papers always in a pocket, touched by a fingertip over and over in a day. Negotiating rent on a shed behind the grocery, an uneven hem, a man looking at him too long as he bent between his legs to measure—anything and everything had brought the fear that made distance and space and sounds uncertain, as if he existed behind a veil of cheap muslin. The townspeople only noticed a colored who stood to the side and smiled a white grimace of a smile until they passed.

The tailor had never thought it possible to die without fear. White men touched him all over, tied his hands behind him, crowded close, their breath on his neck, wrapping arms around his chest and waist to lift him onto a horse. His skin, against his will, soaked in the touch. They arranged his legs, his torso. They backed away into the circle of people around him.

The little girl with her sister's blood still wet on her dress stood among them. He saw in her eyes that she didn't understand what had happened, what would happen now. Her eyes, wide, flat, the green of them washing to yellow, became all the tailor could see, and he prayed for the horse to move before he either felt guilt or found out that he didn't. Under the tailor's thighs, a ripple passed through the horse's skin. Its muscles bunched in readiness to move.

The carrot tops get inside my nose, and my face pushes as near as I can get it. I poke the caterpillar. The yellow horns pop out of its back. From this close, I can see the slime. I touch them and wipe my finger on the hem of my over slip, and it stains, but maybe Mother won't see. The horns flop and suck back under the skin. I poke it again, and the horns do it again. They look the same yellow as what ran out of the sore on Sister's leg. It stunk until Papa put mashed dogwood bark on it. I get my nose closer. It smells sort of bad but not as bad as Sister's leg did. The horns drop into their slits. I hold my breath until the caterpillar starts eating again. I poke it higher up and lower down. This is fun the same way it made us laugh to scratch the place on Papa's dog that jerked its leg. A snake killed him. Papa misses it. Best bear hound ever, he says, and he brought it all the way from the Okefenokee Swamp from before he even knew Mother.

Now I see all the other caterpillars. I could put them side by side and maybe they'll fight. Or get on top of each other like chickens. I pull at one, and its feet suck onto the leaves. I pull harder, and it keeps eating even with the back half of its body in the air. It looks the same all over, even underneath. I poke it.

"Child, stop that laughing."

Mother is just the blur of her apron until my eyes get used to big things. She stands at the edge of the kitchen garden. I watch to see if her hands fist, but they don't. I heard her tell Papa that she's too tired to get angry anymore.

"Are there caterpillar roosters?" I hop to standing and hold one out to her.

"No. And don't move. You've already destroyed enough."

I look around, and I'm in the middle of the garden. I can see the shape of my body in the smashed carrot tops. How did that happen? Mother reaches past me and pinches the caterpillar to death. She wipes her hands on a leaf and holds them out for me.

"I'll have to lift you. Come on."

She grabs me into the air, and it makes my wrists hurt. But she holds me against the little flowers on her apron, against her breasts. I rub my face into the soft places like I used to, but not since Sister got born and then the two babies, this new one and

the one that died. She pushes me onto the ground and turns me
to face the garden.

"Now, watch me." Mother walks down the rows the way we
cross a log over a creek. "See, here and here. The carrots and
the fennel, that's what they're eating. Kill them all." She twists
a caterpillar off its leaf and throws it on the ground. "You can
stomp on them if you want."

I lean forward and arch my neck to pretend I'm a big heron
stalking prey. Flapping my wings for balance, I walk like Mother
did. I jump up and down on the bug. It gets in my toes, and I
scrub my feet into the dirt before I perch with one leg bent up
under my dress and look to see if I've made Mother smile. She's
ripping weeds from around the edges. I make bird screeches
until she looks up.

"Child, you're almost seven years old. Do your chores. Your
papa could come home today, and I don't want to have to tell
him anything about you."

I hold my wings close and drop my head to make low, croaky
sounds. Used to be, this is when Mother might swack me or she
might laugh. I hunch my neck to see into the shadows that her
bonnet makes. She doesn't try to make me wear mine anymore
except on Sundays. Her hands open, and the weeds fall. She rubs
her palms down the front of her apron and lets her breath out all
at once. She almost smiles.

"Do you want fennel cakes for your birthday, or not?"

I make loud, happy heron sounds and stretch my neck the
way they do. I turn my wings back into arms and throw two
caterpillars on the ground and beat them with my feet. I like
fennel cakes. I like the way they smell cooking and the crusty
edges and eating them before they cool and the sour in the
molasses flavor. Sister thinks they taste nasty, and that makes
me like them more. Mother holds me in place as she squeezes

around me. I think she might kiss the top of my head, but she doesn't.

"Every one you can reach. And then go check the dill."

Now, I'm a hummingbird. I buzz my wings and dart from caterpillar to caterpillar and pick at them with my fingers. If I squeeze slowly, I can paint the horn slime around my knuckles like a gold ring or my wrist like the shiny bracelets I saw on the steamboat ladies this last time. Just this winter, the steamboats started going by. The first time was the most exciting day of my whole life. We heard lots of shooting from way down the river, and Papa told us to stay, that maybe it was the war starting, but we didn't, we all ran, even Mother, behind him to the edge of the river. We heard a sound bigger than a bear, bigger than herds of deer crossing the river, almost bigger than the big storms in the summertime. It came around the bend and the slave men at the top stood almost higher than the trees. That first time the boat just had men. They all had guns, every one of them. Otters, all colors of birds, even alligators hung upside down from the side of the boat. We watched, and a man shot another alligator, but this one they just took the tail and the teeth. The hacked-up leftovers floated on the current and got stuck in the cypress knees near our bank. Every day it swelled bigger, and turtles and fish ate around the edges. It stunk worse than my sister's leg and the caterpillar. The next boat, the one with ladies, and some had guns just the same as the men, killed a manatee and didn't know what to do with it and left it behind. We ate good. Even with all the shooting and cutting things up, the steamboat men always have coats and vests with colors on them and bows around their necks. Papa calls them old buzzards baited for widow, and Mother sometimes almost laughs.

Behind me I hear a stick smack on the ground. I kill a lot of caterpillars quick, the way I've been supposed to, before I look around for Mother. And I look for Sister so I can pull her away with me if I need to. But Mother pays me no attention as she beats into a pile of Spanish moss. Dust and sticks and other bits jump under her paddle. I helped pull it off the trees, and I helped wet it every day for a long time. Papa says we can keep some of this batch, and I can sew my own mattress. This winter, I got longer than the one I share with Sister. On the cold days, my feet turned blue and it kept me from sleeping. I'd hear the wolves.

I think I've killed all the caterpillars, every one. The sun has moved and shines all over me and the garden, and today, for the first time in a long time, I'm already sweaty hot even though there are hours to supper time. Sometimes Mother forgets to cook. But not today, I don't think. Mother still isn't looking, so I step into the carrots just a little and try to fluff the tops back into place. I don't want Papa to see what I've done. He said he'd take me with him to town if I took good care of Mother. He took me once before. I was scared, and he says I cried, but I'm older now. I shake the carrots and step back. With my eyes squeezed, I can't tell anymore.

The dill is in the shade. The babies are here too. The one before me and the one after. On this tiny hill under a pine tree. I've never seen a big hill or a mountain. Mother has an old ladies magazine, and it has pictures of mountains with white points like Indian arrowheads. Mother calls it snow. I asked, but she said I'd never seen snow. Then she looked over my head to the wall, like she was talking to the cracks in the logs, like I wasn't even there, and said things about tiny lacey shapes melting into water and making it into a ball that you could throw. Mother doesn't make stories up like I do and Papa does, but how can you make a ball out of water?

The baby graves are shaped like loaves of bread, only bigger. The one next to the sparkleberry bush is the oldest. But I'm the

oldest live one. I dig around a little the way Papa's dog used to
when he looked for hoppy toads. I lift up my dress and sit down
and the bare dirt cools my bottom. This baby wasn't born here
like the rest of us. It was born on the pole barge that brought
Mother and Papa here all the way from the ocean, and then it
died right away, right here, when our house was still trees in the
forest. Papa said it was too tiny. Mother hates those pole boats.
She sometimes says she hates the whole river. She says it took
her away from everything. That she wrapped this baby in her last
silk dress because she wouldn't need it anymore. That once she
and her cousin went to a dance decorated with candles put in all
the trees, and they looked like stars in the branches. Her mind
sounds far away when she talks like this, and it makes me pinch
Sister or take her dollie.

The dill doesn't have any caterpillars yet. Dill smells good,
especially in the pickled cucumbers. I could eat jars of them, but
we only get one a day. Sometimes I can take Sister's, but Mother
slaps me hard if she notices. Sometimes, I just stare at Sister until
she gets scared and sneaks hers to me.

"Are you done? What are you doing on that grave? Stop
daydreaming and come take care of your sister."

Mother grabs me again. She's always grabbing me. My
shoulder pulls apart some as she twists my arm. She lets go and
straightens the tucks on my sleeve.

"Here, let me brush you off." Her hands aren't hard on my
thighs, and she smoothes my skirt back into place. "Take your
sister down to the river and wait for your father." Mother pushes
me away. I look back, and she's kneeling by the grave of the baby
before this one, the one that messed the house with its runny
poop. It screamed all one night until it stopped. I'm sorry that
her babies died. I am. I've told Jesus this, but Mother and Papa
needed to come here. I needed to be born here by the river.

This is my place. I know everything about it—like where to find clams, how not to reach under logs unless you look first, and that the glittery sand at the bottom is farther away than I can swim.

I run as fast as I can, around and around Sister, yelling at her to run with me. She's only four, and her leg hitches up, but sometimes she's fun. She jumps in place, screeching, until I race to the river and she follows, skipping in her lopsided way. She's pretty fast, considering, but her breath gets noisy. I slow down until she catches up. We hold our breaths passing the vat with the deer skins and bark and leaves, but still it smells so bad that I can feel it on my skin. Sister circles around the hide pegged out on the ground, but I leap all the way over.

I'm first to reach the cypress trees. My favorite is big enough to hide a bunch of people behind, but only me jumps out and makes Sister yelp. She always gets scared, every time. It helps that I told about the witch and her pet panther that live higher up in the branches than we can see. At the place with five cypresses in a circle, we stop. We like this place. It has treasures. Sister found her dollie here. The arms and legs dangle too long, but she loves it, especially the black hair on its head. Papa says it has real Indian hair. He cleaned the dollie for her and told us it used to belong to a little girl. It came with a big skirt that had stripes and patches of faded colors. Mother threw the clothes away and instead made a tiny croaker sack dress with a little bit of lace around the hem.

Once, under the mud, we found a piece of cedar with holes in it, and Papa showed us how to blow on the top and make music. He called it a penny whistle. One of the trees has a lightning crack all the way down the trunk, and that's where we keep our treasures safe. Sister reaches for them, but I swat her hand and say for her to poke a stick in first. I do it for her. No snakes or spiders run out, but a sleeping frog has been guarding our treasures. I reach past it to fetch Sister her whistle, and she makes pretty sounds while I look for more beads and shiny shells and broken bowls. Sometimes we find a new treasure, especially in the summer when the storms come and the rain beats away the earth, but not today. I wish we could have played with the Indian children. They had fun things. Papa says that they would kill us if they could, but they won't. He says starting at thirteen he hunted Indians that lived in his swamp. That's how come the government gave us this land and let us move here. Because Papa has a gun and promised to keep them away. But once, I told Sister that the government gave me her pickle. Mother smacked at me and said it wasn't the same. Maybe that's because I don't have a gun. Not yet, anyway. Papa says I can have one when I'm eight. Mother says no. She says maybe to a dog. I want a dog so that when I get my gun it can help hunt. But not too big, so that it fits in the new bed with me. And if it could be white with black around one eye that would be best. I saw one like that on last week's boat. It barked and barked, at the birds, at me and Sister waving, at a man teasing it, just because. I'm going to look for it when we go to town.

Sister and I play the Indian game and after she and her dollie die, we go to the dock. The river water cools the air. The water seems always just what you need it to be. Papa says the temperature stays the same all year, but that's not right because in the winter the water's warm and in the summer it tastes cold. We're not allowed in the river. Papa says the alligators like little children the best. But I'm a good scout and you can see a long ways through the water. I see the green fish with the red breasts like robins. I see two turtles swimming in the wavy plants—the safe turtles, not the lumpy-backed ones that bite with their hooked mouths. Little finger fish squirm circles in the shadow my head makes on the water. But no alligators anywhere, so I jump in fast and out fast. Just to get the heat off. Most usually, Sister knows better than to tell, and I'll dry off quick. We lie together on the hot wood.

We hear the shouting first. "Watch the cinders" and "Hurry your ass with the wood" and "Push us away from that stump." We run to the end of the dock and watch the steamboat fill almost the whole width of the curve in our river. People crowd everywhere and lean over the boat fences all the way up to the tiny top floor. The pilot pulls on the whistle. It screams and steam jumps into the trees. The big wheels tucked in the backside slap the water even louder than Papa making firewood, and smells come to us from the smokestack and especially from the people. The ladies stink like if you cooked Jessamine vines in a pot. The boat turns so near that the slave man on the front pushes his big pole against our bank. His whole body stretches out toward me and Sister. Sister waves, but he ignores her. His hands almost touch ours. The backs are dusty brown. Except for that time I went to town, I've never been this close to a Negro. He grunts over the pole, and the nails turn from pink to white. He's sweating all over.

He doesn't smell bad like Mother says they do. He smells just like Papa home from hunting only with more smoke and less dog. The Negro in town that sews clothes like a woman and stood to the side while we went past him on our way to the courthouse, the biggest building I've ever seen, he smelled like beeswax. He probably uses it to keep his threads untangled, same as Mother, but he's not a regular Negro. Papa says he's one of the free ones. But then Mother says he charges too much.

"Look at those darling forest urchins. Aren't they amazingly dirty?" The lady sweeps her arm out toward us. The whole boat laughs. Sister and I stop waving, and I think that if they all leaned one way the boat would tip over.

The boat goes around the next curve. Pretty quick the world gets quiet again. We lie on our stomachs and lean over the dock. I churn the water like a wheel until we're wet all over our heads and hanging down hair. Sister says silly words in the lady's screechy voice and changes them so that they sound like the big woodpeckers, not the really big ones that just squeak over and over, but the other ones that make a caterwaul through the trees. I stop churning. We turn onto our backs and watch a bunch of little birds fly at an owl and peck its feathers. It just sits there, trying to sleep. The head turns and the eyes blink, but that's all. It could kill them if it wanted to. It must be very tired. Mother is tired. I try not to bother her, like Papa says. And sometimes I don't, but Sister does or the baby. Mostly the baby. Sister points at the owl flying deeper into the trees. We can never hear it, the way you can a hawk. The little birds follow, and, in the new quiet, we hear the sound of oars bumping.

"Hello, the dock. Are those my children?"

Sister and I run up and down. Papa points at the deer in the bottom of the boat. We clap and bounce in place. He throws the line to me, and I catch it on the first try. Papa leaps onto the dock and grabs us up, one on each hip. Warm blood smells sweet and rotten at the same time. He kisses our cheeks over and over. His beard always tickles.

"You two are loud enough to be waking snakes. Have you left your mother in peace? Here, each of you take a part of this." He gives Sister a tiny leather pouch. It has the lead balls and powder for the gun in it. I know. I used to carry the pouch, but now I can carry the gun and the canteen.

"Papa, are we still going to town tomorrow? You and me?"

"And me. Me too." Sister can still make her voice go all high and baby when she wants things. I wait for Papa to say no, but he's tying the other end of the boat, so I say it for him.

"You're little. Little kids don't go to town, just me."

"I'm not little. Baby is little. I go with you, Mother says." Sister swings the pouch against my hip.

"Papa, tell her."

Papa lays the gun into my arms. I stiffen my legs to keep from showing how much it weighs.

"Hush now, children. We're going to the house. No fighting." Papa bends to slide the deer around his neck. The undersides sink in from the guts being gone. Papa wraps the legs across his chest, and we follow him to the yard.

Baby cries and cries in its basket. Mother stands beside it, holding the paddle. I hear Papa take a deep breath.

"Hello, Wife." He slides the deer off his shoulders and onto the ground. "Look at all this meat. I'll salt it to sell in town. How about I get you a new Dutch oven, one with a lid and a handle?" Papa's voice sounds made up and too quick. "You know, that trader has them shipped here all the way from England. They come right across the ocean, and then in a boat up the St. Johns, to the Ocklawaha, and then to our river. Your pot came right past our house already. I'll just go to town and fetch it back."

Mother doesn't look away from the baby. Papa takes the gun and canteen from me and the pouch from Sister and hangs them on their nails. He starts stripping the deer. I want to learn to hunt, but I don't like this part yet, especially having to put the head, eyes and all, in a big pot to boil. He motions to me, and I put some heart pine under the pot to make it burn hotter. All the time he's talking to Mother, telling her the moss looks ready, how he'll just hang some of it over the fence to dry, how Sister and I had danced like water nymphs on the dock. His words help keep away the sadness that blows off Mother and goes deep in our lungs like in the summer when the air gets thick.

She doesn't answer him. Her shoulders look like they've lost all their bones, and her head drops between them. Except for her corset, she might have turned into a puddle on the ground. She says I have to start wearing one soon. I'm not going to, not even on Sundays. Ugly sounds shake out of Mother's throat. Adults cry different than babies.

Papa knows not to hug her, but he kisses the top of her head before he eases around to scoop Baby out of its basket. Baby stops crying. Sister and I stand as still as little water birds hiding in the reeds. Papa looks at us.

"Did I tell you about the first time I saw your mother?"

He has. It was at the ocean and she wore white and carried a parasol with frills and he thought he saw a dream come to life. Mother says she and her cousin had snuck away from her uncle's plantation to walk barefoot on the beach. They heard the fiddling and the laughing and saw a "whole pack of hellions straight out of the swamp, the women just as wild as the men." Her cousin ran away, but Mother went closer.

"There I was, just a Georgia pine country boy camping at the ocean with an even dozen of my brothers and sisters. We went most years to dry salt. That day we were fire roasting some of the turtle eggs we'd dug up out of the sand to take back, my mama loved turtle eggs, and that's when I saw you."

Now he's standing right behind Mother and whispering into her ear, and we can only hear little bits about how she smelled and the way her skin looked. I hear her say that word again—ruined. She yells it at him sometimes in the night—you ruined me. I asked, but Papa says ruined means things like meat that has gone off or Sister's and my blanket after the mama mouse chewed it up to make a nest for her babies. Mother's head straightens and her shoulders jerk Papa away. She gulps a big mouthful of air and takes Baby out of Papa's arms.

"He needs feeding. Supper's ready soon. I'll heat water for you to wash up. And tomorrow you'll have to buy more salt." She holds Baby up into her neck and kisses his nose as she walks to the house.

Papa and I look at each other. He and I remember before. Sister doesn't know better.

"Come, littles. Help me with the fire."

We hand him wood, and he tucks everything in tight. Sister and I scrape the pine straw and oak leaves way away, and Papa kicks the edges of the fire with his feet. Soon we're playing that the bunched leaves are houses, and Papa's the evil giant come to smash them. He lurches around after us until we can't run for laughing, and we roll on the ground together until supper smells come from the house. Papa takes our hands as we walk. He tells us about all his brothers and sisters and how they played tricks on each other with opossums, lizards, and cut off panther heads.

We all stop at the steps, stop walking, stop laughing. We listen. We hear the clang of a pot set down. We hear nothing from the baby. We hear a chair scraping against the wood. There's a place on the wall where the tar fell out from between the logs, and I peek through it. I can't see Mother. Papa puts Sister down and pushes open the door. Behind Mother's back, he walks fast over to the crib and puts his hand down on Baby's cheek. Baby makes his little sleep spit up sounds, and Papa's breath rushes out like when you come up to air after diving in the river.

In the morning, I find out that we have to take Sister. And I have to promise not to pinch her. Or anything else like that. Papa explained it to me, and I do want to help Mother get better, but usually I sit with Papa and help him row. Instead, here I am all the way in the front smashed beside Sister. The moss and the deer meat and stinky hides and bags of honey make strapped down humps between us and Papa. I can hardly see him.

"Watch your Sister. Don't let her fall in."

How does he know what I'm thinking? But I pull her back.

"Keep your body mostly in the boat and then lean over." I show her how the way Papa taught me.

Mist is lace on the top of the water. A little more day and it'll disappear. Sister and I wave our hands into the white, and it spins into the sky like smoke. I lean beside Sister, and we reach our hands until they touch the water and make circles in our reflections. I pull her arm back into the boat.

"Let the water go smooth. We can see through all the way to the bottom." The ripples flatten. Rock caves pass below us. We see fish in their nests on the sandy cliffs. A cooter with its head stretched way out from under the shell twirls its legs to swim away. The underwater plants always lean the same way, and they move like ribbons in the wind.

"Alligator?" Sister grabs my hand.

"No, that's just a long skinny fish with a nose like a stick. See how it floats without moving? Remember, how when we put our heads under, our ears go blurry and quiet? That's because even though fish talk and talk like mockingbirds, people can't hear them. But this fish, it never says much, I can tell." Sister listens longer than she ever has. Maybe she is growing up. Papa keeps telling me she will. So I tell her everything I know about alligators. We pass a tangled mess of fallen down trees.

"There, that's where they live, under there in mud caves. And listen." We hear the funny throat noises that baby alligators make. We look for the gold stripes and little eyes in the lily pads, and Sister finds them before I do. We get close, and they slip under the water and disappear.

"Their mama protects them. She lets them crawl all over her, and sometimes she carries them real gentle in her mouth." I can tell that Sister doesn't believe me.

The light makes the water blue and green and blue again. I stop talking and we both lean as far over as we can. I twist the back of her dress into my fist just in case.

"Don't let her fall." Papa barks down the length of the boat. "You two might daydream yourselves all the way into the river."

"I'm holding her tight. And Papa, we're not daydreaming. We're water dreaming."

Sister's body gets hard under my hand. Her eyes almost touch the water. I look with her, and below us, in the sun-bright green grasses, an alligator, the mama one probably, curves its tail this way and that. She's longer than Papa. I yank us both into the bottom of the boat.

"They can leap out of the water," I tell her in a whisper. My heart jumps into my ribs. "And they don't eat you right away. They push you under a log and wait until you rot." The green in her eyes squeezes into a narrow ring and the black parts turn into shadow mirrors. Trees and moss and patches of sky move across them, only with hardly any color, like night time in her eyes with only the moon shining.

"Hello, the bow. Where are you?"

"Here, Papa." We both raise our heads so he can see us, but I do the talking. "We saw an alligator."

"Well, it won't bother you if you don't bother it. You bothering it?"

"No, Papa."

"That's all right then. But don't lean so far this time."

I go first in looking over the side. The mama alligator is gone, so I motion to Sister. At the shore, a bird beats a snail on a rock until the little animal inside shakes loose. The day is warmer now and dragonflies land all over us—orange and big some of them, others like tiny feathers with gleamy blue tails. When I was young, I ate a pink dragonfly. I wanted to know how to fly. Once, we had an alligator tail for supper. Mother made me eat it. I didn't want to because alligators look mean, and I don't want to feel mean. I lean against the hides to stretch out my legs from kneeling. Deers have soft skin and run fast and have smart ears that listen for everything. I don't mind being like a deer. And fish, they shine and jump into the air and change direction with just a wiggle. That's why I can jump so high, because we eat all those fish. Mother says we eat too many. Every time her belly gets big she can't eat a single bite of fish. Raccoons can see in the dark, but we hardly ever eat them.

We can hear people now. Men, like Papa.

"You buggered cunt of an animal. Get your ass moving."

I don't know what those words are, but they sound bad.

"Don't let the wheel slip back. Whip them more."

We come around the last bend, and there's a landing place and above it, on the rise, a wagon. And oxes, two of them, pulling a wagon, or trying to. One of the wheels sinks halfway deep in the sand. Sister's eyes have gone big again. She's never seen any of this before. I explain it to her.

"They're like big dogs, but people yell at them more. They can pull things. Like that wagon we're going to ride into the town."

"Can the oxes swim?"

"What? No, we take a road."

Sister crinkles her forehead. I've never seen her do that. I thought only Mother did that. I remember that she doesn't know what a road is.

"A road is like a river, only there's no water. You can go places on it."

Sister winces each time an animal gets hit. They stand like stumps.

"Girls, hold on. And keep your fingers inside." Papa bumps the boat against the wood. He jumps out, wraps the line quick around a pole, and runs up the hill to help push the wagon. The men shout more nasty words, and the animals make nose-blowing sounds and step forward. Dust puffs around each of their legs. Now we hear happy yelling, and Papa and the ox man's Negro come and unload our boat. I wonder if he's free or if Papa has to pay him. I hope not. If there's enough, sometimes Papa brings us candies. I like the ginger ones.

Papa finds us a place in the wagon between all the piled up barrels and crates and jugs. He goes to sit in front. The wagon moves in jerks and bumps and the animals talk in rocky voices and the wheels throw sand dust all over. I shut my eyes and slap my hand over Sister's face. The wagon stops again, and I hear a barrel roll and tuck my feet close. I squeeze one eye open. Sand sticks all over my sister, like when we played that Baby was a catfish, dipped him in flour, and were going to pretend fry him. Sister won't stop crying. We shouldn't have had to bring her. Tears make wavy lines over her face. I don't know what to do.

Papa gets in beside us. He pulls off his kerchief and takes his canteen and wets it and wipes our faces, mine first.

"I want to go back to the river. Rivers make better roads." Sister has her hands over her head and uses that baby voice.

"Hide in your sister's lap. We'll be out of this sugar sand soon." Papa blows on her eyes until she smiles.

He wipes her face again before he ties the kerchief around my face. The cloth is dirty with sneezes, but the dust can't get to me. He wraps my arm around Sister.

"Hold on tight to her."

Papa disappears again, and the wagon moves again, and
he's right about the sand dust. I let Sister sit up, and I pull the
kerchief away.

The forest reaches into the wagon from both sides, and
sunlight sprinkles over everything. I see a house and yell at Sister
to look. The forest opens, and the houses get closer and closer
and finally sit right beside each other with little trails in between.
I recognize the courthouse with its white posts as tall as trees. It
has two layers, with balconies, like the steamboats do. I point.

"See, those red stones are called brick. And hear those
women laughing in that house? Papa says not to look at them.
And there's the blacksmith's shed where Papa sells the deer bones
for the horseshoe fire."

"Horses!" Sister stands up to look, but I yank her away from
the edge.

When winter is almost done, the robins come back to our
land. They sit in lines on the branches of all the trees and take
turns flying down to the ground to look for insects. I can count
past a hundred, but not as high as how many robins come to
our land. That's how many people we see here. And they flit
around, just like the robins. Sister gets scared and puts her hands
over her ears from the noise. Our home gets noisy what with
morning birds and pig frogs at night, but the sounds here are like
something that's hitting you.

We stop in front of a house with a big porch. It has a sign.
I can read, Mother taught me, but these letters curl into each
other. Papa walks right in without saying hello or anything. Just
opens the door like he does at home. And another man comes
behind him and does the same thing. And a completely different
man walks out. He's with Papa and has an apron bigger than
Mother's. They come over to the wagon, and Papa lifts us onto

the ground and brushes at our clothes and arms and hair. We make our own little sand clouds.

"Those children under there or sacks of flour?" The man laughs. I don't like him. Papa laughs, too. He sounds different. Harder or something. He hits the apron man on the back.

"These are my girls. That road stays either mud or sand, either way you get stuck." They do loud laughing again. "You two, get up on the porch and stay there while I have a palaver with this shopkeeper. After, we'll go buy things for your mother, and depending on how much this man cheats me for, maybe something sweet."

He hits the man on the back again, and they laugh even more. I don't think they're going to fight. I hear the man whose house this is say something about having some good rum from Cuba, better than that popskull they had regular.

The porch is the most exciting place I've ever been. Everyone goes by. Sister and I wave at them like we do the steam boats, but I guess they can't see us. I count six horses right off. And we're up high, so the heads pass close. I want to touch them. One man in a big hat and with shiny places all over his saddle and his belt, and his belt holds a gun, a short one, he stops and I lean my hand out and put my fingers right in the soft place between the horse's eyes. The man talks to us, but I don't hear him, I just see his eyes looking at me from between the horse's ears. They're like the blue at the edge of a pail of milk. I do hear Papa asking the man what he's doing. I look around at him. Papa has a satchel of meat up on his shoulder like the way he carries us sometimes, and he's standing stiff with his legs spread. The man clucks at his horse and the head moves away.

"Don't talk to just anyone, child. You don't know that man from anything."

"But Papa, I wasn't talking to him. I was talking to the horse."
The horse man crosses to the other side of the road and stops at

the place where they sell the candies. Papa goes back inside with
another load. I turn around and see Sister playing with kittens. I
sit down with her, and two of them run over my knees and tussle
together in my lap. They aren't dogs, but they're still fun.

A commotion starts up. Sister and I shuffle the kittens away
and stand against the railing to look across the street. Papa comes
up behind us. It looks like they're hugging, the horse man and
the free man that makes clothes, but the horse man's arm only
goes half way around the Negro's shoulder, and the hand grabs
hold of the neck and pulls. The Negro tiptoes and stumbles, but
the horse man keeps pushing. Right in the middle of the street
the Negro shrieks like Sister and I did when that snake got on
Baby's blanket with him. I should have just grabbed it, like Papa
did after he ran to us all the way from the river.

People run into the street. A horse pulls its head up and
snaps the leather rope holding it to a post. And a woman in a
shiny dress yells, "He has papers." Maybe that's silk, like Mother
used to wear. Her hair sits way up on her head. The horse man
puts a rope around the Negro's hands and he gets quiet. A man
in a vest walks out of the courthouse and talks to the horse man.
The horse man puts a hand on the gun in his belt and holds out
papers with the other one. The man reads them, steps back, and
shakes his head to the other people. The Negro looks like Sister's
dollie after she forgot it outside during a thunderstorm.

More people come out of the buildings. And I see my dog,
the one from the boat. It runs and jumps and barks at the sky.
Papa reaches for me, but I dart around him like a fish, and he
can't hold on to my dress sleeve but for a second. It makes me
almost fall down the stairs, but I don't. Sister squeezes past Papa
too. She keeps up right behind me. The dog runs to me and I run
to it. This isn't her dog, it's mine. I turn to push her away.

"He has the gun." Lots of people scream and yell. Some of them bump against me, and I fall on my knees. All I see are pants and shoes and sometimes sky. Sister's hand reaches between boots with red swirls carved in the leather and a brown shoe with a rip in the toe. I pull until she's up next to me. The dog sneaks through the people and leans against my thigh. It licks my face. And now everyone is gone and Sister and I can see the horse man's back almost right in front of us and the Negro just past him.

The Negro has the horse man's gun. His hands shake and the rope dangles and dances from his wrists. Sometimes the gun points at the horse man and sometimes at us. I see Papa running closer. I hear the horse man's words, thick and sweet like a persimmon rotting, the same voice he had when I talked to his horse. He says, "Boy, you know you would never dare. Just hand it over." He takes a step forward, and the Negro backs up.

The gun stops shaking, but he's not pointing it at the ground the way Papa says to. I make Sister and my dog get behind me. The horse man reaches, and I hear a shot, and something shoves me until I twist into the air. I fall on Sister and make her breath gaspy. My stomach hurts. Whoever pushed me was mean. Papa kneels beside me. He turns me over and leans me against his chest and holds me like when I was a baby. His arms go around all of me. The dog tucks its nose into my neck. Maybe that's why I can't breathe right. Papa's head drops over me and the sky goes away, and in the shadow I feel his breath wet on my face, his beard on my cheek. My mouth fills with thick sweetness, and I smell blood. Papa is crying.

Sister claws into the loose soil. She's come out into the moonlight, away from her father's crying and her mother's silence. When her fingers touch the casket, she sweeps away dirt to make space enough to fit her dollie. It lies face up on the cypress heartwood. She smoothes the skirt open and touches along the lace at the hem. It takes all the strength she has to push the dirt back into place. She can't remember much from earlier except that the dog screamed when her father kicked it away. But she knows everything is her fault, all her fault. She sits through the night on fresh-turned earth and copies the yips and wails of wolves and hopes they will come for her.

Sister grows up. She knows about the war, but her papa doesn't fight in it. He stays home and hunts deer for whatever army wants him to. A colored troop from Jacksonville comes close and takes food and wagons but nothing else happens. After the war, her mother and the baby disappear. Some nights, Sister and Papa play a game where they imagine Mother back at the sea island plantation she'd come from, her skirts hissing as they brush against mahogany side boards and flowered upholstery. They talk about Baby all grown up and riding horses through fields of indigo. Her father dies, and Sister buries him under the tree with his children.

In 1871, three days of hurricanes flood the deep ruts in sand roads and blow roofs off all the homes that spread out from the courthouse. It also tears the earth away from around Sister's family land. Water and wind destroy the graves, and all she ever finds is the burst open, swollen wood of the caskets. The bodies stay lost to the river. Sister sells the land to a logging company and finds a husband in town who doesn't mind about her leg.

She likes to clean. On the days when she scrubs too hard, and her leg hurts bone deep, and the skin peels off her knuckles, and her fists leak blood inside the pockets of her apron, she remembers. She sits in her sewing room with the door closed and writes on stolen ledger sheets from her husband's store. Her handwriting loops through the ruled columns, careless of the margins and lines. One day at dinner her husband reports that the hanging tree in the square has been cut down. No one knows who has done it. Sister cries all night, and the next day she doesn't make dinner and sits in the dark, in her sewing room, until morning. The echoing shiver of her old flute floods through the house, but her husband isn't someone who cares to notice anything wrong. The sister likes that about him. The doctor told her not to have children, but she does. She dies giving birth to a daughter.

A new century has begun when her widower dies. The daughter who has never known her mother prepares the house for sale, and she finds the ledger sheets folded into a silk-covered box wrapped in a ribbon knotted with cracked beads. The poems tell of an older sister, of knowing, never forgetting, the shouts of triumph as a man hangs, of finding the body of her mother in a backward turn of the current bumping over and over into a mat of spider lilies and pretending that she hasn't, but mostly they are about the river and how to look into it and find the whole world. Her daughter leaves out the blood and body ones and has the rest published. She calls the book by its title poem, "Water Dreaming" and sells them from a display set up on the reception desk of the Silver Spring's hotel where she works.

A steamboat passenger, brought there by the promise of a Florida Cure for his broken health, buys a copy. His mother back in England has an appetite for tales of the colonial wilderness. It travels with him on the Okeechumkee steamboat as it takes tourists back over the aquarium clarity of the Silver River, into the dark waters of the Ocklawaha, and against the tidal saltiness of the St. Johns, a river that flows north like the Nile. From the port of Jacksonville, the poetry crosses the Atlantic. The new owner receives her son and his gift with a kiss and fond embrace. The collection is read once and then passed on to a lady with a publisher husband.

He makes arrangements, and the newly printed book charms a small public with its images of a fairyland of teal waters and glowing green forests of submerged grasses parted by alligators, silver-glinted fish, and graceful turtles. In this old world city of sooty bricks, the citizens have bones that remember their own wild lands in the descriptions of springs bubbling from underground caves that reach deep into the earth. Even after going out of print, the book continues to exist on shelves as a thin spine lost among the leather-bound volumes. The covers fade. Smears of mold form like the fingerprints of ghost readers.

The river is a delirium of freshly-lumbered trees. Discarded crowns and broken limbs hang over the banks. Roots break out of the earth, and the water whitens with the silt of clay, the ash of ancient fires, and the bone dust of mammoths. A wide scatter of feathered needles and their cones rot along the shallows and coat the surface like blood after a battle.

Skeleton Jangle
1918

They label everything. "Florida Industrial School for Girls" is stamped on each of the crates from our fields, our math slates, our sheets, and the gingham uniforms we have to wear. Mine sticks across my back and I reach around to flap it dry. I never used to sweat like this when I was little. And I smell different. It lies on me thicker than before. The morning might still be cool outside, but the kitchen is always hot, and five more bushels of vegetables need preparing. Behind me, at the other end of the kitchen, only seven of us girls wait around the chopping table for me to lift the next crate, corn this time, which means about three fifths of a crate each. I shouldn't complain. Uncle's September letter said the mud in France had frozen that morning. But for me not to worry, that it made it easier for all the soldiers to march through. Before I can squat to lift, I get yelled at from the table.

"Hey, Darkie, hurry it up. We don't get breakfast until we're done."

She's the oldest of us and thinks she's boss. She's from Tallahassee, and they're race mean up there and think anyone, even if I'm just half from Cuba, is colored. I'm not. I ignore her and make up a better formula in my mind. We can shuck an ear of corn every ten seconds and shell a whole hamper of beans in fifteen minutes, but the pecans take forever. I multiply by the boxes in front of me, but the answer can't be right because that would mean we won't finish until midday tomorrow. Maybe I figured the shucking time wrong. And I've never counted exactly how many ears to a crate.

"Hey, mackerel snapper, hurry up."

I hate this Tallahassee girl. I hate her with that consuming fire the Reverend comes once a month and preaches about. I've hated her every single day for a year, ever since the first day they brought me to this sort of prison and she slapped me for crying. And I'm not Catholic. I mean my mami was I guess, but that stopped when she married my father.

"Just because you're leaving today doesn't mean I can't still give you a set to." She's shelling the first crop of pecans. She puts a nut in the vise and cracks it at my face.

Incorrigible—that's what the judge in Tallahassee labeled her. I saw it on some papers in the office I clean. I've grown as tall as her in these past months and weigh more. I could maybe win if we fought. "Don't let anyone provoke you." That's what the house matron tells us. I bend over the crate and recalculate our shucking time while I lift. The corn inside smells the sweet of cow patties. I tighten my fingers around the slats and tassels blow into the air as I huff to standing.

"Watch out, here comes Clumsy." This girl from Jacksonville, she's the nicest of everyone and laughs a lot. Her nicknames aren't ever too mean. We're sort of friends. I can barely see over the corn as I walk toward the table.

"Pull your fingers back everyone and tuck your toes." All the while she's teasing me, my friend is pushing eggplant and okra to one side to make a place for the corn. She burnt down a house and its barn. She says they had it coming and that she made certain to let the horse and milk cow out first.

"Okay, try to aim yourself this way. Just like those aeroplanes, here's your landing field. Wait, someone get that washtub out of her way." Her voice is always cheerful.

I drop a lot of things. When the judge sent me here, my arms had grown long and flung around without me having much to do with it, and, for awhile, I had feet that tripped over plain air. But not lately. And Clumsy is a better thing to be called than Darkie.

"Clumsy. Clumsy." The girls around the table slap their knives on the wood as they chant. Some of them say it in a way that stretches out the middle of the word, and it makes their lips look like fish mouths. Could be my body has gone soft and slower these days, but my mind thinks of things all the time. It's thinking of something now. I wedge the crate hard into my chest to make sure it won't shift.

"Oh no. The box is too heavy." I make my voice high and scared, and I swing to the side. Girls scatter away from the table. I stagger toward them. The nine-year old, she's tiny for her age, has to sit on a stool. I don't think her family fed her much before she got taken away from them. I stop beside her and sway. She covers her head with her hands.

"Don't worry." I whisper it in her ear before I yell out to everyone else. "I can't hold on any more. I'm going to crush her head. Help, help."

As soon as they rush at me, I laugh and dance away.

"You scared the little one, stupid."

The little one giggles and waves her hands around.

"I knew she was joshing. I just acted scared, like in the movies. I was good, wasn't I?"

"Shut up, baby. Everyone knows you're scared all the time." The Tallahassee girl is mean to everyone today. She's always worse than usual on a release day. And she can't be happy that I'm the one going. "And you, Darkie. You think you're getting out, but they're just sending you to Jacksonville to work day and night in a war factory. I heard Matron say so. I'll bet those machines make your hands and arms look like a man's."

She spits the words at me as I squeeze by her to get to the table. They would never send me away from Ocala. This is the only place I've ever lived, and my father needs me. I tilt the crate until corn tumbles over the surface. I count the ears, wait until she's not looking at me, and flip the crate off the table. It scrapes hard against her skin. She grabs at her arm.

"Oh, pardon me. I guess I am clumsy."

The Tallahassee girl looks up from the splinters in her arm, and her eyes make me glad I'm leaving. I drop the crate to the ground and face her straight on, ready. She stares at my chest, and, right as I watch, her face gets even scarier. She's smiling so much that her missing teeth show. She points at me.

"Hey, all ya'll. Look at that. Now her bosoms belong to this place. She'll have to leave them here."

I tuck my chin to look at the thick pleats that cover my front. The printing from the side of the box has rubbed off, and "Florida Industrial School for Girls" letters blur backwards across them. I round my shoulders over until my chest sinks. I've been hiding myself this way for awhile, but today it makes everyone laugh, and the twins, they're twelve and they can take things out of your pocket without you knowing, they bend over and swing their arms down to the floor and stomp.

"Hunchback, hunchback."

If I hit any of them, I won't get released today. "Girls, try to think ahead." That's another thing the house matron says. I think ahead as far as tonight when each of them will be trying to sleep in their cot, in a long line of cots, in a room noisy with snoring and nightmares. And I won't. I'll be at my grandparent's old house, with my father, smelling the vines that grow along the veranda. I inhale until my chest spreads the pleats wide and my shoulders ache from the stretch backwards. I think of my uncle and strut over to the next box like a soldier off to fight the Kaiser.

"That girl, she walks like her chest is leading her around on a leash."

The cook is mostly deaf and always thinks she's whispering. She and the woman that runs the dairy barn were outside having a chaw. They watch me from the doorway, and I pass close enough to hear the smack of them chewing as I walk by. Cigars are nicer. My grandfather worked in the cigar factory, and my mother brought him lunch and one day my father was there to repair shoes. That's how they met. He would tell us that he'd never smelled anything so good. Even when Mami's bosom got black and swollen and she couldn't hardly breathe from the pain, they would tease together about whether the smell of the roast pork or the hibiscus flower in her hair is what charmed him. The cook spits out the door.

They can stare all they want. I keep my chest out and let the new weight in my hips swing me back to the pile of crates. The cow lady puts her hand over her mouth and whispers to the cook. She might know something about me, about the superintendent's plans, so I keep close. Her knuckles are work swollen and leave gaps between her fingers, but I still can't hear.

The milk girl, big as she is, interrupts to squeeze past with her buckets, but the cow lady puts her mouth closer to the cook's ear and keeps talking. The cook's face changes, and I can tell there's bad news, but I can't tell anything more than that because she slaps her hands against her apron and starts yelling.

"You, no more corn. Get the oatmeal off the stove. And twins, one of you fetch the kerosene and the other get the last of the sugar ration. I'm going to dose every one of you." We all groan, except the twins. What is the cook thinking? They will have most of the sugar eaten before they leave the pantry.

The oatmeal throws parts of itself over the side of the pot. I try to lift it off the burner, but the heat from the stove burns up my neck. I hear boots behind me, and the milk girl sets her buckets down and comes to the stove. Some of us don't believe she's not a boy, but they say the doctor examined her to make sure. She's fourteen, the same age as me, but we're not friends, even though, whenever I'm outside, she's always there, nearby, helping if I need it, sometimes when I don't. She lives out in the barn and doesn't even come in when we get taught reading or geography or math. She never says anything. The others say she killed someone, but I don't think so. She takes the opposite handle of the pot and helps me lift, and for a moment we're nose to nose and the oatmeal steam wets our cheeks.

"Good luck, you know, for today." Her voice sounds sweeter than I would have thought.

We back away from each other to keep the pot from burning our arms and swing it up beside the stack of grey bowls. She's gone outside to finish milking before I think of anything to say. The cook always serves, so I go back to the chopping table with the rest of the girls. We're getting lunch ready, not that I'll be eating it. The girls talk about movie stars.

"People say they're having an affair 'cause they always travel together for the Liberty Bond drives." My Jacksonville friend can talk and still shuck faster than anyone.

"They're just patriotic and raising money for the war." The twins are back from the pantry and one speaks and the other finishes. "And, besides, they're married to other people." The cook grabs the sugar and kerosene out of their hands and goes to the back table without telling us what to do next.

"That doesn't matter with movie stars, especially ones like Mary and Mr. Fairbanks."

We all, even me, nod in agreement with the Tallahassee girl. She's right about this. We talk about movies a lot. The sewing matron, she's younger than the others, goes every week and then whispers the whole, entire story—each scene, every word of the titles, hums the organ music—while we're making bandages for the soldiers or repairing tears in our own uniforms, which usually means darning over darning. I used to have a middy blouse. My mother took me to Parkers Department Store and let me pick it out myself. It was white and had blue trim around the sleeves and hem and a bow at the neck. Yesterday, the sewing matron told us about a new movie theatre in town that has a roof that rolls back and you can see the stars while you watch. Across the table from me, the little one walks two tomatoes through the air and makes one bobble to the side.

"I like the story when Mary is the crippled girl and the orphan at the same time. You know, where the orphan girl kills the mean drunk woman. Or the one where Mr. Hawakawa saves the girl from white slavery, maybe that's my favorite. Do you think his voice would sound American or like a Chinaman?"

She's the youngest of us and has never even seen a movie, but she remembers all the stories, every detail. Sometimes at night I hear her talking to the characters like they were real people and right there with her. And a lot of us know about mean drunks. Father is never mean. He just got sad after Mami died.

"Kiss me. Kiss me forever. Tomorrow I go to war." The dim girl from Okeechobee holds the loose morals girl's face in her palms. They tilt their heads sideways and make their eyelashes shake and their lips almost touch before they start laughing. Then the two girls who brag about how they robbed a bank even though no one believes them stretch their arms wide for each other across the corn and okra and tomatoes piled on the table.

I'm here because of the war. When he registered for the draft, my uncle tried to tell them that he took care of me. But then, they came to our house, and Father was home and better than usual. They took my uncle for a slacker and told him he could go to jail or be made into a soldier right away.

"Will you be mine forever, until the stars fall from the sky?" The little one has knelt on top of her stool and has her hands clasped over her heart. Her voice quivers.

Father lost our house. But we moved to where my grandparents used to live before they died. I found two rooms that still had a good roof and made things nice. I even found some linens with Spanish words embroidered on them that I almost remembered what they meant. Then Father left. Usually, maybe in a week, he would come back. But he didn't. I was hungry in an awful way and the market building had food everywhere, hundreds of feet of it. After the man at the booth caught me and called the sheriff, the deputy took me to my house. Since no one was there, they took me to jail instead, and the judge sent me here for not having a home. I have a home. My friend slaps an okra pod against my arm.

"Hey, are you listening? I said you'd better remember that you promised to write." She wags the pod in my face. Sometimes the way she's happy annoys me. And I always think I can smell fire on her.

"If they send you to a factory in Jacksonville, go see my auntie. She cooks for the military there, before they go on the boats, so she'll feed you good. Except, for right now, a lot of them came down sick and they've stopped the trains in and out."

"I'm not leaving my home." I yell it just as the bookkeeper comes in from the main hall. She doesn't look at me even though I help her with the tallies and sometimes we talk like friends. She whispers to the cook, and the cook puts kerosene and sugar in a mug and pours water in and stirs up the slime. She serves us this every time we're sick. And she puts a cloth in the cold water that drips out of the ice box like she does for us when we have a fever. She hands both to the bookkeeper who leaves, still without saying anything. We girls look around at each other, but we're all here. One of the adults must be sick.

"You'll see lots of men in Jacksonville." My friend has sliced the okra and now has a tomato in her hand. I give up on telling her I'm not going away anywhere. "We never see any, hardly. I miss them." Sighs circle the table, but not from all of us. We are divided on this.

The littlest stays quiet. She's supposed to leave tomorrow. When her time first came up, she ran away just before. She got all the way to the far side of Ocala before they found her. They contacted the judge that sent her here, and he said to keep her for longer and he must have told them something else, because now she just goes and sits in the barn and they extend her time for attempting to escape and then she stays.

"Breakfast. Line up." The cook makes a mess filling bowls quicker than I've ever seen. She gives each of us a swig of the kerosene first. I manage not to throw up by saying prime numbers in order. Maybe my uncle does the same thing. His letter said they just put what they have in an old gas can and boil it. And he wrote a joke about rats. I eat too fast and the oatmeal burns the top of my mouth, but they'll call for me soon. After breakfast they let you go. The bookkeeper comes back into the kitchen. Her hair is still in its sleeping braid.

"I need someone to clean my quarters. You." She points at me. "One last job won't hurt."

There's still no special smile between us. I finish the last spoonful and stack the bowl by the tub of soapy water. At least I don't have to wash dishes ever again. Well, here anyway. I get a bucket, rag, and the box of soap and follow her to the room she shares with the house matron. It stinks everywhere, especially from around one of the beds.

"Matron took sick last night. They carried her off to the doctor's, but I'm sure she'll come back soon. Let's make it nice for her." She pats my arm, and for the first time I think she notices me. "I'll be in a meeting with the superintendent. When you finish, come to the parlor and we'll set you on your way." She leaves me, alone. Girls aren't usually allowed alone in the staff quarters.

I take care of the smelly messes right away and put the bucket out in the hall. There's no one around. I stop in front of the mirror that's almost as tall as me, and it tilts. A "Votes for Women" sash hangs from a corner, so I dry my hands before I lift the gold silk away from the glass. For a second, my mother looks back at me. I look like she did. Maybe that's why Father left me. I've shut my eyes, but I open them again. I've never seen my whole self before. I stand sideways and yank the uniform tight around my body. I like it. My body. I rub both thumbs along my collar bone. I drop my hands over where my breasts pouch out under my arms, feel into my ribs, and stop at the sharp ledge of bone above my hips. I press down and things shift and move under my belly button, between my legs, into my thighs. My hips press back and my hands ride on top of them. My legs connect to everything all the way up to the top of my head.

My grandparents danced on their veranda. I didn't know I remembered them. They walked smooth, this way and that, together and apart, and my grandmother waved a fan in her hand. Maybe I'm only remembering a story Mami told to me, but I can see the black lace of the fan. I can see through it to the vines of purple flowers that grew up the walls. Abuela, abuelo—that's what I called them. I raise my hands and turn in a slow circle until I face the mirror again.

The veranda isn't smooth anymore. Last I saw it, roots and heaves of dirt ruined the right angles of the tiles. I hear the teacher calling for the girls to hurry to class. I turn away from the mirror, strip the bed coverings into a pile, keep the blood on the pillow case away from everything else, and that will do for now. I don't want to miss a lesson. I'm at the door before I remember that I don't get to go. I won't work in a factory. The teacher here promised that I could keep going to school in town and that she would make arrangements. I'll be a month late for the classes out there, but I can catch up.

If they're going to call this place a school, they should have more books. But the teacher here makes up better math problems for me just like they used to in my old school. You can do math anywhere. Whenever Father left, I'd leave one lamp on and sit under it all night solving equations and falling asleep and waking when I thought I heard something. I'd think about the numbers until I fell asleep again. Even just before I came here, at my grandparent's, when Father couldn't get the electricity paid, I'd use a candle and be fine.

I go back into the room and pick a dressing gown off the floor and hold it against me. It has pink ribbons threaded through the waist, and my hand shows through the material. A comb falls out of the pocket. I pick it up and put it on the dressing table with the other comb, two brushes and a hand mirror. I pull a blond hair out of one comb. The Matron's. I touch all along the roses carved into the silver back of the mirror. I pick up one of the brushes, but put it down without using it. My hair is too dark. They would find me out.

I arrange the jars on the dresser by size. Each one is the same shiny black with pictures on the lids of glittery green birds whose tail feathers curve way down from their bodies. We have fancy birds around here, I even saw a pink one once, but none that look like this. I hold the oval jar close to my face. My cheek and the white part of one eye show inside the black surface. It smells like tea olives, magnolias, and gardenias all mixed together. No footsteps sound in the hallway so I twist the top off and dip my middle finger in the white cream. It leaves a peak. I spread the cream along the underneath of my arm, up to the elbow fold. It feels like butter. I feel like butter. There's a shiver in the bone between my breasts.

"Are you done? Bring those sheets here." The bookkeeper shouts from down the hall. I've never heard her yell. She hardly even talks to us girls, except for me. I flatten the peak on the cream before closing the lid and rub my finger against my dress. I'm scooping up the bedding just as she comes into the room. She grabs the sheets out of my hands.

"Go to the superintendent's parlor. She'll see you there." The phone rings in the hall, and she throws the sheets on the floor and runs out of the room. I thought she would say goodbye to me.

The parlor is near the front door and we never get to go into it. Except always on the day we get out. No one has ever said what happens. Nothing much, I figure. She'll give another of her speeches, and I'll stand with my arms holding on to each other and my head a little down and nod when she finishes. When do I get clothes for out there? They'll be mission lady ugly, but maybe I'll get a blue dress and it will match my eyes.

The door is wide open. Little tables mostly cover a rug with intersecting lines of big diamonds divided into four equal small diamonds. The brown ones look smaller than the beige ones but I think that's just because of the way the brown smears into the pink background. I'd need to move the furniture and measure to know for sure.

"Come in and sit with me, dear." The superintendent pats an empty wood chair. Her chair is red velvet and has wings around the side for her arms. I'm nervous to sit down in front of her.

"You've done well here, child." The superintendent always looks like she pulled her hair so tight it gave her a headache, but her dress has a nice style of green and black plaid. Maybe she'll give me one of her old ones to wear.

"Now, I'm going to speak frankly. I always do with you girls when you arrive in this room." She taps my arm. I hope she doesn't smell the lotion.

"I must tell you that we haven't been able to locate your father, and I'm a bit out to sea about your future. I think our best choice is to send you . . ." She stops talking. I look where she's looking.

The bookkeeper is in the doorway. She stands as if her insides have melted and left her skin hanging. Her face is grey. She doesn't say anything.

"Well, it seems I must go for a moment. Here's your packet of clothing. You may change, but then wait here." The superintendent's voice, pinched quiet, comes to me from the side as we both stare at the bookkeeper.

She's crying now—messy crying with tears and snot and groaning sounds. The superintendent goes and wraps her arms around her. I didn't know that superintendents did this. They walk, still clung together, out the door and disappear. They've left me alone in the parlor. Why is the bookkeeper so sad? I step from one rug diamond to another until I'm calmer and remember about the new clothes. The string around the brown paper package comes right off.

I unfold knee socks, drawers, and a bodice instead of a corset like I'm still a little girl. But the dress is a lady's. The material is a faded green and softer than our uniforms. I put everything on. The skirt has a nice swing as I walk around the room and touch things. Every surface has a vase on it. I touch a tall blue one with sides thin enough that I can almost see through it. I touch the figurines of ballerinas in ruffled skirts. A china bowl with roses twined around the edges is so white that rainbow colors gleam out into the air around it. I move the rooster bookends tighter against the books. I wish there was a mirror in here. And that I had a hairbrush. I scrape my fingers through my hair over and over until the tangles let go. Still, no one has come back. I lean out the doorway, and the wood floors echo with quick steps, but I can't see anyone. The girls' voices float through the wall. They're reading out loud, all together, from the geography book. We're doing the chapter about Egypt. I step into the hall. I can find my own way home.

I don't have a plan like the Matron always says we should, but I'm at the front door and through it onto the porch before I think about anything. A horse wagon and the Reverend's black car are in the yard below me. I hear the rush of someone in the hall. I turn, but whoever it was has already gone by and disappeared into a room. I step down one step and another and wait for someone to call me back. But they don't. And the long drive ahead of me is empty.

I keep close to the flower border. If someone sees, they might think I'm working. My dress brushes the superintendent's roses. They smell like old eggs and garlic from the poison she puts on them. Still, the leaves have spots and some have fallen. "English flowers, not fit for this climate," my mami always said when we delivered shoes to the fancy houses. I always feel bad when I think of Mami, but today I almost throw up—maybe because of the flowers. They've never smelled this strong before. I can almost taste the petals.

I'm past the barn and no one has yelled for me, and now I'm farther than I've been in a year. At the last fences, beside the boxwood hedge, two men stop their hammering to look at me. The old one's worked here all week. Today there's someone else with him that looks like his son. They've taken the gate off its hinges to fix in new planks.

"Hey, gal, where're you off to?"

"Yeah, you escaping?" The son gets too close and stares at me all over. His face sweats. The skin is white except for grey spots on the cheeks. He flips his hammer into the air but misses the catch, and it falls at my feet. I bend down and pick it up in one motion like a dancer. I lift myself and the hammer all the way up to tiptoes, and inside my head, I'm sticking my tongue out at the whole table of girls calling me clumsy. I offer the hammer back to the son. His face has gone red.

"No, I am not escaping. I'm going home." I stare at him the way those church ladies stare at us girls when they visit.

"Don't you want to go to the river to cool off first? I can show you the back trail just through those trees." He's whispering so his father can't hear, and he lets his hand rub over mine as he reaches for the hammer. "I'm just back from Jacksonville. Did you know the Army's quarantined it? I had to act like a spy behind German lines to get past a whole bunch of soldiers. I could use a good cooling off. How about it?"

I drop the hammer on his foot. I don't like him. Besides, I know where the trail is. Before they came to cut all the trees, I would play on the river. Mami was still alive. Father had the shoe parlor. I had just started school. This is my favorite time to remember. But one day my Mami and I were almost to the river, and we heard a stretched-out noise louder even than a train. We saw men everywhere, and a big tree lay on the ground longer than any building is tall. Sawdust floated in the air. After that we weren't allowed to go anymore—too dangerous, Father said.

"Sorry, miss. He's young, you know." The father shoves his son back to work. He has to hack and spit for awhile before he speaks again. "Do you know your way?"

"Yes, I live in town near the Exhibition Hall." I wince and wish I could take the words back. I shouldn't have told them anything.

"Honey, that's in the old Havana Town. No one lives there since the cigar factories closed."

"I do. With my father." The son rubs his thigh at me from behind his father's back. I walk away.

"Hey, Senorita, maybe I'll see you in town at the Liberty Bond drive." He's shouting at me. I don't turn around. But I do loosen my walk and let my hips wander from side to side over my legs. He shuts up. His father coughs even more.

Once I'm around the bend, I change to skipping, but hear crying before I'm up to full speed. I follow the sound to a clump of palmettos and see a small shoe sticking out. I get as close as I can to the little one, but I don't want to dirty my dress, and she's sitting right on the ground getting redbugs and ticks. I squat beside her.

"You know, everything is all arranged." I put my hand on her back and rub in circles until her head stretches away from her shoulders like a turtle coming out of its shell. Her face is filthy. "You just have to go to the barn and wait with the milk girl there. She doesn't scare you, does she?"

"No, she gives me milk and sometimes corn pudding that she steals from the kitchen. I like her."

"Then why are you all the way out here, crying?"

"This time they might make me leave. They made you go. And there are lots of loud men in the halls." She huddles closer to the ground. I pat her back.

"But they didn't make me leave. I ran away, sort of. Are they looking for me? Did you hear anyone say my name?" I shake her shoulder just a little.

"You ran away? I don't think anyone knows. You could come back."

"But I want to go." I almost tell her I'm going home, but she's too little to keep a secret. "I'm going on a big boat down the river. Remember the map? How the little river here goes to a bigger river and that one meets up with an even bigger river and then you're in the ocean and maybe I'll go all the way to England or France. I'll drive ambulance cars like the English ladies do in the war movies."

"I've never seen a movie."

"Well, someday you'll want to leave here and go see one."

Her head whips back into its shell and the crying starts again. I've said something wrong.

"But that's years from now when you're grown up and you'll go wherever you want to." Still, there's crying. I'm going to just leave if she doesn't stop. "Or stay wherever you want to. Maybe you'll become one of the matrons or even the superintendent."

"I can sew good." The voice is still wet, but like after the rains have stopped.

"Yes, you can. And I've heard the sewing matron say so. She'll probably need your help for a long time. Now, run back. Don't go by the gate though. Just sneak through the fence right here. Go on. Go now."

She's not moving fast enough for me. She looks back over and over. I want to yell at her, but I smile and wave her on. I wait two heartbeats after she's out of sight before I skip the rest of the way to Ocklawaha Boulevard. Oak trees crowd both sides in both directions, but right where I am the light gets through. Either way I look, all the way down the tunnel of road through the trees, is empty of people. I hear a mockingbird and crows complaining the way they do, but no sounds of people. Once my teacher brought a crystal to class and showed us how sunlight has all the colors in it. My hands lift into the sunbeam and it makes rainbows along my skin. I twirl in place until my skirt lifts and air spins up my legs. I hop up and down, higher and higher, until everything on my body shakes, and my feet kick over the tar and rocks.

At the school, our sewing teacher brought ladies magazines. She said for the designs, but we all looked at the pictures and read the captions. One said "Distinctive Fall Millinery for Misses." With the back of my hand under my chin, I tilt my face and walk sideways up the road just like the women in the ad. Another picture showed a lady in breeches like a man, and it said she traveled in the Sinai and Persia. She stood with her hands on her waist, her elbows out, her legs spread. I try it. It feels good. I spread my legs some more. I bend my knees, and now I'm the ballerinas in the superintendent's parlor with my hands over my head and my feet wrapped around each other. I'm on my toes and spinning and dizzy, and I hear music, real music.

A drum, trumpets, and something higher pitched than a songbird sounds from the river end of the road. I run behind a magnolia tree to watch. A motor car, more of a covered wagon with an engine, jerks and bounces and kicks up rocks out of the slag. A bunch of men sit in the back. They have red uniforms with brass buttons and gold trim around the sleeves. Gold braids of rope hang down from their shoulders. Their music is wild and jumpy.

The car is close enough now that I can see a fat man playing a clarinet and a tuba hiding the skinny man behind it. I laugh, and the car slows until the spokes of the daisy yellow wheels flicker light through in a revolving pattern of triangles. It stops beside me, and right in front of my face, along the wood sides, it says "Silver Springs Inn" in orange letters. The men pass liquor around. One of them leans way over the side and holds out the jar.

"Hey, aren't you a choice bit of calico. Want a snort? Better hurry before those teetotaler loonies make it illegal." He has a beard and his lips show up wet and pink inside it.

"Honey, ignore him. You know you want a tuba man like myself."

"Are you kidding? Everyone knows a girl likes an oboe the best." The first man tilts his instrument over the edge and plays a trill of low notes.

"Come on, hop in. Really, we're safe." The accordion man leans sideways to reach a hand out. They're all old, but he's the oldest. "We're the best musicians south of Jacksonville, or we were until all our young un's got drafted. Just us geezers now."

"And us." A woman's voice comes from up by the driver. She turns in her seat and smiles at me. She's holding an instrument all brassy like a trumpet, but with a circle of pipes. "Don't worry lassie, we'll keep these old men in line if you need a ride." She pats the driver on the arm, a woman driver. They both have on uniforms—pants, shiny buttons, hats—with everything the same as the men.

The men shift around to make room. The big drum gets hung off the side. They seem fun and dangerous, and I'm not scared of them. I grab a hand and they pull me over the wood slats. I kick someone accidently and see one of them curled onto the floor of the car, his flute over his knees.

"Oh don't mind him. He laid out all night with a piece he's got across the river." They all laugh, even the women.

"Hey, are you escaped from the girl prison?"

"No, they let me go."

"Look it here, men. We have an actual convict in our midst. What did you do little gal?" The trumpet player shakes his finger at me.

They're teasing me. I put my hands on my waist, Sinai desert pose, and look straight at the trumpet player's face.

"I killed a man for playing off tune."

No one says anything. The car engine hiccups.

"Whoo hee." The man with the cymbals hits them together. "She smacked you like Babe Ruth on a ball."

The accordion man and the women start laughing first. A movie star who says all the right things and makes men admire her must feel like I do right now. A hand wraps around my ankle. The man lying on the floor coughs and coughs and holds my foot tighter each time. I try to shake him off, and the other men reach down the best they can between the knees and instruments to pull him away. We hit a rut, a space opens, and I see blood on my feet.

"Miss, don't worry. I'll get that." The oboe man flips a handkerchief out. He bends down and wipes my foot. He takes a long time, and I didn't think any blood got on my ankle. But it doesn't feel bad, his palms and fingers on my skin.

"Old man, keep your blamed hands to yourself." The woman's voice is sharp, and it snaps the man away from my foot. But he grins at me on his way up.

The road smoothes to pea gravel, and I know we're close to town. From this high up, I can see past the iron gates to the big houses. They have pointy roofs sticking out from all over and turrets and bay windows in no set pattern that I can figure out. But the railings around the porches are carved in perfect matching shapes that repeat and repeat. We pass the street where I used to live before Father couldn't take care of things anymore. A man from Poland has the business now. Next comes the courthouse and its square filled with people. I see women wearing clothes like in the magazines—silk skirts that look like water rippling, plaids trimmed with black fringe. The men have on suits and their dress oxfords, expensive ones. Father taught me how to tell about shoes. The car keeps going to the west side of town. As soon as we get to the colored businesses, the pavement gets rough again. I can run to my home from here.

"Stop. Let me go. I want out." I hit the driver on her back.

"Whoa down, champ. We're all getting out here to start our march back into town. The bank swells have paid us to put on a big show for their war bond sale."

I'm on the ground before the car stops. I run until the shrubs change from squared-off hedges to the bougainvillea and jacaranda my mami grew in our yard. The road passes half torn down houses and empty lots. Vines make carpets of rust red over old stoops, and blue wasps with spotted wings swirl around yellow and red oleanders. I stop. I know I'm in the right place, but I wish I wasn't. The roof hangs off the side. The walls lean and ripped-up sticks of wood cover the yard. One day this summer the matrons stuffed all of us girls in the pantry. Because of the tornado, they said. But it missed us. Here the papaya stalks are purple and broken. The fruits lie on the ground, split open, with the orange insides smeared everywhere, and they stink. My grandmother grew these. I can see her fingers drop a piece in my baby mouth and feel it soft on my gums and sweet.

I remember and remember that time when someone fed me, someone took care of me. I close my eyes and hold it in my mind until I can't anymore. Eyes open, eyes closed—all I see is everything ruined. Pain sets into my bones, into my elbows and my calves, and I'm on my knees in the matting of vines. I call for help. I call out for my father, and my voice sounds like a baby's. I cry until I choke. My skin itches all over like wool, and the crushed flowers under my knees smell heavy and make my head ache.

Flat on the ground, my hands covering my face, I remember other things. How the rats sounded when I was alone all night and the next day and then another night. And I'd find my father right here in the yard asleep with vomit all over, and I'd have to lift him best I could. I should be sadder than I am. I should be worried about my father. My hand holds my throat where it feels charred. I'm not little anymore. I know my father is gone. I know that even if my uncle came home we couldn't live here. Last spring, at the school, a deer got caught in the barn. You could hear her kick and throw her body against the sides. Dust shook out of the slats every time she hit. That's how I feel inside.

From far away, outside my head, I hear a drum, an accordion, a trumpet. I sit up. I reach around me and twist vines until their stems break and fill my arms with yellow, red, and purple. I weave them into a circle that fits on my head and wrap others over my neck and around my wrists. I touch inside petals and rub their gold dust on my palm. I remember more. Mi abuelo smelled like burnt wood from his rum, and Mami loved vanilla custard. I stand and flowers fall around me. I leave their house and run toward the music.

The band people have on white gloves now. Toots, bleats, and drum rolls echo back and forth. The accordion wheezes. Each hat sits at the same angle—thirty degrees, I think. I stand and wait for them to notice. The skinny man gets inside his tuba. His head pokes through the circle, and he sees me.

"Well, here's our very own fairy princess." He blasts four notes that shake in my ears. The rest of them look at me and join in. The sounds are loud and mixed up, and no one's playing any one tune but still I dance like I think a fairy might. The sick man got left in the car. He calls me to him and unwraps the gold ropes from around his shoulder.

"For a belt, don't you think?"

The rope fits twice around my waist, and the leftover tassels brush my thigh. The band quiets down. They rub their sleeves to make a final shine on their brass. Some wet the mouths of their instruments. Others finger the levers and buttons silently, practicing. The tuba player stretches his neck in all directions and stamps his feet in place. The lady holds her horn so the big mouth swings over her hip. She winks at me.

The driver has the biggest hat of all. She stands in front, facing them, and claps and makes "hut, hut" sounds like the rest of them are horses. They look at each other and shift apart, even the drinking ones, until they form a perfect rectangle of people. They raise their instruments and white sunlight glazes back from the metal parts. The driver says "Skeleton Jangle," and the trumpet starts, the trombone slides in and out, and all the other

instruments make sounds that circle around the trumpet. The
driver marches in place until she puts one foot on tiptoe behind
her and pivots. She steps forward, and everyone steps exactly like
she does. I run to catch up, and the perfume of flowers comes
along with me. My bones still hurt, but I ignore them.

The music excites the air. The coloreds all come out from
their shops. The butcher's apron is as white as his skin is black.
We pass the dry goods store, tailor, bank, drinking place, and in
front of the dentist's I see the Negro lady doctor that helped my
father once when he cut his head from falling, even though we
aren't colored. I wave, but she doesn't recognize me. Children
dance around us, around me, and I copy the way their elbows
wing out and their knees bounce up and down. I lead them in
wavy lines through the band rectangle until we get closer to the
square and they drop away.

The driver holds both her hands up and the band stops
playing and walking. My heart keeps running fast, and my
breath won't stay even. She says "Over There," and they start a
new song. The tune is simpler than the first one, and it makes
you want to swing your arms like a soldier. I try, but I have to let
the band go on without me. For awhile, the coughing won't stop.
I count each one, and at twelve it stops and I can breathe again. I
run up the street and walk behind the band. We've gotten to the
brick buildings, every one of them fresh built after the fire from
when Father was little. He calls it the worst tragedy, and says he
remembers the way the sky lit up red all night.

"Johnnie get your gun, Johnnie show the Hun." People sing
and clap from both sides of the road. "Over, over there, over
there, send the word that the boys are coming." Some of them
lift their knees and step right on the beat, like soldiers. My band
keeps playing all the way to the center of everything. We pass
the gazebo with a man yelling a speech that no one can hear and

coveys of ladies in hats that wing off their heads and through men in serge suits with Liberty Bond buttons on their lapels. They close back in behind the band, and I'm part of the crowd. I let it take me this way and that, in and out of conversations.

"What about this last draft, do you think they'll call up those young ones?" "They might, what with the flu killing whole tank corps." "How much are you buying this time? Liberty Bond, my arse. This is more like blackmail, the way they make us well-to-do pay for the war." "Hush. They can arrest you for talk like that. Besides it'll be over soon." "Do you think that girl's well? She's got dead flowers all over her. Are those fever spots on her cheeks?" "I'll race you to the German ears."

This last bit of talk comes from one of the two little boys that screech past me. The men that said mean things about my flowers keep looking at me, so I follow the boys through the crowd. They skid through people, kicking shins to open a way, and I'm right behind. They stop all of a sudden, I bump into them, and they hit a display table. It shakes and everything rattles until the soldiers behind it swat the boys away. I slip into the space they leave. The banner says "War Relics." I pick up a piece of fringe splattered though with a brown stain.

"Young lady, what you have there is a bayonet tassel, right off a dead German. But it looks like he got one of ours first, doesn't it?"

I think about my uncle and throw it out of my hand. It flings into a man beside me. No, he's a boy. He's big and blond all over, but he's a boy like I'm a girl. He looks at me from under his almost invisible lashes and sees me looking at him. I stare back down at the table. I look at handkerchiefs with the same brown on them as the fringe, eagle buttons, medals with foreign words, and a spiked helmet. The boy's arm reaches in front of me to pick up a German coin. The sunlight angles and shows up the fur of white hairs on his forearm, and I can feel blood beating up my neck and into my face.

"Yes, men. You can bring home souvenirs like these. Remember what the sheriff said—'Go to work, go to war, or go to jail.'" The old soldier holds up a shriveled piece of something and waves it in the air. "You, you look old enough." He grabs my boy's shirt and yanks him over the table. "Don't you want to slice the ears off our enemies? Get on over there and sign up." The boy says something too low for me to hear.

"Not old enough. Well, you're a big one for your age, aren't you? Smaller boys than you have lied to serve their country. But I think we can all tell that you're a timber man. Came up the river from the camps, didn't you?" The old soldier smacks the boy's shoulder and sawdust clouds around it. "Your country needs that wood. Do you have any papers on you?" The boy shakes his head. "Well, you need some, looking older than you are. The sheriff in this town is tough on slackers."

The other soldier, the younger one, gives an up and down eye to the man on the other side of me. He pinches the man's lapel between his fingers.

"And you, my good man. It seems these United States of America have allowed you to prosper. Where's your Liberty Bond pin? We don't like shirkers of any kind here in Ocala."

He sounds hard, but he looks at me and smiles a little. His eyes go back a long ways, and around them are lines that usually only older people have.

"Hello, my fair maiden with a rose in each cheek. Did you want to try on this helmet? We machine gunned the Germans across a field in France in a slaughter that filled us with pity even as we kept killing. I took this right off the head of one of the Kaiser's favorite boys. Here, let me help you."

He adjusts the strap under my chin, and I take flowers from my neck and wrap them around the spike. The blond boy and I smile at each other. He's about to say something, but someone pushes and I'm shoved to the side. The soldier yells for his helmet. The boy holds his hand out to me. Our fingers touch. During a storm this summer lightning hit almost in the classroom and books jumped off the desks and the teacher screamed and my arm hairs raised up and tried to pull out of my body. I feel it all the same way now, only more.

People move forward between us, and he's gone. The crowd pushes me through to the edge of the square. My breathing takes awhile to level off. If I hunch my shoulders and bend over, it comes easier. The helmet falls off my head and drops to the ground. I shake out my hair, lift it up off my neck, and wish I had a cool cloth. Air moves across the back of my neck and slides under my collar. I shiver. He's behind me, the blond boy. I feel him, but I don't turn around. I know he'll follow me. I take him toward the music.

My band stands in place on the grass, playing, and people dance all around them. The tuba man waves while the clarinet winds a long ribbon of music around me—around me and the boy. I smile, and the smile connects to a place behind my belly button, and all of a sudden I know things about myself, things that I want. I want to dance with the boy. I turn to him.

He pushes the sleeves of his shirt up past his elbows, hangs his hands loose at his side, and his feet stomp out the music. He dances that up and down way that my father's people do. I hold my arms out, curved, and make slow, swinging circles with him in the center. The skirt of my dress brushes against him. His feet go still, and I feel like summer heat, like cane syrup, like velvet. The music slows, and all around us the dancers embrace.

He stands close. He's going to touch me, but I don't know where. My body wants him to press against me. I think of how, in the night, I'd roll over in my cot and bunch the sheets between my legs and just hold them there, tight, and hope the other girls didn't hear my gasps. Purple flowers drop out of my crown and fall against my neck and belly. I catch one and put it behind my ear. I close my eyes. I feel a hand on one shoulder and fingers wrap through mine. We move. People sing to the music as they dance.

"Moon of the summer night. Your silvery beams bring me dreams." The voices sound sweet and sad at the same time. "Could you only tell them all that I'm safe tonight?"

We keep a small space between us, but I imagine it gone. I imagine the brush of flannel against my arms and that the denim catches on my dress and lifts it along my thighs.

"That's her." I open my eyes and see the two men from before. They have the sheriff and his deputy with them. The deputy recognizes me and says something to the others that makes them put their hands over their mouths. He yells at me not to move.

I jump into the crowd and shove through people. My boy is with me. He stays close to my back, and we slip like one person, like birds flying, with his breath on my hair, all the way to the far side of the square. We can't stay in the open. I lead him down side streets that run the same way—parallel they call it. We run behind the Jewish church, up the alley at Loy's Laundry, past the gun shop, and under the water tower. The buildings stop, the side roads end, and we're back to the boulevard where I came from this morning. We stand at the edge. I don't know what to do now. I'm too hot to think. I look at the boy. He came from the river. We'll go there, to the head of the river, to the cold spring.

The quickest way means back to the school. I run the best I
can, but I'm not as strong as this morning. My legs hurt all the
way through. We pass the last of the shops and the churches,
and before the fancy houses end, I have to stop. My chest hurts,
worse even than once when I burned the trash and a sideways
wind pushed hot air and embers down my throat. I hold my
knees and pant. We're alone in the road. Blood rushes through
my ears. It burrs the outside sounds and forces heat through my
skin.

I raise my head from my knees. He's looking at me. It hurts
my breathing in a different way. I walk to him and stand in
front of him. My sweat thins the cloth of my dress, and when
we touch I'll be slippery against him. He smells like pine trees.
He doesn't move or speak. I lift my arms. They ache all the way
through, in every muscle. I don't care. I want to touch along his
shoulders where they turn down into arms. I want his muscles
under my hands. I want him to press so hard into me that the
buttons on his pants push under my belly, and his fingers press
into the spaces along my spine. I lift on my toes to put our faces
close. His lips are pink and just like my uncle and father, he has
a mole in the dip under his nose. I'm going to bite his chin and
then his bottom lip.

"Papa, Papa. What is that girl doing?"

We jump back from each other. A child in a yellow dress
with a blue ribbon around her waist flounces her skirt back and
forth. Three more girls, in a variety of heights, rush out from the
iron gate. Their dresses are blue, pink, and green, and they have
matching sunhats with satin bows. They point and chitter and
hop up and down like baby chickens. A woman runs out behind
them holding a hat with blue trim.

"You just fly off, half unmade. Here Daughter, put this on
before the sun darkens you. Oh."

She sees us. I wipe hair out of my face and pull the last of the flowers off my neck. No one says anything. A big man in a black suit closes the gate behind him.

"We're late. I'm due to make my speech and all you women of mine have made me late. Are we finally ready? Why are you all in a huddle? Go on, girls. Your mother and I will be right behind."

The man says all this while he's looking down to pinch the crease in his pants. He smoothes his mustache and notices us.

"Who are you? Girl, are you from that place? Get on back there before I fetch the Sheriff."

He comes too close. I move out of his reach. He takes a big sniff, and I know he can smell what is between the boy and me. We run. The man shouts, but the pipping voices of the little girls are what I hear for the longest. I run until I can't. If the father rushes to town, that will take ten minutes. He'll have to find the Sheriff, ten more minutes maybe, but they'll probably use a car to come get us so that will be quick. My mind tries and tries to add this simple tally, but I can't keep all the threads in my head. But I know we should hurry.

At the turn to the school, I hide behind a palm tree with a trunk messy and wide from ferns and the stumps of broken off fronds. I listen but don't hear hammering or any chatter. The only sound is the slow, stretched out noise of a hinge that needs oiling. I motion us forward.

The gate is making that noise. It swings skew whiff from one hinge. I step through on an open swing, and my feet kick through spilled nails. Farther along, near the boxwood hedge, a hammer lies on the ground. Above it, breaking the hedge halfway down, is a body. The feet splay out onto the path, and a face lies turned up to the sky. Pink smears around the mouth like cake icing. The old carpenter is dead. Branches stick into his clothes and pull the pants up over his calves. His ankles have gone a purple sort of blue. I don't go near him. I listen for his son, but instead I hear the cars coming from town.

I run into the cornfield. The cars stop and rev and men shout. I run until the engine sounds barely leak through the stalks. I breathe loud breaths that squeak and hiss. The boy stays behind me, and I feel more than hear the rhythm of his lungs. It matches and soothes mine, and this time I don't cough. Still, deep in the field, I hold in place. No one follows. The cars travel on to the school. Girls get lost in the corn all the time. I listen and hear crows and a cardinal and finally, faintly, cows. We can follow the sound of them to the barn. The milk girl will help us.

The barn smells like always of trampled hay and muck, but no one's remembered to untie the cows after their morning milking. They shake their heads and moan as we pass. There isn't anyone anywhere. The heat of the boy's body follows behind me. Together we look though the gaps in the siding, squinting into the light until the main house comes into focus.

The milk girl walks onto the porch. They've let her in the house with her dirty boots still on and an overall strap falling down her front. She hangs a black crepe banner off the railing. We had one on our door after my mother died until one night Father ripped it down. I found him lying on the kitchen floor with the black shreds tangled around his body. The Matron must have died. But she wasn't even sick yesterday. I don't see anyone else, so I step up to the edge of sunlight at the barn entrance. The milk girl raises her head and looks right at me as if I had called to her. She points to her side. I lean farther out the barn door and see two deputies standing wide legged at the end of the roses. Each of them has a shotgun hanging down from under their arms. I step back into the shadow. I didn't steal anything. And I left right on the day I was supposed to. And why do they watch into the house and not away from it?

The boy and I stand together in the shadows. The milk girl hangs two more banners, white ones. A baby who lived on our street cried like a car horn for days and then they hung a white banner on their door when it died. White for children, my uncle told me. I have to lean against the stack of hay. I feel like a barrel with nothing in it, no heart, no lungs, empty. I shouldn't have sent the little one back. Or if the Tallahassee girl has died, I shouldn't have hated her so much. I decide to only think about how to get to the river. I add up the number of feet between us and the back of the main house and how fast we can run and figure we'll be out in front of the men for at least fifteen seconds. They're sure to see us.

The milk girl holds up her hand. Wait, she's saying. She moves to the front steps and coughs. She does it more and louder. I look back through the gaps and see the deputies stand straighter. She comes down one step, and they back up. She coughs more, and it sounds real. She takes another step. The deputies lift their shotguns and point them right at her. They don't shoot, but still the milk girl falls into the gravel. She doesn't even put her hands up to protect her face. She should be in the movies. The men have backed up enough that they won't see us leave the barn. She's given us a chance.

I can't move. Each time I try it feels as if my muscles rip apart. I look to the boy for help, and in my eyes he fades until the light from the cracks in the walls comes all the way through his body and over mine. I blink and blink and he's back. He motions to me, and I follow him past the building, past the kitchen garden with peppers fruiting in a mass of red, yellow, and orange, past the wood shed, and into the wildflower meadow before the woods where dotted horsemint grows to my waist. My skirt sweeps it away as I run into the forest and scrabble down a thicket of holly and sweet bay into the marshy edges of the water.

The creek isn't much of anything right now, so the boy and I can walk the middle. I take off my shoes and stockings and tuck them in the gold cords of my belt. The water comes up around my ankles, and the cold soothes them. My mind feels sorghum thick and my head almost too heavy to hold in place, but I can follow the creek. That's all I have to figure out. I watch my feet kick through the water. It reaches up my knees and weighs down my skirt. The banks get high and the water deeper and I look for a place to climb out. A fallen tree has branches spread like a ladder, and I grab and pull and dig my feet into mud that feels like satin between my toes. My uncle comes into my mind as if we're one person or I'm in two places. He huddles in a hole cut into the bank of a river, and explosions spray water up into his hiding place. Yellow smoke smells like the powder on the superintendent's roses. It makes him vomit. He buries his face in the mud so no one will hear. The bombing slows, and he runs. Just before he leaves my mind, I hear a bomb and feel the earth under his, our, feet heave. My boy whispers from just out of sight above me.

I thought I would remember the way Mami and I took to the spring, but all I see are the flat circles of cut down cypress trees. I crawl onto one and stretch across it like a diameter, but I only reach to the middle. I'm a radius. I smell the bite of cypress and the rancid fumes of left over machine oil. I try counting how many times I cough, but they run all together. We used to take the train on Sundays to the spring and ride the glass-bottomed boats and swim, and I would dive deep into the water again and again. I grab for mouthfuls of air like I did then. The coughing stops and I lay flat on my back.

The cypress used to go up almost farther than I could see. Now I see open sky. The light comes in sideways through small leafy trees and flares across the ground in long lines. I think I see the boy far away in a gold streak of sun. I know he wants us to keep going. He's right, but I have to think about sitting for a long time before my body moves. I roll off the stump and land in a stew of ripped branches mixed with sawdust and brown muck, and I think that maybe these are the tree tops that used to sway and curve into the sky. I stumble through them. The boy stays always ahead of me in a blur of sunlight.

In one step, the woods end, and I'm on a lawn, sleek and green. Benches with hearts carved in the back face the river, and all of them are empty. I can smell cool air and wetness. I see the white curve of a small beach. My teeth shake. Inside, everything is scorched. I pant dry breaths that blister my throat. I am tinder, kindling, like the center of a pine tree. I unlace, unfasten, loosen, and my clothes drop around me. I should be in the water. That's where the boy is waiting.

But it is my grandparents who call to me from the water. They are dancing, and she turns under his upraised arm in a gentle circle. He looks over her shoulder and smiles at me. "Mi vida," he says. They dance down the beach. Maybe my mother is with them. My feet stick to the grass and drag with each step until they sink into the sand and I can't lift them anymore. I sway from side to side and the ground lifts and lowers under me. My boy is behind me now, and his arms steady the earth.

I remember how to raise my feet. My legs wobble and dip my body almost to the ground. The water smells close. I force my legs to move me and don't stop until I'm wet over my knees, and the water clouds from mud dissolving off my feet. Steam leaves my skin and rises into the sky. I look for my grandparents, but they're gone and instead two wood ibis scatter away from me. I walk thigh high into the spring. Another step and water pushes through the curls of hair between my legs. I fall, and the wet goes deeper into me, cooling me from the inside out, and I float with only my toes and breasts and face in the air. My head drops until my scalp wets through. The pain behind my eyes goes away.

I remember Mami washing my body with a soft cloth, and my muscles loosen away from my joints. Above me, the clouds lift into their afternoon towers and their bottoms singe with pink. Underwater grasses stroke down my back and bottom. Minnows gum at my heels. The water pushes me into the shallows, and I'm left sitting waist deep. Spikes of red flowers surround me. Mating dragonflies float through the air like jeweled bracelets. Yellow swallowtails flicker around my nipples.

I lean against a half-sunk log to stand. It bobs under my weight, and a metal oar lock slaps into my palm. The canoe is a tree hollowed out down the middle and burnt in places. The oar locks screw into the old wood and at the bottom used to be a hole, but someone's put a piece of glass over it as a patch. My foot slips in the mud, the boat tilts, and I fall into the well of the canoe. Heat sparks and flares behind my eyes. My insides explode. My head snaps back. Bubbles fall out of my mouth. My legs jerk against the wood over and over, and I can't stop them. The boat moves into the river. My legs collapse, and my body curls around the bottom of the canoe. Sleep presses down on me.

The light has mostly left. Mosquitoes hum over my body, but I can't feel them. Ribbons of grass pass under me. A fish kisses the glass. I can see myself in its eye and in the glass and in the water. My eyes are circled in black like a raccoon or Cleopatra of the Nile. I cough more than thirty times and the mosquitoes scatter and blood smears over the glass. Beyond the blood are rock caves and long black fish that hold still in the cliffs. I close my eyes.

The moon has risen above the trees. The white, almost round circle lights the sand under me. It lights turtles and the silver of fish scales and shows up the red eyes of alligators. Water smacks against the side of the canoe. I'm thirsty. I lap water from the seams around the glass, but I need more. I can break the glass. I raise my arm, and it falls with no power except for its own weight. Where is my boy? My mind goes away.

I'm on my back now. My head hurts. Even after I open my eyes, a veil lays over them. I listen in my mind and around me for the murmur of sueno con los angelos in my ear at bedtime or the tap, tap of soles being repaired in the shop below me. I hear the night wail of a limpkin. I hear owls clack and chatter. When I was little we heard wolves at night. I'd like to hear them again. I hear water churning and my boat shivers. Voices come through the dark.

"See that canoe. Get your pole on it and pull it over."

The boat and I jerk and turn in the current. A fire hangs in the sky, and underneath I see the shadow of a steamboat. My mother and I used to see them on the river. I didn't know they still came. Maybe this steamboat has come for me. I see the upper deck with its fire pan that lights the way. The bent over outline of a man throws logs into the fire. His arms stretch out and a log falls and makes sparks fly into the night. I am hotter than that fire. Maybe they will put me in the water.

"She's a girl. She doesn't have clothes. Someone must have hurt her."

"Look at the feet. They're black. She's dead from that flu. Don't touch anything, don't even breath the air off the body. Let the boat go."

I try to sit, but only a hand waves into the air.

"She's still alive."

"No, don't pull that boat any closer. She's too far gone. Push it away." The canoe and I are released.

The big boat sinks out of the moonlight and wavers like mist into the dark. My canoe bounces through its wake, and we turn in wide, slow circles.

Branches hang over me, and their moon shadows flicker on my skin and on the white iris blooms that lean into the boat. At my feet the bow rocks against the shore and a kerosene glow swings above me.

"Who all's out there? Say your name, or we'll just shoot on account of you disturbing our fish."

The lamp shines into my face and down my body. It lights the tiny cones on the cypress tree, the curled stalks of baby ferns, and my hands that I hold out to the lamp. My fingertips have shapes the same as the ferns, the cones, the moon—the same pattern, the almost round pattern. I can hold it in my mind and everything fits within it and now I am inside a math equation. I feel a hand touch my leg. The touch pulls away with a hiss.

"Wife, move away from her. She has the scourge of sinners. We must pray down the illness. The angel of death is pouring out his cup on the great river Euphrates."

The light shakes. Another voice speaks.

"Oh Lord, support us all the day long, till the shades lengthen and the evening comes." This voice, soft and female, covers my body, but the man's voice interrupts.

"Behold, the Lord will come with fire. God in heaven spare your chosen in these times. The great and terrible day of the Lord is at hand." The man's voice rises in harsh excitement. "If this be the end, take us to our reward." The light moves to my feet. In its circle I see a boot raise and push against the bow.

The boat is set free again. The river takes us down its center. I hear the woman's voice spread out over the water.

"The busy world is hushed, and the fever of life is over, and our work is done."

I gulp and gulp for more air, but the vise in my chest tightens until my spine breaks. I am cold now and no matter how far inside I listen, I'm alone.

.

The moon is gone. The night is almost over. The boat has come to rest along a bank. I can hear the snapping of crabs running along the mud. My dancer lies next to me, and he matches every curve of my body with his. He wraps his arms around me and his breath cools my neck and the pain in my bones goes away. I remember that I know the shape of everything in the whole world, and I think about it deep in my mind until it makes itself into music. My head stops hurting. I don't try to breathe anymore. I can rest.

In the glass we watch the stars blink into the water, sometimes in the eyes of fish, sometimes like candles in a distant window waiting for the last person to come home for the night. We watch until the water lightens to metal grey and the stars fade into the morning. A turtle swims close by my nose. Spirals decorate the fringe of its shell. The day is almost here. Flecks of glimmer green show below us.

In the summer, cardinal lobelia grow in sunlit eddies of the river. The stalks of open-mouthed flowers shake with the black and white stripes, powder blue, oranges from tawny to tangerine, and yellow gauze of butterfly wings. Butterflies taste and smell through their feet. A quick touch on a leaf, a tickle of air from underneath, or a brush of pollen—each is a message, a discernment, a gathering of knowledge.

Half-Boy
1932

Manatees taught me how to swim. Everyone should have such good teachers. Our bodies aren't dissimilar—round, thick, born with no legs the same as me. Every year they, even the babies, swim from the ocean and up the rivers, one hundred and sixty two miles of rivers according to my study of Father's *World Atlas*. The manatees use their paddled tails, but my arms reach longer and flex more. It seemed reasonable that I, even with my body, should learn to, at the very least, float in an eddy.

The manatees don't come here in the summer. Right now they're in the Atlantic Ocean eating kelp and scaring fishermen as they snort to the surface, fishermen who will report that they saw a mermaid. But still, I lie on my back in the water, drop deep into the river, and pretend that I'm resting beside them. White sand puffs into the current wherever I touch the bottom. The eel grass slides into my hair, wraps under my arms, and tickles along my back and into the folds of my body. The trees that hang over the river glaze above me. If I would ever let my breath go, I could stay here forever. But I don't. I never do. The reasons not to change, but today's reason is that I want a drink. My lungs ache in a final way. I race to the surface and gasp for air.

The rum is in the boat. I swim toward shore until my hands can touch bottom. They pull me through the stalks of pickerel weed going to seed. Dragonflies are disturbed into the air. Black wings with flashes of smoky red, and needle-sized sparks of blue dip and soar around me. I flip to sitting in the patch of dry ground beside my boat, and strands of wet plants hang out from my arms as I reach into the stern for the jar. The toffee brown rum with its flecks of gold coats the side of the glass in slow waves. I swirl it again before I unscrew the lid. My usual corn liquor only slaps against the glass. Five quick gulps and my lungs burn until sweat and the smell of clove and burnt wood pushes through my skin from the inside. I drink half-way down the jar. The world goes soft.

It was my twenty-ninth birthday, the night I first watched the manatees. I'd just read the newest Virginia Woolf, *Orlando*, about the man who woke up one day as a woman, and while my parents sang to me I thought about the Cemetery of the United Hebrews of Ocala. Four years before, my father, mother, and I— what was left of our family—pulled the covering off my brother's tombstone. After that, I never left the boundaries of our garden. Before, as a girl light enough to be carried in my mother's arms, I went with her to shops and civic dedications. We had picnics and listened to the bands that played on the square. Sometimes a hand clamped down on my head, and a white-collared man or lady with glistening eyes, their other hand raised to the sky, cried out to their Jesus for my healing. Nothing worse than that happened.

People's reactions changed once I matured the way women do. I'd follow behind my mother, walking on my gloved hands, my hips tilted just up off the ground. My mother sewed the hem of my skirts closed for modesty but still they outlined the shape of my waist and bottom. I had a bosom and long eyelashes and people's pity hardened. They gasped, ran away, or peppered my mother with questions as if I were an unusual breed of dog. One woman screamed. I went out less and less.

But that evening, on my birthday, with the drapes closed over the windows and the lamplight pink against the flowered wallpaper, the ceiling lowered and pressed into my mind. Chairs, sideboards, lace things everywhere crowded too close. I have never screamed, but that's what I felt in my throat. My mother cut the apple cake, and my father suggested I should give my birthday charity money for the education of Negros, perhaps to Howard Academy just down the road. My mother agreed with him. My hands went to my face, one on top of the other, and pressed back the swelling inside me. I bit my lip until it was safe to uncover my mouth. But I had to leave. My parents watched, forks poised, as I dropped off my chair and left the dining room.

I went up the stairs and into my dead brother's room where the dust kicked up around my hands. His clothes still hung in the armoire. I pulled a pair of pants off its hanger and unbuttoned my skirt. The pants legs tied into a knot underneath me. My blouse tucked into the waistband. The straw-banded sailor hat that he had thought the elephant's eyebrows of fashion covered my bob. I went down the stairs fast enough that I somersaulted the last few. My mother rushed to me, but I pushed away her concern, resettled my brother's clothes around me, found the hat where it had tumbled ahead of me, and left, really left—through the iron gate and onto Ocklawaha Boulevard. The full moon lit my way. Men's clothes made me brave. I went farther than I ever had, first down paved then dirt roads to a trail that narrowed. The hard sand under my hands softened, changed to forest loam, to mud, and for the first time, I saw the river that had been there all my life.

I had one moon-shined view of tree branches rugged with ferns, of underwater grasses bent by current, before clouds covered the light. I sat in the dark on the edge of a small bank. Even through the winter air, the plant smell lay thicker and more layered than anything in our garden. Frogs, higher pitched and louder than I'd ever heard, called to each other. Blisters had split open over my palms, and I patted my hands into the warmer-than-air water to sooth them. My eyes relaxed into the night, but I heard and then felt the soft blowing against my palm before I saw the baby. The clouds moved past the moon, and in the creamy light, a mother manatee hovered beyond its child. The baby dropped away from my hands, and they both sank under the water. That night I stayed too scared to touch under the surface again, but I watched the manatees' slow risings and fallings until the first light pulled a mist up out of the water.

I left for home before the roads filled with people. My mother still sat in her parlor chair, asleep with a book open over her lap. I shouldn't have worried her, but I knew I'd do it again. She woke and saw the way the soft Italian leather gloves from my father's store hung in blood-tinged shreds. She bathed my hands in marigolds from the garden while she chatted about her clubs, the food drive she was organizing, and how hard my father worked. She asked me nothing, but the next night I found a pair of her garden gloves laid out on my bed.

That first winter I returned to the river every day and petted the noses that bobbed beside me. I studied our atlas to trace the manatees' voyage. I watched for the long time they could stay on the bottom without breathing and tried to match it and made my lungs stronger and stronger. Through the next year I read everything I could about swimming. I memorized books with complicated diagrams. I practiced in my bathtub and on my bed. I watched how things work on the river—where alligators choose to feed and where they don't, that turtles mostly scare away, that the silver-backed birds can swim under the water. That next birthday, in private celebration, I stripped and slid otter-like down the bank.

Sometimes not having legs is an advantage. The mud was cold against my bare belly and slick enough that I skimmed far out over the water. Then I sank. I hung face down under the surface with my arms spread. The winter sunlight rifled through the water past me and lit up the geometry of a turtle shell in the underwater grasses. When I felt the first pull in my lungs, I arched the middle of my body and vaulted through the water. I was swimming. The babies came from behind their mothers to see me. That day, for the first time, I felt their stiff whiskers on my belly and smelled the spoiled plant smell of their breath when our heads lifted out of the water together. My father saw me come home that evening. He saw my wet hair, the disarray of my clothes and all he asked me about was the path I took to the river. The next day he left a rowboat on my bank with a backrest nailed into the seat for balance.

I'm in my boat. The bow has wedged into downed branches. It happens sometimes when I'm drinking, this not remembering what I've just done. I'm in the boat and I'm dressed. The overall straps twist over my shoulders and the shirt tail sticks up my back. I check to make sure I've wrapped my breasts flat. The light filters low through the trees, and soon the alligators rise to hunt. I reach for the oars, but don't mange a firm grip and they twist out of their sockets. My hands smash against each other. The booze sloshes in the jar, the boat wobbles, and I tilt to the side. The boat takes in a splash of water but rights itself. I jerk backwards, and it floats free into the river. I have no destination or plan. I'm tired. I cross the oars in front of me and drink more. The current turns the boat. The late afternoon air is thick with heat. It presses my eyes closed.

"Lookee there. Half-boy is passed-out blotto. Hey, half-boy, you row that boat over by here and give us some of your moonshine."

I keep my eyes shut since I've found it best to ignore little boys. The shaft of the oar dents into my forehead where I'm bent over. Cicadas sound like a thousand sewing machines. The clacking rises and falls and pulls through my head from one ear to the other in sheets of sound. Without moving, I'm dizzy. Sweat has stiffened my clothes.

"Hey, freak show. Wake up."

Clay splatters over my cheek. One of them has a good aim. My eyelids stick as I lift them. I reach into the water and splash it over my face and around my neck. The boat gives to one side, and I put a hand over each edge to steady. I'm facing the boys and watch while they dig into the bank for more ammunition. My arms have gone numb. I work the sleep out of them until I can grip the side of the boat and swing my body upright and back to center. Still in the air, I shake until the layers of cotton batting my mother sews into the closed-off overalls fall into place underneath me. I drop onto the seat and reattach a buckle that has come loose.

"What'cha doing?"

I've forgotten about the boys. And the river moved me too close to shore. The bigger boys reach over the water and can almost touch my boat.

"Is that some sort of cripple dance like in the circus? Hey, you got any man parts left under there?" The boy's voice has been show-off deep, but it cracks high. His friends turn to poke and tease him, and while they do, I slip the oars into the water, brace against the backrest, and paddle away. They notice.

"Half-boy, come back here. Come on, we'll show you ours."

The line of them have unbuttoned their pants. They waggle small penises and laugh. I'm on my second generation of little boys. It seems that any of their parents who remember that I'm a woman haven't told them. No one's yelling Mockie or Jew boy, so this particular batch doesn't know about that either. They might not be local. Last year just men arrived here, dusty and hungry, and settled in Hooverville shanties near the railroad, but the paper said more and more boys travel on their own and they've become packs. I row until I'm out of sight.

My head still hurts. During all this, the jar has rolled into the bow. I don't remember any sound of glass breaking, but I lean over to make certain. My copy of *Room of One's Own* kicks out of my bib pocket, and it falls into the puddle along the keel line. I grab it up before the cover soaks through and shove it back deeper. The river lifts over a fallen log and the jar clatters out of the bow and rolls back to me. I take a sip, and another, and my head improves. There's very little left. A business friend of my father's came for dinner and after, when he had gone, I came out of my room and found the rum bottle on the china buffet. I poured half of it into a jar. But now I'll need money to buy more.

Only liquor helps with how my shoulders and arms hurt. It works as a salve deep in my joints. I started by watering down the stock my father kept for company, but one day I looked up, nervous, from pouring, and saw our gardener watching through the window. The next time we passed in the yard, he offered to supply me, for a price. I'll tell my father I need the money for books. Last time, I hinted at new undergarments, and he blushed and almost threw money at me. I'm becoming more skilled at this. I suppose stealing is the honest word for it. One time, early on, I told him I needed new pens. That was a mistake, because he sells them in his stores. He brought a set home made of orangewood and carved with the shapes of alligators playing violins. Before the alcohol, before I needed so much of it, I would have been enchanted. Nevertheless, I pretended well enough to please the both of us.

One more sip, a last-for-now sip, and one more sip. I screw the lid back on. The boys are two river curves out of hearing. I find an eddy to rest in and boat the oars. Virginia Woolf waits. The river water warped the cover, but the pages stayed dry. Still, my eyes blur the letters into wavering doubles. I squint and blink and can make out words, but sentences elude me. Besides, Virginia Woolf doesn't understand my life. I already have a room—on the ground floor, behind the kitchen, away from the rest of the house, and with a separate door to the garden. My father had a downstairs water closet and bath combined built next to it. "So the stairs, they're not a bother," he said, even though he knows I lift up the porch steps with no effort. On generous days I think they just want me to have adult privacy. But I don't need a room of my own. I need the rest of the world.

Sometimes in summer, like today when it hasn't stormed, the heat holds on into the evening. Soaking my wrists in the spring water cools my blood. I lift up handfuls to drink and splash on my face. I loosen one button of my shirt and slap a wet hand against my chest. Water drips down and under my breast bindings. I dip my hands in the water one more time, shake them dry, and pull men's work gloves out of my pocket. I found them and a man's broadcloth shirt in the back shed where my father keeps his grandfather's old tinker's wagon. The "source of our family fortune" he says. The boat drifts into the woods where the river has overflowed its banks, and the evening swarms of mosquitoes descend from the shadows. They sting along the pulses in my wrists, and I pull the gloves as far up as they can go. I flip the shirt collar and set my work cap low. I unscrew the jar's lid for another sip.

Mosquitoes I can guard against, but people, mostly I avoid them. I roam at night. My parents never say anything, but a Rayovak light appeared in my room, and then overalls, and then, outside my door, a board with wheels, like a flat bed rail car, only just big enough for me to sit on. My father keeps talking about getting me a wheelchair. "So light, they fold, these new ones, you can push yourself even." I don't argue with him, but the board works better. I think he just wants me up higher. As if my head level with people's chests rather than their privates will make me normal.

I only use the flashlight during the new moon. I don't like being visible. In the dark I've seen night riders, packed six to a car with rifles sticking out the side, wind over the dirt roads looking for Negros too far from home. I hide from them in the palmettos and sometimes there's the rattle of someone else doing the same. Once, I saw a woman in a green silk dress dance with a man in the headlight beams of their car. A portable phonograph on the seat of the convertible played a smooth voice singing about his sweetheart. Breezers, my brother used to call those cars. He wanted one. I watched the man's hands slide over and under the silk and understood more about my brother. A lot of sex happens. I've heard sounds from the inside of everything from broken down flivvers to Cadillacs. Around bonfires men on their own smoke herb and talk about bitch kitties and vamps. Other nights, dogs and wild pigs chase after me.

The mosquitoes swarm around the uncovered space under my ears and where the material pulls tight over the back of my arms. It hurts, but in a distant way. Ossified, embalmed, owled, plastered—that's what my brother called it when he'd visit with me in my room after a night out jiving. Mosquitoes fly into the corners of my eyes and others try to catch my breath before it even leaves my nose. I brush along my face, but hit myself more than them. They won't follow me to open water. I row out from the forest and toward the other bank.

"Great arms, boy."

A white man's voice, unfamiliar, and not from around here, comes from behind me, from the far shore. I button myself to the top and backwater the boat until it faces and stays away from the bank. Two young men stand at ease with their long legs and a sureness of their place in the world, in this forest, on the river. They both have hair brilliantined back from their faces in a long black shine. One has a shirt banded in purple and red with white diamonds patched into the pattern. The colors glow in the low light, and a scarf flows down his front. He's a Seminole Indian. I've only read about them, but he's a picture in a book come alive except he's not wearing a skirt, just pants same as the other man. I really want to see if he's wearing regular boots or moccasins, but he's not a picture in a book, so I stop staring at him. Both men hold sacks down away from their bodies. The bags squirm, and I know snakes when I see them. The white man has the widest chest I've ever seen. This must be who's setting up a reptile show near the head springs. The paper said they're going to have Indians wrestle alligators. That made Mother talk again about how it used to be that only the finest people, royalty even, visited Silver Springs. She says they came from Europe to escape their

wars and their coal-tainted air and find a sublime experience
with nature. Mother always lets her eyelashes flutter when she
says "sublime."

"Hey, boy. Do you need a job? I could use a good snake
wrangler and you sure have the strength for it."

Of course I've never had a job. These days even able-bodied
men don't have jobs. He's missing a few things about me. I'll start
with the no legs part. I let the boat drift closer, so they can see
over the edge. I fish the Lucky Strikes and my lighter out from
a pocket. This way I'll not watch them while they figure things
out, and they'll have a little privacy to rearrange their faces. I tap
a fag out of the pack and bend my head to light it. I cup a hand
around my face to protect the flame from a non-existent wind.

"Share a coffin nail?" The white man's voice sounds regular.
The Indian isn't saying anything, but in the westerns I've read,
they don't talk much so his silence might not be shock, just his
way. I snap the lighter shut and look at them. I can tell they
haven't seen, so I row close enough to offer them both cigarettes.
They loop their sacks over a tree limb and come sit on the bank.
Behind them, the snakes struggle and stretch the cloth to its
limits, and the bags spin in the air. The white man sees me
looking.

"Rattlesnakes. I've got this idea to milk them and make an
antidote. I'll ship it to doctors. And then I'll can the meat and
sell it to fancy food stores in the cities, even over to Europe. No
matter what, even now, rich people want their special stuff and
have the money to pay for it."

His resentment makes me lower my eyes.

"In the meantime, there's my show. Have you heard about
it?"

I nod.

"Just this week my anaconda arrived from Venezuela. She's twenty feet long and a real bear cat. And no dumb oil can of a female, either. I can tell she's thinking, all the time, of how to best kill me. A young buck like you could get in the pool and wrestle her. I mean I'll do it most days, but you could be my relief. Those tin can tourists would go ape over it, and you'd get paid decent. And Joe Jimmie here says best thing is to train them young. He wrestled alligators from when he was a bitty thing. Not that you'll get that sort of training. They keep it in the family. Don't you, friend?"

I hold out the lighter, and the Indian leans into the boat. Our eyes meet and he rolls his as the other man keeps batting his gums about snakes and how their venom is orange and thick like orange juice. So, maybe this isn't so much an Indian thing. Maybe this Joe Jimmie just never gets the chance to talk. He smiles at me. They don't do that in the stories. He lowers his head to light his cigarette and sees into my boat. Now his face goes the stoic way they describe it. He sits back on the bank. I need to say something.

"A woman in town has a cooperative canning factory. I'm sure she can accommodate your rattlesnake meat." I shouldn't have said this. She and my mother were suffragettes together, and she knows who I am, that I'm from wealth, that I'm a woman. This is getting complicated, but it doesn't matter. In the next minutes, he's going to figure out the body stuff and take back the job. But I'm already ahead of anything I've ever done just talking to an Indian who wrestles alligators and this guy who's snake crazy.

"That's swell news. Hey, Joe Jimmie, this boy is already earning his clams, and he's well-spoken to boot. Now, an anaconda is a constrictor. Not that they won't bite you and it hurts like piss, but there's no poison. And as long as she doesn't get more than one coil around a leg, you're okay. And I'd be right there to help if she got away from us. How about it? Want to give it a bash?"

He leans into the boat for his light and sees me all over. His eyes stop as they reach where my legs should be. He drops his cigarette, and in the last light of the day, in the perfect, clear water, we both watch the white paper go translucent and show the flakes of tobacco underneath. We watch fish poke it from side to side as it drifts to the bottom. He sits back onto the bank.

"Sorry, son. I can't hire you. I know the freak shows are popular, and there's even that movie about ya'll they just made, but, no disrespect, that's not the direction I want to go in. I'm trying to be as educational as we are entertaining. Like Joe Jimmie and me, we're going to do a study of alligators in the wild. No one really knows much about them. Anyway, sorry again. So, are you visiting up from Tampa way? What's that town where ya'll circus people live? I went there once to fish and met the Giant on the river. He and his wife are good folk. She's only half, same as you. I saw her do that show where she climbs ladders upside down. Hey, are you related?"

"No, I live locally." I gulp, hold my breath, press my tongue into the roof of my mouth, but still, I'm about to cry. To be fired, I can't believe how bad it feels. And, for me, it was only for two minutes of my life that I was a person with a job. I lower my head and pretend to reset an oar in its lock. I make myself think about everything he said after he fired me. What movie is he talking about? And there's another woman like me just a few hours away? I've never left this place, but I could. On the maps, Tampa isn't far. My father could hire someone to drive me. My ex-employer keeps talking about lobster boys and midgets, and I arrange my face to look as if I'm listening. Maybe my father can find the movie and set up a showing at our house the way he did for my last birthday when he handed me the newspaper's theatre listing and said to pick one. I chose the Marx Brothers, even though I really wanted *All Quiet on the Western Front*. I thought it might explain what happened to my brother in the war. But it would have been too hard on my parents. Instead, we watched *Animal Crackers* twice through and laughed all night. My ex-employer has come closer and holds onto my bowline. I pay attention.

"But, if I think about it, I need someone to strip skins and chop the meat for canning. All you'd need different is a table with its legs cut down." He slaps the bow and the bottle of rum rolls down the length of the boat. I snatch it back. Now I have to offer some to him. Men do this. I tilt the jar his way, and our fingers cross over each other as he reaches. I've touched men before— my father, my brother. Doctors have touched me. In books, characters say their skin melted into his. I never understood that. I've never wanted to hold on. I stretch my arm toward him to keep our fingers together for as long as I can. He tilts the jar and closes his eyes in appreciation. I watch all the small movements of his face. His temples flatten, his cheeks suck in. I follow the rum down his throat and see the cording of his neck.

"Whew. That's fine panther sweat. And smoother than anything I've been getting around here."

"Rum from the West Indies. They have speedboats that come across to Jacksonville and then all the way up the rivers. This could have come from Jamaica or Trinidad. Or the Bahamas." Now, I'm talking too much and my voice sounds too high. Is he giving me some sort of job back? I offer the jar to the Indian. He shakes his head. I think maybe he knows that I'm a woman. And I shouldn't have said that about the booze. West Indies rum is expensive. He's only offering me a job because he thinks I need one. And that I'm male.

"How about you come by my place midmorning, and we'll see about it all. That is unless you make a habit of this giggle water here."

I shake my head and wedge the jar behind me. If I have a job, I'll cut back.

"I hear say that they're going to repeal that law pretty soon, and we'll be buying it in stores again. Who are your people around here?"

I don't want to answer any questions. I slide the oars through the water.

"So, tomorrow. I'll be there. Thanks for the job. Much appreciated." I need to row away. These days, at thirty-three, I'm losing my boyish good looks to wrinkles and a womanly softening around the neck. I see it whenever I look into the river. He'd have noticed in full daylight, which it will be at some point tomorrow. Although people just see what they want to see. I'm not going to think ahead. Even if he fires me at first look, it doesn't matter. Tonight, I'm an employed person. I leave the men sitting on the bank and only paddle around the next curve. I can still hear them.

"Life sure took that boy for a ride." The white man's voice is matter-of-fact. "Now, how about your mother? Do you think she'll agree to ya'll moving the village here for the winters? I'd have chickee lumber already cut. And I'd throw in a couple of pole barns for her sewing machines. You know it'd be a good situation."

Two owls chatter to each other for awhile before the Indian answers.

"I've heard it gets colder here in the winter than in Big Cypress. She might not like that."

"Okay, blankets. I'll promise blankets."

Another pause. There's the long splash of an alligator sliding into the water.

"She always says that children need meat to stay healthy."

The white man, my boss, replies right away.

"Hey, the newspaper this week had an article about the over four thousand deer around here, more than in a long time. And loads of turkeys. That will do you, don't you think?"

"My mother says this is unfamiliar land and not friendly to Indians. And she mentioned many times how much the tourists like our palmetto dolls and carved canoes and how fast her children can make them. And that this would be the most north our family has traveled since the wars."

"Oh, man, your mother sure knows how to jew a deal. Let's see. I can provide a meat serving a week, but wild pig mostly. And I'll go fifty-fifty on the craft sales. And I'm hiring a bunch of her men for the show. Now don't tell me that's not the best deal of any of the exhibition places."

This pause is the longest. The river stays quiet.

"Did you know that my great-grandfather fought against your American Army right here at the Springs? When we ran out of ammunition, we hung water moccasins from the trees with deer hide straps."

"Is that a yes?"

"My mother will say. But you've answered all her questions. We need to get those snakes back."

I let the river pull me farther down stream. If I'm too close to the headsprings, the glass bottom boats pass by with all their tourists crowded around the edges. One of them always notices me, and then come the whispers and suddenly their boat lists to one side from me having become another oddity to stare at. Some days I just think of myself as a wonder of nature like an alligator covered in her babies or a scarlet hibiscus rising eight feet out of the swamp and festooned with butterflies. Tonight I row under an ash tree until I'm hidden. There's no hiding from the mosquitoes, but I'm covered except for around my face, and the cigarette smoke will take care of that. I'll wait here until the moon rises to light my way home. In the meantime, there's a jar of good rum to finish.

What would Virginia Woolf think about all this? Or my friend, the one who sends me my books. I've always been tutored at home, privately, except for one year when a colleague of my father's, they were much more observant than my family, anyone is more observant than we are, had his daughter study with me. They didn't want her around boys. I gave her the heebie jeebies at first, but we started talking. Neither of us had ever been to the movies or to a dance, but she shopped in stores and had picnics by the river and wore a dress with a zipper on the side. I'd never seen a zipper before. In return, I impressed her with the books I'd read and that I'd voted once. I told her all about it. How my mother made them let me that first year women were allowed. That the poll workers tried to stop me the way they did the Negros with the poll tax and the reading test, and they said the booths were too high for me. I didn't want to be there, but they spoke rudely to my mother, so I read everything they wanted me to and then translated it into Latin and then Greek. I pulled a chair over to a booth, flipped up into it, and voted. My mother cried. I don't think it was about me. She never marched with a gold banner across her chest, but my mother opened her home for meetings and gave money. And then, less than a year before the amendment passed, so many of her suffragist friends died from the flu. The paper filled first with obituaries and then, later, because there wasn't enough space, just lists of names. We don't talk about it. I've never read about it in any book or magazine. You might not know it ever happened.

That story made us friends. It was strange to be the worldlier one in some ways. Our favorite book is still *Kristin Lavransdatter*. We read all three volumes together. We gave each other pet names from the story and still use them in our letters to each other as if we were both women in medieval Norway. Only, even at my age, I'm stuck before *The Bridal Wreath*, and she's deep into *The Mistress of Husaby* with her children and estate to run. Her family moved to New York where there were more like them, and they found her a man almost the same as in the old days when my grandmother came from Lithuania to marry someone she'd never met. My friend says she's happy. Her husband works at a publishing house and provides her with books to send to me. My whole family, including the cook, loves the mysteries. If one is wrapped separately in brown paper, I know to open it in my room. Once it was *Ulysses*, and right here, on this little river, in this row boat, over an entire winter, I read a proscribed book. She told me she promised her husband not to read it, just to wrap it for me. She's fierce with him about my books, and it seems that if she stays in certain limits she always gets her way. Emma Goldman's autobiography is why I always carry a book with me everywhere. Not that I expect to need something to pass the time while I'm in jail, the way she does. The last brown paper book was *The Well of Loneliness*. Neither of us said anything to each other about that one.

She's the only person I've ever kissed. It had been in August, and we lay across my bed almost in a faint from the heat building in advance of the afternoon thunderstorms. When lightning glared through the room we startled and turned to each other. Her lips tasted of sweat and the mint tea we'd been sipping to keep cool. Maybe that's why I've never told her about dressing like a man or about drinking and smoking and staying out all night on the river. I tip the rum and drain the last drops. I reach into my overalls and think about the kiss, about the small twists of hair on the snake man's knuckles, about how men, close up, have a smell that catches in the throat. I finger down into the places that feel good, but I've drunk too much. I light another cigarette off the one that's almost gone.

The moon is high enough that light scatters through the branches screening me from the river. Pig frogs grunt near the shore. The muscles in my face fall lax until the cigarette droops, and my eyes close to slits. I could sleep now, just for awhile, before going home. The frogs hold their breath for a moment, and I hear a low growl. I think alligator until I hear the slow rhythm of an engine, and a speedboat sneaks around the curve. The polished wood of the hull shines slick in the moonlight, and the white stripe painted along the water line reflects and wavers in the river. The men behind the wheel are the darkest-skinned of Negro. The boat slips back into shadow. The engine shuts off. A cigarette butt glows with each inhalation like the single eye of an alligator, and I smell its foreign perfume. I let mine hiss into the water.

I've heard of these rum runners. Grenada, Montserrat, Jamaica, and the Saints—Kitts, Lucia and Vincent—Cuba, Haiti, Tobago . . . The names from the atlas circle my mind in their miniscule script. I duck behind more branches. Wood scrapes against wood, water splashes, and men speak in whispered French. I can read French and speak a little. "Pardon me." "Nice night." "I mean no harm." I should know how to say all this in French. I hold my jaw tight, press my fingers into my cheeks, my temples, but not a word comes to mind. Their boat drifts back into the moonlight. There are guns. One is held loosely at a thigh, and the other wedges into a belt while the man tries to pole the boat upstream. I'm thinking clearly again. I remember *bonsoir* and *excusez-moi*. I understand that they've planned on coming up the rest of the way silent, but don't know about the river being high. The boat slips backwards in the current. The second man puts his gun in a pocket in order to lift another pole over the side. They'll have to get closer to shore to find a bottom to push against. They figure it out, because the engine starts. The boat heads right at me.

I close my eyes like I did as a child to make myself invisible. I hear a pole finally scrape bottom and a grunt as the man leans into it. The engine shuts down, and the weight of their boat moves water under mine and I rock. I brace for the touch of our bows, for the yelling. I should at least open my eyes and take whatever comes like a man. That's funny. I work hard not to giggle out loud. The French words for "don't shoot, I'm a woman" stick on my lips. I open my eyes just as a pole reaches through the branches and scrapes against the side of my boat. The man hesitates. A frog sounds like a finger running across a comb. The man lifts his pole. I close my eyes again.

The gun is louder than close thunder. I wait for it to hurt. I wait for hands to grab my boat. I wait for the next shot. It comes, as I now realize the first one did, from behind me. It sounds far way, but is close enough that air pushes against my cheek the same as when a flock of ibis fly past. I don't hurt anywhere. I open my eyes, and a man on the boat is flung backwards and tumbles over the side. I don't hear the splash, and I didn't hear the shot. Something half smothers my hearing. But I can see. A long line of moonlight follows his body down into the thicket of underwater grasses and glows orange against the plume of blood that spreads downstream.

The other man is nothing but a gun tilted up from behind the hull and pointed at me. His fingernails press white around the grip. Gunfire passes around me in waves of burnt air and brown smoke. I can hear again as a voice shouts for me to get down, but I can't stop watching. Bullets hit over and over into the side of the speedboat. It spins from their impact and jerks back into the flow of the river. The boat moves downstream as fast as if the motor had caught. It rounds a corner. The shooting stops. A great rush of movement sounds along the bank behind me. And the final boat man must still be alive because I hear the motor start.

"Clovis. Big Al. Go get the skiff and pinch him between our boys waiting downstream.   Don't sink the boat until we get the load off it." The bushes snap and crush. The voice is familiar.

"What about the ofay girl there?" This voice is unknown to me.

"I'll take care of her."

Our gardener, in a tone harsher than I've ever heard, has said these words. He wouldn't hurt me. He and my father are friends best that white and black can manage. Both their boys fought in the Great War, both made it back, and both died sort of because of it. His son got shot outside a jive joint mostly because he came home from fighting and didn't remember the way things work around here. Or he did remember and just kept pushing until he got someone to kill him. He wasn't much different than my brother, who came home half-dead in his mind and then finally hung himself. The gardener cut my brother down from the attic rafter and kept the secret from outsiders. And my father paid for his son's funeral. He wouldn't hurt me. But I should row out of here.

I put the oars in the water, but he grabs the stern and slides me close. He speaks over my shoulder in that same voice, like he's the boss.

"Miss. Those there were bad men and these be bad times. There's no allowing strangers to jack business away from hard-working locals. You're drunk. You can't be sure of anything. Best

for you if you just go on and unremember all this. And your
father would want you to forget. Do you understand what I
mean?"

His breath heats my neck. It smells of cigar and bacon. No
Negro has ever spoken to me in this manner. What does he mean
about my father? I nod my head.

"All right, then, miss. Now get on home and bury your head
in those books. Your mother is a kind lady. You shouldn't worry
her so much." He gives my boat a hard shove, and branches
scrape around my head and shoulders until I'm in the open.

I'm free. I row against the current as hard as I can and slide
backwards through the moon shadows of trees. Fish jump and
silver through the air. Before, I would have thought that I was
the only person on the river. The lightning-scarred cypress, the
one too damaged for loggers, marks the edge of my landing. I
turn the boat until it scrapes onto the narrow curve of sand. The
jar rolls under my seat, and I lean down to it. I unscrew the lid
and lick inside the rim for the last drops before I rinse it in the
river until it doesn't smell of anything. Sometimes my father uses
the boat to fish, and I tell him the jar is for bailing. He's already
had too much pain from his children. What did the gardener
mean that my father would want me to forget?

My board is where I left it. I settle on top, drop my hands to
the ground, and roll my shoulders forward for leverage. My body
slides through my arms, and I lean forward again and push again
until the wheels underneath spin into a steady hum. Usually I
rest many times during the trip home, but tonight I pump my
arms until the casters flutter and skid the board over the road as
if it could fly. I don't stop until I reach the front gate. I lean on
the wrought iron vines wrapped around the pickets. A light still
shows from the living room. The gate is well oiled and quiet, and

I slip into the shadow of my father's Studebaker and slow until
my wheels are noiseless on the macadam path he had laid around
the house to my back door.

I can see just their heads through the window. If they're up
this late, it means my mother is almost to the end of her mystery,
Dashiel Hammet this time, and won't stop until she finishes. My
father will never go to bed without her. He has the newspaper or
a ledger book open over his lap and pretends to read. His head
drops against the back of the chair. Like that, with his mouth
open and his face slack, he looks old. I count up the years. He's
sixty, and the almanac says on average men don't live past their
early fifties. His head drops to the side, and I feel sick all over.
I rush to a far corner of the yard to throw up behind the hedge
of yellow anise. The smell of licorice from the leaves calms my
stomach. Average means half which means many men live much
longer. I go back to the path and look one more time through
the window. My mother stands over my father. She kisses his
forehead. I move past the window, around the corner, and pause
on the top step of my door. An owl sounds from the chinaberry
tree, and I moan and pull at my clothes as if my father were
already gone.

When I know anything again, I'm leaning against the door
in the deep night. I open the latch and fall into the room. A
light has been left on, and newly-altered clothes perch at the
end of my bed. I take off my gloves and hat and touch the vase
of fresh-cut red and purple salvia on the dresser. I imagine my
mother and the gardener, companionable and talking about
mulch and soil and aphids, cutting them for the house—our
gardener who bosses a gang. I slide the bar until it locks into
place on the outside door. A gang of thieves. I roll into bed and
push the new dresses to the side. I loosen the binder around my

breasts. The bedside light has an orange tinge this time of night, a brighter orange than the hue of blood under water. Thieves and murderers. I turn off the light. And my father might be involved.

I can smell coffee from the kitchen. I'm still in my clothes from last night. It doesn't bother me anymore how my mouth feels after drinking or how thirsty I get, and without fully waking up, I know to rush to the bathroom. I manage not to vomit, but I sit surrounded by white porcelain and rock to the beat of pain inside my head. All the small bones in my hands ache and my shoulders hurt enough to make me whimper. I'll stay in my room today. I'll finish Virginia Woolf and then read my father's Tarzan novel while he's at work. I wish we had stronger vines in our trees. Mid imaginary swing, I remember. I have a job. How could that not have been the first thing I thought this morning? I need a bath.

I unbuckle my overall straps and feel the grit of gunpowder under my fingers. The gardener's voice is in my ear, as stern as a white man's, and I remember the rest of it. I wish I knew more about the world. I'd know more of what to do, of how to feel. Will this make getting liquor easier or harder? I feel immoral thinking this way. That I have a job is more real to me than seeing someone shot. I can't make that be more than a story in a book. The gun becomes a piece, the liquor, tarantula juice, and death is the big one. The dead man is a stiff and no more than one of the minor characters that the author added just for a little excitement. We're not supposed to care about him. And besides, they were criminals. Is it even illegal to steal illegal goods?

I strip down and run the hottest water that I can even though the summer heat has held on through the night. It will soak

the booze smell out of me. It will make me clean. I ease into
the water, and it burns into the scraped places and bruises. My
mother has lined the edges of the tub with jars of perfumed salts
and oils, but I can't risk smelling that sweet today. A soaped cloth
lifts the dirt from my body. It floats into the water and grips the
edge of the tub in a grey line. The steam fills with the smell of
lavender from the soap, alcohol sweat, and gunfire, and my head
spins until I'm too dizzy to lift out of the tub. I open the drain.
I run the cold faucet even though I know the water will stay
lukewarm and have a musty smell. Still, I splash it over my body
until my head clears.

The air hangs almost as wet as the tub water, and I can't get
dry even sitting in front of the fan. I open the outside door for
ventilation and there, on the top step, a whole gallon jug waits,
one of my mother's zinnias wrapped around the handle. I reach
a bare arm out and bring it inside. I've seen men in the night,
around a fire, twist a jug until its weight rests on their shoulder
while they drink. I brace against the pull of my muscles and, with
an awkward tilt of a forearm, the liquid pours into my mouth. It
smells like a doctor's office, but my body eases.

With the door open a handbreadth, I sit in the narrow breeze
and sliver of sun until I'm dry. I put cream under my breasts
where the fungus gets them in the summer and wrap them in a
fresh, tight binder. Flattening isn't the style anymore, but they
still offer them in the ladies' catalogues. I put on a blue silk
blouse with a gathered bodice and bunched sleeves that hide my
arm muscles. Today, before I leave for my job, I want to spend
time as the daughter of my family, to sit at the breakfast table
with my parents and talk about the day to come, the world,
the neighbors. I walk to the dining parlor in ladies' gloves, blue
to match my blouse. From the hall I can hear them discussing
the morning paper with each other as they always do, but their

voices weigh heavy with an odd formality. My father speaks as I enter.

"Sholtz might win. If you don't mind, the butter please. Imagine, a landsman as governor."

"I've read that he's in tight with gambling interests, dear."

"Wife, they all get their money somewhere. The difference is what they do with it. I'd think you'd be for him since he's strong for education."

I lower my body. Moving is easier if I tilt it up behind me, but it bothers them. Not proper, my mother says. And I walk around the table rather than under it to get to my seat. They both go quiet and avert their eyes until after I've climbed into the chair. I used to think they looked away because I repulsed them, but now I don't think that. I think, in their minds, they are always considerate of me. I take off my gloves and fold them fingertips to fingertips.

"Some coffee, Daughter?" Her voice is more tender than usual. I worry that she knows something she couldn't possibly know.

"Yes, Mother."

I avoid her eyes and reach for a piece of the newspaper that they've folded and put to the side. For weeks, each of us reading silently, then putting the paper down silently, we've followed the story of the Great War veterans camping out around the Capitol demanding payment of their bonuses. The pictures of those tired, aged men—is that how my brother would look now, if he had lived? Today, there's a photograph of a tank with the White House in the background. General MacArthur keeps threatening that he's going to "clean out" the camps. What's he going to do, shoot them?

I flip open the paper to the article below the picture and skim through it. This can't be right. I go back to the top and read every word and still it says that American soldiers gassed and shot and rolled tanks over American veterans. The edge of the paper crumbles in my fist.

"Here you are, dear." My mother pours the coffee and adds three spoonfuls of sugar without a comment about my teeth. We look at each other, each through our own gauze of tears. My mother turns away and smoothes her page of newsprint flat.

"Parker's is closing their store. 'No other way out' they say. Every week another one. I'm so glad you didn't get caught up in all that land speculation, dear. But be honest with your family, do we need to conserve a bit?"

While she chats, Mother reaches around the table and weighs down a plate with eggs, fried turkey, mayonnaise muffins, and a dollop of smoked whitefish that she taught the cook to make from the flounder shipped here from Tampa. Maybe I could take the fish truck to Tampa and find those people like me. Mother has set the plate under my nose. I crumble off an edge of muffin with my fingers. I know from experience that if I can eat this, I'll feel better. My father reaches over and pats my mother's hand.

"We shouldn't be ostentatious. Just not to attract attention. But we're not to worry. Think of what we've already survived— the big fire, the freezes, the phosphate mine bust. This is nothing. Here in the paper, look. The new commerce secretary says the depression has run its course." He lifts his hand away from my mother's and fingers through the gap in his vest to fiddle with a button from behind. This particular gesture means he's lying.

Mother and I look at each other. Her eyes glaze, and I know she's trimming the house budget in her head. I'll do my part. To begin with, I'll suggest that she tell him to hold off on the wheelchair. I smile and eat a piece of fried turkey. We divide the rest of the paper between us. My sheet has three Olympic swimmers, women, with their arms around each other—

breaststroke, one hundred meter free style, and spring board diver. I'd be good at the breaststroke.

"Tell me, Wife. Do you think Roosevelt will save us? I'm not sure about all the handouts he proposes. Maybe I'll vote Republican this year."

My mother bristles and shakes her knife at him before she realizes that he's teasing.

"Applesauce. You, who give credit to every family in Ocala and have hired so many extra servants that I don't know what you do with them all, and I know you send food down to the shanty town by the railroad. Don't talk to me about handouts."

"People will do anything necessary for their families, no matter what the law. So best give them food or a job. It protects us. Even with the patrollers at the Georgia border, more sneak by every day. I met a man from Idaho and another from Rhode Island and another from Oregon. And sometimes, women on their own with children. Don't get that look, Wife. You are not to go there. The danger is too great. Even I only go with the gardener and a few of his friends."

My fork stops mid arc between my plate and my mouth, and fried egg fills the view of my half-lidded eyes. I picture my father at the lead of the group of Negros. My hand shakes and eggs drip onto the tablecloth. Through the daze of leftover alcohol, last night is not just a story. My throat closes against a sudden nausea.

"Daughter, are you ill?"

"No, Mother. Just hot." Did a man really get killed in front of me? Does my father know?

"Cook, bring some cold water from the Frigidaire. And here, have some iced pickles." My mother can be loud when needed. Although, right now I'd prefer quiet more than a cool cloth. "You must have care, my dear. Remember what the doctor said about having fewer sweat glands, and this is a terribly hot summer."

My father pays a lot of attention to buttering his muffin. Both he and I would always prefer it if she didn't talk about my sweat glands. Without raising his head, my father shifts the conversation.

"Here's some good news from Germany. Remember that man Hitler who ranted about 'national honor?' He didn't get enough votes to be Chancellor. I worry when politicians become nationalists. But this one has had a setback."

"Cook, the ice." My mother yells again. My father calls this her Baltic fishwife voice. I sip water to settle my stomach but everything smells of gunfire.

"Mother, I'll just go lie down."

"Daughter, wait."

"Yes, Mother?" Can she tell what I'm thinking? She used to be able to.

"Don't forget your gloves. A woman needs to keep her hands soft."

Sometimes all I can do is stare at her. We both suffer when the fantasy daughter she holds in her mind leaks through. But I take the gloves that she's handing down to me, put them on, and scurry under the table and into the hall before she can say anything else. I do go to my room, but only to change clothes. I won't think about last night. I have a job. It won't last. I know this. But I might not be found out for awhile. People prefer not to acknowledge me. And it sounds as if he's going to keep me hidden from view. I wonder how long I can pass as a boy young enough that his voice hasn't changed. It doesn't matter. It doesn't matter. I fill my hip flask from the jug and hide the jug in the hole under the steps. The flask is pretty, scrolled silver, with a cap that flips open, but it holds less than the jar. That doesn't matter. I'll be drinking less today. I have a taste before I screw the cap. My joints need it. I say "hello," "good day," and "sure, boss" in lower and lower voices. It doesn't matter because whatever happens, it will happen out there in the world. Remembering Emma Goldman, I put Edgar Rice Burroughs in my breast pocket alongside the flask in case he fires me right away or was joking about the job or I find out he's the sort of unmentionable type of man that my mother worries about. And if he catches me reading, Tarzan is more a boy novel than Virginia Woolf. I pull the jug back out and refill the flask up to the top. Now, I'm ready.

On the way by the kitchen garden, I snap a mint stem. It will mask the smell. My teeth grind the mint into a pulp while my eyes jump from side to side until the muscles around them ache. I'm watching for the gardener. I'm uncertain of whether I'm hiding from him or looking for him. Either way, he isn't here. I spit out the pulp and head toward the gate.

At the side of the house are the orange trees. My father told us that before all these tall, sprawling houses were built, before the big freezes, acres of orange groves grew farther than a person could see. My brother and I would lie on the grasses under our small, remnant orchard and imagine ourselves back in a mixed-up time of Indians, confederate soldiers, Spaniards in shiny armor, and lonely frontiersmen with long rifles. We felt washed by the smell of the blossoms.

Through my memories, interrupting them, is movement and the sound of humming. The gardener comes into view swinging a scythe and half-sings, half-grunts in time with the snick of the blade. The metal shines into my eyes with every lift. I'm breathing to match its rhythm. The blade stops mid arc, holding my lungs in place, and the gardener looks up as if someone called him. He catches me watching. I see my father come out the side door and approach him. I can't hear what they're saying, but my father's face flushes. The gardener lifts his head in my direction. My father pivots and stares, and now he waves at me, once. He leaves the gardener, and I wonder where I'll tell him I'm going, but he veers away from me and goes into the house. The gardener turns his back and hums again as his arm lifts and falls and the blade cuts the summer growth of grass between the trees.

Many stories could make sense of what has just happened, including that my father is angry about how high the limbs on the magnolia tree were pruned. I heard my mother complaining. It could be anything. I turn my back to the orange grove. My breathing has become my own again, and I have a job waiting.

The way to the river looks different in the daytime. Sunlight blurs through the weight of the air, and I can't open my eyes more than a squint without the glare making them tear. The humidity runs like oil over my skin. And people use the road. Cars jerk and swerve even though there's plenty of room for them to pass. I don't know that I've ever gone out during the day without a parent. At least the depression means that no one drops spare change down on me anymore.

I reach the path and the cold river smell meets me half-way down. On the other side of the water I have a job. I tuck my board under a thicket of beauty berries, lift my body high behind me, and run fast enough that I make my own breeze. I hand over hand into the boat and row upstream and to the far bank with long, efficient strokes. The high water has spilled over the landing, but I weave through the cypress knees until I find a place to tie up. I secure the boat and pull my gloves tight around my wrists. I'm ready.

I can hear little kids yelling to each other. Women squeal and men make that half-laugh, half-yell they do. I copy it under

my breath. The Indian must be wresting the alligator. I'd like to
see that. Maybe he has to practice when there's no one around,
and I'll watch. And maybe, well, all sorts of maybes are possible.
But this won't last. Too many people around here know me and
my family. Even if they don't tell the snake guy, my boss, I enjoy
saying it, my boss, they'll tell my father. And that will be that. I
have to take everything in as if it was only for today. Only this
next hour, maybe. Even if he already knows, I have now, this
moment. The tourists go silent. I hear a mockingbird copy a
phoebe's trill, a cardinal's peep, a jay's caw. The tourists yell and
clap. He must have put his head in the alligator's jaws.

I circle away from the people until I get to a batch of outlying
sheds set up on piers. One of them has its door shut, but inside
I can hear my boss talking to someone. I wait for a pause, but he
keeps talking. I climb the steps and knock.

"Come in, but get a wiggle on and shut the door behind
you."

I pivot inside on one hand, shut the door with the other, and
finish off facing forward.

"Oh, here you are. Sorry, I didn't mean anything personal by
the wiggle part. And don't be worried. She won't bite."

He's staring at the pine floor between us. I hear something
like the sound of a quick broom over sawdust before the snake
slides all around me. The body gathers and expands as it looks for
somewhere away from me, away from him. Black scales flicker
blue whenever it passes through the light from a window.

"Look at her. Nine feet, don't you think? And these indigos
tame up really nice. We'll drape her around the breasts of some
pretty girl in a bathing suit and have them walk through the
crowds. Those tourists will think you're the bee's knees, won't
they? Calm down, darling. How about we find a nice frog for
you?"

No one else is in the shed. He's been talking to the snake for awhile.

"You're not scared, right? I mean that snake must look even bigger from your point of view."

Alcohol sweat pops out my skin, but the fear smell, the one that makes wild pigs charge, disguises it. I hope.

"I'm fine. Do you want me to catch it?" I remember to lower my voice

"That a boy. What a trooper. No, we'll let her get tired, and then I want you to handle her as much as possible. Be her friend. Get her used to this new life. Tell her she'll have food and someone to help scratch whenever she's ready to shed, and a heat lamp in the winter. And she'll do a service for her own kind by getting people not to kill every snake they can."

The head rises to the height of mine as it goes by another time. A black tongue stabs into the air like a split claw, and I see the red along its chin and throat. She is beautiful and fierce, and I don't see any sign of friendliness on her part.

"Come on. Let me show you the set up."

I keep my body tucked down and close as I move farther into the shed. The blue snake twists on itself and comes at me, and I startle and bump into a barrel, and the barrel tips, and the man jumps and reaches over me to steady it. From inside the barrel are thumps and a thousand rattles.

"Oh, man, oh, man. We don't want all these angry rattlesnakes let loose on the floor."

I look around me and plan. That cane-bottom chair will take me up onto the table with all the glass jars and, if needed, the cabinet beside it has enough clearance between the top and the ceiling—I have an escape route.

"Sorry." I don't remember to lower my voice, but I think he'll put the pitch off to the circumstances. It occurs to me that

he might fire me now. I've heard my father talk about having to
fire people, but I never paid much attention. When do you have
to be fired? Are there set rules? How many mistakes do you get?
Sometimes I don't know the simplest things. Watson bumbles
things all the time, and Sherlock Holmes still works with him.

"No problem. I got all excited about my new sweetie here."
The indigo makes another flailing search for a way out. She gives
up and finds a shadowed corner. "I should have given you the
tour right off."

Half an hour later I know to feed the green snake her crickets
and to keep plenty of water in with the mud snake, and have
watched a bright orange snake eat a mouse slowly and whole.

"Okay, then. Almost time for another alligator show, and
I'm going to spot Joe Jimmie just in case. Take care of all my
sweethearts, and I'll send over some grub for you later."

He slips out the door, shuts it, gives a test shake, and now
I'm alone. The barrel rattles. There's a thump from behind
the table. I'm not exactly alone, and I can't remember a single
thing he told me. I go around the room touching things. Water
snakes, especially cottonmouths, are the only snakes I know
much about. Cottonmouths don't back down, so on the river
I've gotten a long look at them. I reach the bucket with frogs in
it and remember that he said to feed them to the garter snake.
I slide the board off the top, snatch a frog out, and put it in my
bib pocket alongside the book. It kicks its legs against my chest
and pushes its head up past the snap. I shove it down again and
drag a chair close to the table and climb. On the table, inside a
glass box, is a snake that could make me fall in love with snakes.
Four feet of gold and turquoise ribbons ripple over a side swath
of spring water blue, and the colors shift depending on which
stripe touches another and where the light falls. Here are the
colors of river water contained inside a skin. I drop the frog in.

I don't watch and am back on the floor before I hear the first alarmed croak.

The frog continues to protest as it dies. My hands go over my ears. The orange stain of blood in moonlit water hazes over my vision. I work it in my mind until the image flattens into a story. It becomes just another article in this morning's paper, set in smeared black type the same as "Negress found guilty for selling liquor" or "a smartly dressed girl taken for a ride and dragged into a clump of bushes" or the results of the baseball game between the Limerocks and the Phosphate City Lads. I drop my hands away from my head and look around the shed. In front of me are cages of crickets. They jump, hit the sides, jump again. Mice scramble in a box. A toad grunts once. I don't know what to do next. I'm sure someone with a job isn't just supposed to sit around. I hear feet on the steps and understand for the first time what it means to try to look busy. The door opens a finger width, and a voice says "safe" in a question.

"If you're quick."

The smell of beans comes through the door first and next a young Indian holding a plate. The light falls over her features, and I think Negro, but she has one of their skirts on so an Indian for sure. She looks into the room past my head and searches. I clear my throat, and she goes on tiptoe and backs up before she sees that I'm not a snake. She hands down the plate.

Now she's going to look me over. I'd do the same. Like everyone else, she starts at my hands and follows my arms up. I've always found it easier to look away, remove myself, let them just have their time with my body, but today I feel too real in the world to be erased. Her eyes flick up and down, especially down, along my skin and clothes as if she can only take it in small doses. I watch her looking at me. I decide not to make it easier for either of us and stare at her right back. Her skirt is striped with reds, yellows, and blacks like a coral snake. Her poncho is a solid brown, and the strands of beads around her neck pile up on top of each other until they rise almost to her chin. Her hair hangs Indian straight. The bangs lie flat on her forehead and the rest pulls into a smooth bun. And now we both look into each other's faces. I recognize the careful blankness of expecting to be stared at. I think she does as well because her head tilts and her lips go sideways into a crooked smile. I smile back. She sits on a box nearby.

"How many are loose right now?"

"Only the indigo."

"Oh, she's as sweet as a fawn." The girl pats her hand on the box in a complicated rhythm, and I hold my breath as the snake sticks its head out of the shadows, licks at the air, and moves past me. It slides onto the girl's lap. She lifts it around her shoulders and soothes it with her hands.

"Why does he think this snake isn't tame yet?"

"Oh, I come in at night. My grandmother would never let me perform. Sewing, making fry bread, and letting people stare at me while I do it—that's what I'm allowed. I tell her, well not directly, I just say it into the air or tell one of the children when I know my grandmother can hear, that our whole lives are an exhibition. And I wouldn't put on a bathing suit like the white ladies. It would be dignified and respectful. But she ignores me. I think she doesn't trust me because I'm white educated. It took everything just to get to come on this trip with my uncle."

The snake circles down her arm and puts its head on her wrist.

"Have you ever seen a bathing suit, you know, to hold it in your hands?" She's whispering.

"My father sells them in his stores." I try to bite back the words. I've said too much. She keeps talking.

"How is it sewn? And they seem thinner than wool these days. Are they cotton now? And how do they fit so well?" The snake is bothered by her inattention and leaves for another corner. "And the colors. Do you know where the dyes come from?"

She's talking darts and support and width of straps, and I know I could help out since my mother once thought that sewing was something I could do. I was terrible, but still I know things. But a man wouldn't. I just stare at this young woman with her wide nose and skin the color of leather on good books. Every time she gestures her skirt ripples all its colors.

The door opens quietly, and I watch my boss watching her. She keeps talking until a breeze from the outside reaches us. She shifts to look over her shoulder. He smiles at her. She stops talking, lowers her head, and slides past him and out the door. She shuts it, and I hear her test the latch.

"Was she talking to you?"

"Yes, sir. Brought me some food." I remember to lower my voice, but the effort makes my words slur. Now he'll think I'm drinking again.

"These girls aren't supposed to talk to men they don't know. Well, more the other way around since men they don't know shouldn't talk to them. It shows disrespect."

"Sorry, sir. I didn't know."

"This is not your fault, boy. I've never heard her say a word. I've known the family for years, and only every now and then her grandmother will say something directly to me instead of passing on her orders through her sons. That's how they do. The women run business things. People don't know that, and it gets them into trouble. I can't believe she talked like that. What did she say?"

"We talked about snakes, sir."

"Well, after lunch try to clean the place. I want it nice in case the Hollywood people look in. Don't tell anyone, but I think they're going to make a Tarzan movie here. I'd be great for the stunts, don't you think? They say they're going to bring in monkeys and elephants. Hey, have you made any progress with the indigo?"

I put down my plate and tap the floor in the best copy of the girl as I can remember. My hands shakes from the drinking last night, but I think it helps. I let my palm tremor against the floorboards, and the snake moves toward me. It stops. I reach out a finger, and we have a whisper of contact before it flings itself into the mess of potato sacks at the other edge of the shed. Only the snout shows. I wonder what its weight would feel like over my breasts.

"Fantastic. You're a natural. After you clean don't do anything but work with that snake. We could have her in a show by the end of the week. Good job, boy."

Each time he calls me boy, I'm aware of the afternoon sun. It has filled the building and taken away all the shadows. It lights up each wrinkle on the back of the hand I have stretched out to the snake. It makes a mockery of the word boy. I lift the plate and bend my head. I scoop up beans. I hunch even more and feel the flask press into my chest bindings. I wish I'd had a nip before he got here.

"I'm still curious about the girl talking to you. Maybe there's an age rule. Maybe you're young enough that it doesn't matter."

The indigo rattles something under its table, and we both look. Or I do. He's staring at me straight on, in the face, for the first time since he saw that I didn't have any legs.

"But you're not that young, are you?"

I keep my head up. I watch him put the pieces together.

"I asked around about you. No one said much but that you went around at night on that cart, and that kids tell stories and scare each other by making the sound of your wheels screeching.

They looked at me funny when I said I'd hired you, but I just thought they were being ignorant about the crippled. But they knew."

He will fire me, but I will still have touched a snake and talked to an Indian maiden about bathing suits. I'm ahead of anything I've ever had before. But I want more. I hold onto my breath and to hope. Maybe he'll hire a woman.

"Miss." He looks ashamed.

My job is over.

"I'll be going." I don't alter my voice. "Thank you for this opportunity." I want to plead. To say that I'm a good worker.

"Boy. I mean Miss. You know I have to let you go. Too many men need jobs just to eat and support their families."

"Of course. Again, thanks."

I'm already at the door. I balance on the top outside step and make sure the latch catches. I'm going to sit on the river and read and drink and swat at mosquitoes until dark. And I'll scare as many children as I can on the way home.

I walk hand over hand through the hammock and down the slow incline to the water. The oaks and maples and sweet bays give way to the cypress knees and the old, flat stumps of the logged trees that must have grown bigger than anything I've ever seen. I swing up onto one and sit on its edge. The center collapses into decay, and cinnamon ferns unfurl from the muck. I take off my gloves to lay my bare hands on the wood. Cypress trees, spindly, short, with feathered branchlets and grey scaled trunks, lift up out of the swamp forest. They lean over the giant stumps of their former selves and sprinkle the sun over me.

A voice comes off the river. Through the trees, I see one of the glass bottomed boats. They use an electric engine now and can sneak up on you, or could except for the tour guide. In a loud and sing-song voice, he tells the story of the old trees and the railroads built to haul them out and the rafts that floated down the river to the Ocklawaha to the St. Johns and then to the saw mills in Palatka. He tells them to look around their houses when they get home. That almost everyone east of the Mississippi has furniture made from cypress trees, maybe even from this very river. He shows them the split hull of an old dinghy rotting in the underwater sands and in a made-up story, proclaims it one of the steamboats that used to come up the river.

Once, my father took my brother with him on a business trip, and they traveled to Jacksonville by steamboat. My brother told me about the bad smells inside and how men stayed up all night playing poker, how the fire pan on top of the boat lit the way during the night, and how, from the top deck, he could see through the tops of trees and almost touch the stars. He made us laugh at the dining table for years, until he left for the war, by copying the accents of tourists from England and Germany and New York when he asked for more potatoes or butter. My brother could tell stories better than any novel. And the real wreck of a riverboat is down near the mouth of the Ocklawaha. I've seen it.

The boat captain's voice fades as he turns back upstream to the park where his passengers will buy celery trays made in Japan that say Silver Springs or tin alligators made in Germany, or soon, if that girl's grandmother agrees, corn husk dolls and tiny replicas of ancient canoes. That was the last run of the day. I can go now.

But I'm crying. I brace my arms against the cypress stump while my chest shakes against its bindings. Tears pool in the cracked seams of the wood. I don't drink or light a cigarette or cover my mouth with my hand, and sobs pour out of my throat. I cry out for my job, my brother, the old veterans, the forest that

used to exist here, for all the times that have passed. I grieve for
things I don't remember, the things I've never known. Inside me,
in the air around me, I'm many women, women mourning. The
broken bark scrapes against my skin as I shake. My arm flails
into the spider-webbed, mossed center of the trunk. The women
cry with me until I empty. I think I will lie here forever, but
they press against me, into me, become me, help me take one
shuddering breath and now another and another until I fill with
the peppered smell of the young cypress.

I exist. My strong lungs gather air from around the trees and
return it to them replenished. I exist in this world. I sit up from
where I've lain over the rotting trunk and drop down onto the
lattice of cypress roots layered over the muck. The messy, mixed
smell of life and death rises around me. It feels good on my skin.
I walk along the roots as if they were a tightrope and I was a
world-famed and beloved performer. I balance with one hand
on top of a cypress knee and swing to the next. That Indian girl
didn't seem beat down by working as an exhibit. I could work in
a circus. I somersault along a downed trunk and lift my hands
high and wide and smile for imaginary applause. All that crying,
and now I'm silly like a girl. I scurry the rest of the way to the
boat and don't stop until I'm back out in the center of the river.
I reach for the hip flask.

The spout touches my lower lip, and I see my life the way it
will be forever if I take this sip. Tomorrow I'll wake up to thirst
and the comfort of a stack of books to read and an almost full jug
under my back steps. My mother will keep altering my clothes,
and my father will bring me stories about customers from his
stores and fresh gloves whenever he notes I need them. We will
exist in our delicate place of unspokenness until they die and
then I will stay in the house forever. I have a choice. I can know

what will happen, or I can not drink and not know everything. I put the flask in my pocket. It warms against my chest. I pull it out, flip the top, and pour the booze into the river. Its weight swirls like clear oil over the river's surface. My fingers feel along the flowered scrolls one last time before I drop the flask into the water.

I do know some things. I won't ever live in a circus. I will never ask my father about the gardener and look for a lie in his gestures. But there will come a day that I make us talk about my brother. I'll read every day and learn. My friend will love me with her letters and packages of books. The river is mine with its alligators and snapping turtles, and each winter the manatees will let me swim among them. Others should be so lucky. I have a life. And I will find work to do. As I've had pointed out, I don't need a salary. I could write for the paper. Or talk on the radio. No one would have to know who I was. I could sign off as Orlando.

Another rowboat floats into view, low in the water line. The man has on fashionable clothes and a bowler hat, but they're frayed. Even sitting, he's terribly tall and thin. He's bailing water out with his hands.

"Evening." I touch the brim of my cap.

"And a fine day to you, young sir." His voice isn't from around here. "Do you know where I might best catch a fish?"

He waves a stick of bamboo that dangles a too-short, unraveling piece of string with the end tied onto a nail. An impaled worm writhes around it.

"In the shadows, under some branches, is your best bet. And watch for snags." I keep my voice low. I'm getting better with practice. "And here, this might help you bail."

I throw him the jar from under my seat, and he catches it. He smiles at me.

"The gods will bless you and this river and the ones that come after as they have the ones who came before." His voice has a tender music in its accent. His oars bump and angle too high as he tries to row closer to the shore. The boat tips, but the man sits straight and true in its center, as if he floated in air. He whistles a slow tune as he rides the current around the next bend in the river. Over his head, three swallowtail kites veer and dip in wide circles.

The day has lasted long enough for a final swim before the alligators come out to hunt. I could have told my boss a lot about alligators. Maybe I'll write my own book about them before he can get his done. It wouldn't just be about alligators. I'd share everything I've seen on the river in these years of watching. I'd have a chapter on manatees, of course. And one about limpkins. How they knock snails out of their shells. Their shyness. How the soft spots along their neck and back help disguise them as dappled shadows along a river bank. How in the spring they become bold and flap from tree to tree and scream in metallic voices.

A palm tree has fallen in a long stretch over the river. I wrap the bow line around the trunk, unbuckle my straps, and let the denim fall around me. I set my cap on the front seat and scratch through my hair into mats of sweat and shake my head until everything tingles. I loosen my bindings, and they drop away. With a hand on each side of the boat, I lift up out of my clothes and, in what I imagine is circus fashion, flip from boat to tree trunk and end with a belly flop on the water. The cold always burns at first, especially on my breasts and through my underneath parts where they've been blanketed by cotton. I take a breath and somersault into and through the river. The light runs gold over the grasses. I follow it as far down as my breath will allow. A small spring pushes out through a rock ledge, and it blurs the water upwards as if it were smoke from a chimney. I pirouette inside it and coil and release my center until I'm flying up to the light. I launch through the surface and into the air like a mullet.

"It's a sea monster come up from the ocean."

"Stupid, look at the face. She's a mermaid. With bosoms. And see the tail."

"Where?"

"Look under her. See the blue and green with gold shines in it?"

"I see it. I see it."

The boys are taking the river colors and inventing a tail. For a moment, I am their mermaid, and I feel my fringed and graceful tail.

The boys are a line of dazzled spots in my vision until I blink the water away. The number and size of them look the same as yesterday's group. They stand along the palm trunk and teeter back and forth as they point. The palm dips under the weight. One of them gets in my boat.

"Come on. Let's go get her. She'll be ours to keep."

"We could play with her."

"Even better, we could put her in a show and make money. We'd get rich."

"Or we could . . ." The biggest boy makes squeezing motions over his chest and all the rest of them laugh. I drop under clear-as-air water that won't protect me. They're fumbling with the bow line.

It takes my strongest, Olympic-level breaststroke to swim upstream and to the bottom. My hands dig into the sand over and over until a cloud of white rises around me and sweeps downriver. I swim within it until I'm under my boat, hidden in the curve of the keel. I gasp as quietly as I can. Most of them are in the boat, but not all. When they all get in, I'll reach up, tip the boat, and be gone into the woods before they can swim to shore.

"I can't see her anymore. What's that stuff in the water?"

"I'll bet she can change shapes. See that long fish over there? Maybe that's her."

The boys' images throw out over the water in the long, late-day light. Like shadow puppets, elbows crook up out of the sides, heads bob, arms rise until they reach half way over the river. The palm fronds at the end of the trunk shake and dip into the water, and the smallest shadow collapses in on itself.

"Hey, pipsqueak. Why are you hugging the tree?"

"I can't swim. I never even saw this much water before." His voice is skinny and breathless.

"Me neither, nancy boy. And I'll bet none of us can swim. But don't worry. Look how close the bottom is."

This is an optical illusion. I still sometimes reach for things that seem right at my fingertips. The boat rocks and sinks lower as another one gets in. The water reaches almost to the gunwale. I give up on the plan. I can't drown them on purpose. Even my brother probably tormented strange things when he was young. I swim to the bow of the boat. I'll go under the tree, get behind them, and disappear into the woods. The palm fronds shake again, but sideways, and a snake slides out onto the trunk. It raises its head and the mouth opens. I can't see the cotton mouth white from my angle below it, but the boys can.

"A snake." The boy's voice screeches high enough that the 'k' sound is lost. The bow smacks my head as the last boy vaults into the boat. It lurches and water bursts over the side. I grab the bow and try to keep it trim, but the boys are stupid about boats. Arms and half-bodies lean over one side and now the other in movements awkward with fear. I stay low and move between the

palm trunk and boat, brace my back on the tree, and try to hold
the boat steady from underneath. Up above me, the boys yell.

"Untie that rope."

"I'm not reaching close to the snake."

"Here, let me up there. I'll cut it with my knife."

The boat lurches, and a boy jolts over the side face down.
Our noses touch. Even red from the sun, his skin is perfect, his
lips smooth and full. His eyes go big, and no wrinkles spread
into his temples. Who could think I was a boy? This is a real boy.
He's recovered enough now to scream and fall back into the boat.

"She's here, the mermaid. Right there. She touched me."

The boat tilts up away from me as they all scurry to the far
side. They're going to capsize. I scramble until I can just get my
fingers over the edge of the boat. I hang and hope my weight is
enough to stop the boat's roll. They're all screaming now.

"She's rocking the boat."

"She's coming in."

"Do something. She'll eat us."

The current pushes the boat against the palm trunk with me
pinned in-between. Maybe I can twist and get up on the tree. I
turn my head, and the snake is closer.

"Look, it wants to help her. She's a witch mermaid."

"Give me that knife."

The bravest of them all comes to my and the snake's side of
the boat. The boat lowers and scrapes my back against the palm.
My face rises into their view. I'm pressed even tighter between
the tree and the boat. The boy holds the knife up. His fingers go
tight, but he hesitates. Another boy yells at him.

"Quick, before it speaks. They can hypnotize you with their
voice."

The boy slices the back of my wrist, but almost carefully. Still, blood drips down to my elbow and into the water. He cuts again, one wrist and now the other. He does it again, one and the other, each time deeper. Blood sprays into the air. I try to let go, but my fingers have locked around the edge. The boys' voices change from screams to the cheering I've heard coming from ball fields, only wilder. They all move closer. Blood slicks under my hands and my fingers go loose just as the boat rocks away from the tree far enough for me to drop into the water.

The river pulls me under the palm and out into its center. I float, face-up, away from the voices. My arms cross over me as I sink. In sunlight, blood plumes red rather than orange. Sometimes I rise to the surface, but more and more and for longer I stay under the water. My skin dissolves, becomes liquid, but my eyes see everything. The fish they thought I had changed into swims alongside, longer than I am. Grasses brush down my back. A minnow fills my vision. It passes and becomes small again. My face breaks into the air another time. I breathe. I drop again. The snake swims over me, at the surface, her belly dark and water rippling around it. She swims with her head raised into the sky. Above her, past her, I see the low branches of trees and stacks of clouds, their bottoms tinged grey and pink. From under the water their edges bulge and distort like the view through my mother's magnifying glass. She will be sad that I've gone. Bereft. I used to think they'd be relieved somehow. That's not true. They'll grieve that both their children are dead before them. And if they find me, with my wrists cut like this, they'll think I killed myself as well. It will break their hearts beyond healing. This must not happen.

The snake has veered off to the muddy edges that she prefers. With the strength that is left to me, I follow it under a tangle of downed oak branches. I touch into the underside of the bank and pin myself between the roots and limbs where alligators store their food. Should he have kept me on, I could have told my boss this. I will never be found. The mud stirred up from my efforts clears. There is no more blood. I become one thin line of sunlight shining into the river.

A dragonfly naiad lives under the river. She breathes water through her anus, and each exhale propels her forward in a sudden, powerful spurt. She's a skilled hunter with a folded lower lip that can spring out faster than a snake strike. It captures worms and snails and mosquito larvae and provides for a long insect life in the muck of the river bottom. But when the day comes to change, the naiad doesn't hesitate. She climbs out of the river onto a stem, hooks her claws tight, and swallows air until her skin splits and wings unfold.

In A Chamber of My Heart
1996

Lawdy, the noise in here is almost worse than anything. Someone dropped another tray on the floor, and the staff never stops yelling to each other down the hall. Well, now I'm lying to myself. Nothing's worse than the pain or even how it itches inside the cut on my stomach. Abdominal incision the doctors call it when they come poke. Opened me up, closed me up. Seems they could have known there was nothing for it without all this. But their drugs work okay, and Demerol's my favorite word these days. I could use some now.

"Here's your lunch tray, ma'am."

He's rattling his cart on down the hall before I can tell him not to leave it. The Demerol makes me slow. Cheap deli meat, too much mustard, a hard slice of cantaloupe on a lettuce leaf—I can tell from the smells what's under the plate cover. I wouldn't eat that on a day I wasn't sick in my stomach.

"Excuse me, ma'am."

So much ma'aming. I don't seem to have a name anymore. But she's waiting for me to answer and hasn't walked in my room like it's a broom closet and I'm the broom. Whoever she is, I'm disposed in her favor.

"Come on in. And who are you?"

"Ma'am. I'm a volunteer for the County Historical Society. We want to put together a book of oral histories from long-term residents of the area. Your chart says you were born here. Is that correct?"

Everyone seems allowed to read my chart except me. But she seems nice enough.

"Well, not far from here, right across the river. Used to be that meant what 'across the tracks' does now."

She's not paying attention, yet. She's rummaging in her big purse. The color matches the linen suit. Periwinkle, they call it. That, with the pressed white shell, means she's one of our Ocala society ladies, most we have them. I can feel the pain ripple around my spine, and need to brace before it attacks. I close my eyes. This time—just a quick bite and let go. I look over at the woman again.

She's sitting on the edge of the fold-out chair that my gal sleeps in sometimes. A spiral-bound notebook covers her chest like a shield. She twists a finger through her necklace and a cross flips over her neckline and dents into the blouse. The cross is a tiny thing, so she's Methodist most likely, and I'm a good work. I wonder if I'm her first. That tray must have warm mayonnaise on it.

"I'll make you a deal. You take this food out of here, and I'll talk to you. At least until my gal comes."

She looks at the tray like it might give her something, but she summons up a sense of duty. While she's gone, my favorite nurse comes and squirts the nice stuff into my IV.

"Here you go, dear. I'm going to load you up the most allowed before you leave tomorrow. It'll make the trip home easier." She holds my hand.

She's got one of those crushes people get on old ladies. I'm only seventy-six but I guess with my hair mostly gone and weighing as little as I do and smelling like I'm rotting from the inside, my time of women wanting me for real is over. But I'm not going to let her think I know that. I tickle my fingers inside her palm.

"Hey, watch that lady. I'll tell on you to that jealous girlfriend of mine down in Radiology. You'll have to watch out if you get another scan."

She's still wagging her finger at me as the historical society lady comes back in the room. We stop laughing like kids getting found out.

"If you need anything else, just buzz." Her voice goes professional, but she winks over the woman's head as she leaves. I like her so much. I like the historical lady. I like everyone when the drug first goes in.

"Ma'am, are you awake?"

My chin rubs on my chest. There might be drool. I give it a wipe on the sheets before looking at her.

"Where do we start? Do you ask questions?"

"However you'd like, ma'am. I do have a basic information form to fill out, but otherwise I'm just here to record whatever you have to say. We're not to judge or censor. But I will say that most people start with their parents."

"I'm a bastard."

"Excuse me?"

"Write it down. I'm a bastard."

"Now, that's not a word we use these days."

"Aren't you supposed to let me tell it my way? And in 1920, when I was born, people used that word. I heard it a lot."

She studies her notebook even though she hasn't written a word. She looks at me again.

"Write it down."

And she does, best that I can tell.

"My mother ran a jive joint during the Prohibition. A whisper sister, that's what they'd call women like her. Our family had always had a bit of land across the Ocklawaha, out of the way of city law, and people could drink right in their boats and listen to the bands. Negroes and whites both played, sometimes together. So many people had died, in the war, from the Spanish Flu. My mother said something wild and desperate got in their hearts."

It feels so good, the drug. I stop talking to enjoy the moment like all the cancer society pamphlets say to do. I think they meant loved ones and sunny days and kittens and such, but they should have included the drug rush. I hear the sound of linen against vinyl and know she's thinking of leaving. I find I don't want her to go.

"My mother was beautiful all her life. She'd grown up out there on the Ocklawaha and didn't care much about the proper way of things. You add that up with how soft she felt toward strays and hurt things and mix in all those broken-down boys coming back from Europe. I figure one of them for my father. And with my skin darker than hers and hair that never would lay flat, not that you can tell that now, I've always thought there might be some mixing in me. My mother said no, that he was a Jewish boy, but she'd say that no matter what, wouldn't she?"

The woman's pen stops. She's staring at me. I give her my old lady eye, and the pen moves again.

"She said he died. But Ma always took care of me. Especially those first years when the money just poured in. Hah. That's a play on words, get it?"

I know I'm laughing too loud. The drugs do that. But I'm not strong enough for it to go on very long. I finish with a tired squeak and pant for awhile before I speak again.

"So, she sent me to school with books and nice clothes. The other kids called me names, but I looked good. Better than some of them. Ma made sure of it. Then came the Depression time, in the middle of that Prohibition ended, and the money disappeared, all of it. My mother said that she made good money but spent gooder. We'd have been hungrier if not for our garden. Ma's grandmother had taught her about roots and such, so we'd dig up the arrowhead plants in the water and roast their tubers. And people don't think they're good eating, but you can roast a long skinny gar fish to tender right in its skin. Do you fish?"

"Oh, no, ma'am. But my husband does."

"If I felt better, I'd teach you. You can have a lot of fun fishing. And I think you should always know how to feed your own self." I smile at her and feel my lips go too wide. I must look like not much more than a skull. She holds her notebook tighter and poises her pen.

"Anyway, one day, after another meal of roots that left our guts sort of messed up, Ma washed in the river, put on the best clothes she had left, and told me to stay put until she got back from Ocala. When she did, she moved us into the quarters of a big house, and Ma did for the family. A friend owed her—that's all she ever told me. After I grew to a full woman, I understood the looks that got passed back and forth between her and the husband of the house. They knew each other from before, I could tell. No prouder woman than my Ma, but still she used blackmail to keep me fed and sent back to school, at least for the months they kept it open. Did you know the government closed the public schools to save money?"

"Really?" The woman writes as fast as she can. My stories tell better than those pornographic romances I'll bet she reads. She probably has one in that big purse right now. She flips over to a new page and fills half of that before she catches up.

"Still, I managed to do pretty good, and when a teacher decided I was smart enough for secretarial training, the money showed up for that. Ma hated working as a servant. Not that my mother hadn't always worked, but when she had me she came down with the sugar diabetes. It came back later, and lifting wet laundry made her bone-tired. The very day building started on the Cross Florida Canal and those six thousand construction workers moved here, pretty much overnight my mother quit that house and went back to her old business. It was legal now, sort of, and crazy busy. She came home at night just as tired, but happier. I was fifteen and, I'll just say it my own self, good looking, so Ma kept me close. But she didn't need to worry. I studied hard, and I never had eyes for men anyway."

I raise an eyebrow at the historical society lady. She smiles.

"We need more nice girls like you these days. The young women now don't do much but try to imitate the half-bits of clothing music stars wear."

"A nice girl. Oh my, if my gal heard you say that. Anyway, life looked up for a year. Then the government money got cut, and the canal work stopped mid-construction. Overnight, those men left. But the Depression had turned Ma into a saver, and we lived off the money from that year for a good while. It lasted just long enough for the war to rescue us."

I'm staring at the ceiling, and the past moves over the squares of pitted tiles like a movie, and I'm just the narrator. But that last bit sounded bad. I look over, and the woman has stopped writing again.

"Don't stare at me like that. Of course, it was terrible, especially what happened to those Jews over in Europe, but we didn't know anything about that then. I was twenty years old, and for me it meant a good job."

"Yes, ma'am. Of course."

The pen moves again, and I rest my voice while she catches up. The pain drugs have leveled out, and I'm not just saying whatever comes into my mind anymore. I can pick and choose. The war started my life and, in another way, stopped it. But I don't know if I'll tell her about that. I stare at the ceiling. My pilot's face looks down at me, and she's mad that I'd leave her out of my story. She was the one always so careful, so hidden. If she wants this, who am I to get shy at this late date?

"Okay. I've decided. I'm going to tell you something I've only ever told my gal. Have you got enough ink in that pen, because I'm not saying this again?"

"Yes, Ma'am. And I have another one right here in my purse."

She flips to a fresh page. I've got her interested, I can tell. Let's see if she keeps writing.

"Over on Highway 200, that's where Taylor Field, the airport, used to be in the Forties. They brought in military boys and taught them to fly. Lot's of local people worked there. My secretarial school got me the job, and I ended up handling the payroll, about fifty thousand dollars a month if you can believe that. They don't tell you this, but a woman pilot helped with the training. Did you see the picture in the paper yesterday of the Army helicopter pilot, that black woman, setting off for whatever it is they call Czechoslovakia, no Yugoslavia, these days?"

"Bosnia?"

"Yes, that's it. She had on the cap covering her head, the bug-eye goggles, and a hard-looking set to her face. Serious, just like my pilot when she came in that first time with some problem about her pay. And let me tell you, they paid her so much less

than the men, not that she questioned that. Her zoot suit fit too
big on her, so she had the arms rolled and the waist cinched. The
way the cloth billowed, she looked like the Sultan of Arabi, but
with hips. Those pilot goggles sat on top of her head, and hair
stuck out the sides of them. She leaned in and put a hand on
my desk to point at her pay stub. I had to wring my hands into
each other to keep them from cradling hers, it was that sudden.
She said later it felt the same for her, but she had that military
training. You could never tell anything just by looking at her. A
few WACs worked at the airfield, secretarial pool mostly, and the
women had their own barracks. I started dropping by there after
work, and the best memories are how we'd jitterbug to Benny
Goodman in those narrow aisles between the bunks. My pilot
kept care that she and I didn't dance together more than with
anyone else."

Up on the ceiling, my pilot smiles at me like she would on
those days she got a weekend furlough, and we'd pretend to fish
along the Silver River. We're remembering together the place
where the river curled around on itself. Behind an old lightning-
scarred cypress, we found a bank hidden from view. Pain kicks at
the backside of the drugs and mixes with an old grief I thought
I'd left behind.

"Ma'am? Are you tired? Should we stop? Ma'am? Ma'am?"

Her words come from far away. I can't see anything. Will this
sadness about my pilot be what I take with me? I wish my gal
was here, but this will do. I relax into what is to come. I wait. But
I keep hearing the noise from the hallway, and all I feel is cold
metal hurting against my ribs. I open my eyes. I've slumped into
the bed railing. My arms are just strong enough to push back to
center.

"Ma'am, should I call someone?"

"No. I want to get to the end of the story."

I manage a deep breath and figure it might be my last. I'm going to run as many words out on it as I can.

"The first time I took her to the river was in winter but I knew the water would be warm. We had to push through bushes of purple asters all in bloom, and they scratched against us, but we didn't feel it. We stripped bare and jumped in, and when she came and laid her body against the whole length of mine in water so clear that we could see ourselves all the way down to our twenty toes, it hurt like a scald and then it didn't."

I breathe again. It seems I'm going on for a while longer.

"After that we came together whenever we could, and sometimes when we shouldn't have, like in my boss' office during lunch or the one lady's bathroom. Oh my, these medications make me say all sorts of things."

"Ma'am. Perhaps you need some assistance."

The woman has her face tilted up and pinched, as if she smells something bad. Maybe I shouldn't have told them to take away the machine that pumped out the smell of wintergreen. It tried to cover up the cancer smell, but it didn't, and it ruined me for Lifesavers.

"No. You need to listen. No one remembers her anymore but me and, secondhand, my gal, and soon it will just be her. This is important. Write this down."

I've got my eyes shut against the pain, but I hear a pen scratch paper.

"On the river, we could take our time. She told me about her parents dying of the Flu and how an old aunt had raised her and how on the exact day of her tenth birthday a flying circus buzzed over her town, the planes doing loop-de-loops, dives, and barrel roles. She ran after them, along with the rest of the town, to a field where the planes circled and landed, and she waited in a long line for the one dollar joy ride. A Curtiss JN-4 biplane—I still remember the name because of how her face looked when she said it. Her aunt died, and my pilot took the bit of inheritance and spent it on flying lessons. We'd talk about the future and how when the war ended we'd live near an airport somewhere close, she understood that I couldn't stay far from my mother, and she'd work flying, even crop dusting if she had to. It didn't matter, we'd be together. The war got bigger, and orders came for her to join the other women pilots in Texas to ferry bombers out to the west coast. We'd always known she'd have to leave for awhile. That last day she gave me her flight scarf. The white silk had dark areas where her neck sweated against it. We only kissed that day, but over and over, me pushed up against a pile of broken wing struts lying in the back corner of the hanger. I never heard from her again."

I fumble through the sheet until I find the call button. I have all sorts of hurt coming through the drugs. I close my eyes against it until my nurse comes. I hear her talking to the historical lady.

"Perhaps you should go. I think she's talked enough."

"Oh, certainly. We're not supposed to intrude."

"No, she needs to stay. Just give me another dose." I've grabbed my nurse's wrist, but I let go so she can do her work. I hear the flap of the tubes against the IV pole and feel heat race through my body.

"There you go, lady." She cups my fingers with hers and whispers. "I'll send in the aide to help you with that little accident"

From far away, I feel the wet under me. You'd think I'd be ashamed, but that's all done with now. I open my eyes, and the historical society woman's nose is still wrinkled. She should get used to it. Sick people smell.

"I waited for a long time. You couldn't just call or send messages over the computer like now. And showing too much interest wasn't safe. They watched for that sort of thing in the women. I wondered if she had left me, if everything had been a lie or a dream. When the paperwork came through our office about a plane accident and asking for her records and my pilot's name had comma deceased after it, for a second, just a second, I felt a strange relief. I had been loved. What came next wasn't pain. Instead my hands were on hers, gripped on the rudder. They felt the stutter and drop that sent clouds rushing over the cockpit. We saw the curved horizon of a blue sky drop into a swirl of first browns, then greens, then the details of branches, a stream, a field of purple and yellow flowers. I heard the great noise of everything ripping apart."

The historical society lady wipes her eyes. But I feel good— and not just from the Demerol. Talking about it out loud makes me know that sadness got left behind years ago. My pilot salutes me from the ceiling tiles and fades into the speckled paint. The historical society lady concentrates on her notepad.

"I fell down right there on the floor behind my desk. They found me and took me to the flight surgeon who decided I was pregnant, so they fired me. I didn't argue with them. I didn't care. I ran all the miles to the river, but I couldn't even put a hand in that water. I couldn't for years after that. I'm not proud of what I did next."

The aide comes in with linens under her arm. She shakes the curtain, and the hooks rattle along the ceiling track. The historical society lady becomes a shadow in the material, but I think she'll stay. I've left her with what those books call a cliff-hanger. The aide loosens the corners of the sheet and rolls me to one side. She's never rough, never skimps on her job, but ever since she mentioned that I'd be going to meet Jesus soon and that I might want to wash my sins beforehand, and I said that I'd never been to meet any man and wasn't about to start now, she's made a show of putting on gloves right at the door. Even with them on, she holds everything by the tips of her fingers, like dirty diapers. And she never calls me by name. Her tag says "Dolores," but I refuse to even think it. The latex squeaks along my skin as she loosens the ties on my gown. I'll be damned if I don't say this next part of the story just because she's here.

"I ran away. I left my mother. During all those times of dancing in the barracks, the girls like me would talk about New York in a sideways, sly way. They'd say how open people lived, how free. So that's where I went. With the war work, regular women walked around the town, alone, with their own money, and it meant us girls didn't stand out. In Ocala we'd had a least two of everything—Chinamen, Lebanese, Cubans, even Indians—but New York had whole neighborhoods, and the way I looked I could walk down the street and fit in lots of places. At least until I opened my mouth. In the bars they called me 'The Cracker' and said I probably had grown up with pigs living in the house. I didn't."

The washcloth slaps cold on my behind and drips, but the aide is good at what she does and finishes quick.

"Although when I was about four we had Daisy, a Dominicker chicken, all black and silver, and I loved her and had her in the house with me whenever I could. I didn't tell any of those New York girls that, of course. But when you got some of those WACs up to your bedsit, they'd stop pretending. A sergeant from Ohio would talk about heifers over an illegal hot plate breakfast, or a bomb assembler would bang her leg against the table in the dark and say shit in a drawn out way like the Carolina mill worker she used to be."

Did I say all that out loud? The aide rolls me back to face up and stares at me like I'm something bad about to happen in one of those chainsaw movies. I guess I did. I don't care. This is my life, or it was. When do you start using the word was for your life? I've heard other old people do it, but I never have. I don't think I'll start now. This is my life.

"Sorry about that. The cancer, you know." That usually gets them to excuse me anything. Except for my gal, she doesn't let me get away with it. The lady's voice comes from the other side of the curtain.

"Of course. I'll just take that part out." I hear the pen scratching and picture her hand swishing back and forth and the black ink getting thicker and even ripping through the paper and leaking onto the next page. Oh, well.

"Ma'am, do you go to church or have any other religious affiliations?"

"No, my mother either. I guess not going to church was our tradition. I mean we had a Christmas tree and presents, and Ma told me her grandmother had words she said over the corn when it came in, and my mother gathered river water every new moon and made me drink it. Is that what you mean?" Now I'm just messing with the poor woman.

She doesn't answer. The aide snorts. Despite everything, we sort of have the same country sense of humor. We found that out one night when she bathed me while Jamie Foxx was on the TV that hangs from my ceiling. She gathers the dirty linens and swishes back the curtain on her way out. The historical lady's pen dithers over her form.

"Well, we don't really have a box to check for that. I'll just put Christian. When did you come back here?"

"Fifty or fifty-one. The man my mother lived with died. He had one of those cat boats that worked the river picking up big logs off the bottom and selling them to lumber companies. That's all that was left of the giant trees. Ma helped him with the hoist rigging—Spanish windmills they called it. Anyway he died, and it was getting so Ma couldn't stand on her feet much anymore. I still had a job, but not for long with the soldiers back and the war factories shutting down. And the police cared again about what us women did. And did you know that all over the Northeast, billboards, bumper stickers, and signs on sides of buildings told people to come visit Silver Springs, same as if it was the White House or Grand Canyon? It was like being haunted. And the cold weather wore at me. So I came home and helped Ma in her new business. That Depression had made my mother into a careful planner, that's for sure. She'd always quilted, but now she made things for tourists like pine straw baskets and trays, even candlesticks. I'd go out to the places long-leaf pines still managed to grow and gather the needles off downed branches. She'd weave them around tray bottoms that had pictures of orange trees and said Silver Springs or Weeki Wachi. When her eyesight started to go, I helped."

"You know, my husband's family has one of those trays. Maybe your mother made it."

"Or I did. Spider web weaves, fern and pop corn stitches, inside cover lips, flared sides, and Indian wrap handles with fagoting support—I could do it all. It turned out I could see something in my mind, and it would form between my hands. I got hired on to help the potter they had out here at the Silver Springs Park. And that's all I did for awhile. I put my pottery first and let the loose ends drag on everything else in my life. Except for taking care of my mother."

"Tray pick up." The cafeteria man yells into the room and makes the historical society lady drop her pen. I wave him away and wait for the pen to be ready before I talk again.

"Every day I worked in a studio close enough to hear the glass bottom boat captains pointing out geysers and fern gardens. They turned the odd shapes of underwater rocks into tragic stories of bridal chambers and lover's lanes. Every day, I didn't go to the river, didn't even look out over it until the winter Ma got real sick. When I thought she might die, I'm ashamed to say it, I almost ran away again. I had it planned, the suitcase packed. But that day, after work, after getting my pay, instead of going to catch the Greyhound, I left the suitcase in my studio and walked to the river. The asters bloomed in great sprays everywhere. I walked through them, and they cut over my face and hands. Blood stung into my eyes and tasted sweet in my mouth."

I'm still shamed from knowing that I almost left my mother. I look up at the ceiling for awhile. I don't think Ma ever knew, but I guess she does now. The lady rattles her form. She wants to leave. I don't want to be alone. My gal will be here soon. I force another breath and talk as fast as I can manage.

"I fell down at the edge of the river, and my face splashed into plants, mud, and water. When I rubbed my cheeks, I felt clay. My hands searched into the underside of the dried out bank and found more clay. I scooped armfuls into my shirt, carried it dripping back to the studio, and dumped it into a bucket. I didn't know what the heck to do with it. Roots, shells, snails, even chips of old pots crumbled all through the muck—nothing like the clay we had delivered. As wet as it already was, I found myself knowing that I should add more water. My hands stirred the clay thin. They felt the heaviest things drop out to the bottom. I sat at the wheel and watched all night, remembering every memory of my pilot, while gravity cleaned the clay. At dawn, I skimmed off the top layers and worked them. All day I pressed the clay, pressed out water, pressed out air bubbles. I knew it needed tempering and ran to the park's beach, through all the pale-skinned tourists, and scooped up a bucket of that brought-in sand."

"Silver Springs had a beach?" The lady's voice is a surprise. I'd forgotten she was here.

"It sure did. It got closed with integration same as the swimming pools."

She writes that down. I don't know if she's been writing the other stuff.

"I worked the clay into a pitcher. I can't tell you how long it took, but I didn't sleep, even during the drying. I only went home while it fired. After the bisque firing, I brushed it first with sky colors and then poured coils of coneflower yellow, sponged prairie iris purples, and sprayed streaks of tangerine earth around and around in a rush of color. I fired it again and slept, maybe for days. I bathed and washed my hair and got dressed pretty before I opened that kiln. The pot seemed perfect. I knew what I had to do next and went and pretty much stole a boat. I found our place, me and my pilot's, and dipped the pot into the river. It filled for the first time. It didn't crack or leak, and the colors glittered in the water. I kissed the rim, took a long drink, and let it rest in my arms. Two hawks screamed out from over the trees and circled each other until they wrapped talons together and somersaulted toward the earth. Around me gallinules bobbed and strutted over mats of plants, frogs called for one another, and manatee noses broke the surface and huffed. You know, it broke my heart when they built the dam, and manatees couldn't get here anymore."

I pull my mother's star quilt over my belly. I'm always cold. The pain is close again, but talking keeps it still. It quivers like an animal ready to leap. I don't look at the lady. It would give her a chance to interrupt with some made-up excuse to leave.

"I was all right after that. You know, those women in New York, I don't regret anything, I met some wonderful people, but that was about grief and me looking for my pilot in each new woman. Understanding that helped when my mother died, and I didn't have to leave this time. But I worked. It felt good. Every day my hands made something real. When the potter retired I took over there at the Springs. He'd studied the Indian way of making pots some place up north and added to that. I added some more. The way yellows hold their color thick on the pot, that was my doing."

"Ma'am, did you ever marry?"

"What? Aren't you listening? But I did sort of go out with a man once. But no one knew. It would have been trouble if they did."

"I don't understand."

"About a year after my mother died, I took a ride on one of the glass bottom boats, resting my arms for a bit, breathing in the smell of the water, ignoring the tourists packed around me. Right over what they called the Turtle Meadows, one of the boats from Paradise Park came alongside."

"Paradise Park?"

"Don't tell me you don't know about Paradise Park? Has it been that long ago? It was like Silver Springs, owned by the same men, but for the Negroes. A line got drawn in the water and each side reflected the other—same boat, same fish underneath, same number of screeching children, but all white in one boat and all Negro in the other. So anyway, the boats passed each other with not five feet between, and I saw her. I watched how people moved around her and listened to her and clapped her on the shoulder, and I knew they thought she was a man. The way I smiled at her she knew I knew she wasn't and that I liked her."

The historical society lady just stops writing. Well, you can't push people beyond what they can handle. But I'm going to make her listen.

"Turns out she started passing for a man during the Depression to get work and just kept at it. I think she was more man than anything, no matter what her outside parts looked like. She taught herself about engines, and ended up a boat mechanic for both the Parks. After that boat ride, she took up lingering behind my studio. I'd come out and sit on a bench to get some air, and she'd lean against the palm tree beside it and wipe her hands on a cloth while we spoke about simple things. She smelled like the oil Negro men wore in their hair then. Now we weren't each other's big loves, but we had some good times. We'd get dressed to the nines and go dancing in Negro clubs like the Manhattan Casino in St. Pete. Once we saw Sarah Vaughn there. I'd just brush my hair out big and keep my mouth shut and people wouldn't ask too many questions. We liked that mix of danger and fun. If I'd thought better about it, I'd have realized the danger was mostly hers, but we kept ourselves in a sort of bubble. When the civil rights movement came to Ocala, she left me."

"Oh yes, the civil rights movement. Our society is very interested in that." The lady has her pen ready to go.

"She joined up with the Hunt and Fishing Club. That was the only way blacks—you know, I can't hardly call people that. When I was growing up, it was such an ugly word to use about colored folk. My mother would have smacked me. Anyway, blacks, that had started to be the polite word then, could only own guns if they belonged to a hunt club. But this club didn't hunt anything much, except white men, I guess. They'd guard outside houses and churches where racial activists spoke. They never had to shoot anyone that anyone knows about, but she had some long nights. The only way we saw each other was if she snuck up the back way to my house in the early morning. One day she said she wouldn't be back. It had gotten too risky. She was right about the danger, but I think she also had shame about being a black man dating a white woman. Well, that might not be all of it. I'm dying after all, I should serve up some truth. She might also have known about the photographer."

"Excuse me?"

"Do you remember the show Sea Hunt? They filmed a lot of it on our river. I met Lloyd Bridges and his little sons once. Not that that meant much around here. It was pretty regular to have run across Gary Cooper or Esther Williams or even maybe have seen Jayne Mansfield in her see-through bathing suit or at least to have cleaned the guy who played the monster from the Black Lagoon's hotel room. I know this one old waitress who still blushes when she talks about having taken Johnny Weissmuller's order for a grilled cheese when he came in off a shoot still in his loin cloth. On rye, no pickle—she remembers everything. But the camera crews interested me the most. That's what they called them, a "crew." The first time I saw my photographer was in springtime when the limpkins screamed and flapped across the river in their lustful ways. I'd been making mold pottery all week, getting ready for the summer rush. Stamping "Silver Springs, Fla." on piece after piece made me squirrely, although I might have had more patience for the work if I'd known about the plans to hire it all out to China. Anyway, I took a break to watch them make an episode of Sea Hunt. The underwater photographers look at everything like a painter does a landscape only with movement. One of them that day danced her camera around. She'd pivot and pirouette, and I watched until she rose out of the spring. Water streamed down the slick of her wetsuit and when she shook off her cap, red hair spread out into the sunshine. The crew filmed Sea Hunt all over—the Bahamas, Cypress Gardens, Nassau, California—so she traveled a lot, but we'd date when she was in town. She didn't seem to mind how much older I was than her. Still doesn't."

I'm glad I've talked past most of the hard times. The pain chews at me right through the middle, but I'll win against it. I'll die, and the pain will have to die with me. And my gal will arrive soon. I lick my lips so I can keep talking until she gets here.

"So that short time when the mechanic was leaving me, but hadn't quite yet, I guess you'd say I cheated. She got married not long after that and died back in the eighties. I waited for the big hullabaloo when the funeral home got a good long look at her body, but there wasn't anything but the regular 'loving husband for twenty years' in the obituary. So many people have died. Mae

West was my mother's favorite, and Kate Smith—my pilot was mad for her singing. I know they're just famous people that I never met, but each time they pass I lose another piece of the world that Ma and her lived in."

The drugs make my mouth dry, and I can hear my voice fail. She does too.

"May I pour you some water?"

"No, I'll wait. My gal will get here soon, and she's promised me mint tea from our garden. She mixes lemon balm and spearmint and drips in a little honey. And she'll have her camera. She keeps taking pictures of me. I complain, but she says I'm more beautiful than ever. She better arrive soon. That nurse that comes on in the evenings makes her leave at the end of visiting hours like she wasn't family."

"So you had a child."

"Bless your heart ma'am, but you're missing a few things. Last I checked you had to have had relations with a man for that. Of course, we could have adopted like the girls do these days, but that never happened."

I stop talking to the woman because my gal is at the door, her silver hair lit from behind by the fluorescent lights in the hall. It still has sparkles of red in it. She has stems of spider lilies and cardinal lobelia in one arm and a pitcher of tea in the other. She sets the pitcher down and leans over to let the flowers fall around my body. She kisses me and kisses me and rests her forehead against mine, and we breathe each other's breath. How she can stand the smell, I don't know.

I look to see how the historical society lady takes all this. She's out the door, in the hallway, and the pages in her notebook are half-ripped off their black plastic coils. My aide passes her, stops, and says something that I can't hear.

"Oh, we can't use any of this material. You know that." The historical lady has one of those whispers that carry.

She tears the papers through the last coils. The aide's hands twitch, and I wonder if she's about to snatch those papers right out of that white lady's hands. Of course, she doesn't. She sees me looking, and we have a moment, I don't quite know of what, but for sure a moment. She moves past my doorway. The historical society lady pushes her pen through the top of the notebook and holds the papers down at her side as she disappears in the opposite direction. I hear the lid of a metal trash can raise and drop. I hear her ask if the man in 213 is well enough for an interview.

I don't regret talking to her. And here's my photographer pouring me tea out of my pitcher. The purples have faded and there's a chip along the rim, but this is still the best work I've ever done. My gal tilts the plastic hospital cup to my face, and I sip. I wish I could enjoy it. But I pretend that I do, and am remembering the taste of fresh-cut mint from our garden as my throat snaps shut.

My arm flings out and smashes the cup into the air. My legs shake against the sheets. Something tries to rip through my spine. Telling stories distracted me for too long, and now I'm helpless inside the pain. I grit my teeth not to scream. My gal runs out of the room, and she does the screaming for us. The room fills with people, and they talk over my body about whether they should do anything, and my gal hisses at them to just give me something for the pain. Someone must have listened because the drug overflows into my muscles like the river after a summer storm. The evening shift nurse says anyone who isn't family has to go. My photographer tells her to fuck off, those Hollywood people always had the worst language, and climbs into bed with me.

She's still here beside me. Best you can tell in a hospital, another morning has come around. I feel better than I have in weeks. Today I'm going home. My nurse comes in and puts coffee beside the bed and wakes my gal and tells her to drink it quick, that the doctors will make rounds soon. She's a slow waker, always has been. Her arms spread in a long stretch that ends up as a hug around my shoulders. She kisses my mostly bald head and goes into the bathroom. While she's in there, all the white coats gather around me. My gal stays in the bathroom and listens. They know she's there, but the compromise covers them legally. I nod and smile to everything they say just to be pleasant. I'm going home no matter what.

The doctors leave, and I work myself to sitting while my gal packs up around me.

"Here you go, my old lady." She hoists me the rest of the way. She's sixty-five this year but still the athlete. "Let's get some real clothes on you."

"Wait. I've finagled one more dose of the good stuff for her. Then I'll take out the IV. It'll make things easier." Our nurse comes to my side. She's brought a wheelchair.

My skin tugs as she pulls out the needle, and part of me is scared to be without it. The two of them stand on either side of the bed and slide pants up my legs. Our nurse shows my gal how to roll me from side to side to get the waistband over my hips. She turns away to get one of the menstrual pad things they use for "leaking" as she delicately calls it. My gal takes the moment to give me a squeeze back there, and we smile at the memory of our desire. They lift my arms and pull a sweater over my head. The nurse flips the one wisp of hair I have left out over my collar, and she winks at me. A few days ago she took care of my gray roots as a going home present. "We girls have to look good," she said as she ripped open the Clairol package and shook the bottle. Our nurse hands my gal a bottle of pills.

"These aren't as strong, but they'll hold her until Hospice gets to your house and sets up the IV. And here's our favorite radiology tech with all the supplies we could put together."

I can hardly see the tech behind a wheelchair piled with those diaper things and pads for the bed and all sorts of basins and who knows what else. She gives my gal a hug and comes over and kisses me on the cheek. I guess now that I'm going home they don't have to act as professional. I want to tease about just how well her girlfriend took care of me, but I'm still too high to say anything. The aide comes in and the room goes quiet. The radiology tech takes her hand off the wheelchair with the stolen supplies.

"You wanted these discharge orders. Does she need anything else?" The aide stands in the doorway. My nurse shakes her head. The aide stares at the wheelchair. The tech looks at a wall, at the ceiling. The aide, Dolores, reaches onto the shelf and adds a bottle of skin lotion to the pile. "Her backside needs this. And you should rearrange that so nothing falls off." Dolores is out the door and probably into the next room before anyone says anything.

"Let's get you out of here." My photographer lifts me out of the bed as if I were her bride.

I don't weigh enough to hold down paper in a wind, but I know that later she'll complain about how I ruined her back. I'll pretend to hide my pain drugs from her, and we'll joke about my drug addiction. I put my head under her chin and rest in her arms. This is how it must have been with my mother before I can remember. But my body remembers, and I hear my mother singing and feel how it used to make a breeze through the hair on top of my head.

Our nurse pushes the wheelchair closer, but we stand like that together for a little longer. She's so gentle that I hardly know I've been put down. The nurse tucks pillows around me, and my gal wedges the pitcher into the crook of my arm.

"Can you hold on to it?"

I can. I'm coming out of the drug haze, but the pain only licks at my back. This is my best time. My gal pulls something long and beige out of her pocket and wraps it around my neck twice and lets the ends fall into my lap.

"I thought she'd want to keep you warm on this trip."

The silk has gone yellow, but I smell my pilot on the scarf.

We head out into the hall with my gal holding my hand and our nurse pushing the wheelchair. The radiology woman whistles and pretends she doesn't know us as she rolls the supply-loaded wheelchair a few feet behind. We must be quite the caravan.

At the car she lifts me again, but we're all business this time. She doesn't have a back seat or much of a trunk in her Alfa Romeo, so supplies get tucked in all around. She bought a stupid car for around here, but there's no getting the Hollywood out of my girl. She got it from some actor whose movie sales went south and says it wasn't that expensive. I never pressed her on the exact price, because I like being driven around town in a yellow convertible with a black leather interior. It looks good on me.

"Now, we'll come by tomorrow. We'll bring dinner, and I'll check on things. You've got my number, right?" The nurse hugs my gal and now she's hugging me. And now she's crying. My gal reaches in and fastens the seat belt around me and the pitcher. She smoothes the scarf over my neck.

"A seatbelt?" I cock my head and give her the look I do when she forgets that I'm dying.

"Well, for the pitcher."

She drives much slower than she can usually manage and turns to check on me over and over. I want to snap at her to watch the road like I usually do, but that good feeling I woke up with rushes out of me. I don't hurt yet. This is something else. My skin doesn't hold me anymore. The heart of me moves out through it, and all the world comes inside. I've never felt this way before.

"It's time."

"What, do you need a pill? I can pull over right here, and I brought water."

"Darling, it's time."

"No, no, no. We're almost home. I had a hospital bed delivered and put downstairs right where it will look out over the garden. We'll take that quilt there and put it on top. I have the new portfolio to show you. It tells your story, our story. I have plans. We have plans."

"Don't take me home."

"What? Should I turn around? Okay, we'll go right back to the hospital. I can still see it in the rear view mirror. They probably haven't even stripped your bed yet. Do you need one of these pills first?"

She's like a soon-to-be father losing all sense.

"Darling, take me to the river."

"What. Oh no. That's too much to ask. And you'll ruin my back if I have to lift you again. And the park has river access locked up tight. We'd have to pay, and I can't see them letting me carry you in past all those tourists."

"I'll show you. There's a back road through to where Paradise Park used to be. We're going to scratch up your car, maybe even knock it out of alignment. It'll be something for you to remember me by."

"Shit. You are so damn stubborn. And mean to the last. Where do I turn?"

I show her, and soon we're driving through an opening that almost remembers it used to be a road. The loose sand pulls at the tires, and red bays slap against the sides. We roll down the windows, and my scarf flickers around my neck. The smell of new leaves washes the rot off my body. The car nose dives into a pit of sugar sand and stops just before where the river makes a sun-bright gap in the trees.

She carries me to the shore and there, as there needs to be, an old canoe, its aluminum beat up and stained, waits for us in the marsh grasses. We're in one of the old stories where the hero is provided what he needs as he needs it. She lays me on the bank in a meadow of blue-eyed grass that spreads between the cypress knees until the blossoms drip down into their own reflections. My love gets the pillows from the car and stacks them into the bow of the canoe. She nestles me among them. She spreads the quilt and puts a cap on my head. She tucks and folds and rearranges things until she's satisfied I'm comfortable. But those sorts of feelings—warm, cold, the press of a rivet against my side, pain cracking my bones—don't matter anymore. She puts the pitcher into my arms, and it rests between my breasts.

We stare into each other's eyes as she leans forward to wrap her arms around the stern and launch the canoe. It slides into the water, and at the last moment she hops in and kneels in front of me with her bottom perched on the center strut. She uses the oar as a pole and pushes us away. That moment when you leave land, when the boat floats—there's no mistaking it. Through all the cushioning and drugs and death that is so close, I feel it. My love paddles and looks over my head. She sees what comes. I see what passes—patches of star rush in the shadows, the green, blue, white of hemlock puffs. Swallowtails leave pickerel weed blooms to unfurl their tongues over the red triangles on the quilt. I see a wood duck with her Cleopatra eyes. At first it seems that the wind fluffs out her feathers, but she swims out of the grasses, and I see the babies snuggled into her side. The ancient potters that lived here, right here, attached small figures of animals onto the sides of their pots—adornos. I saw one once in a museum. The duck has adorno babies.

We hear voices, splashing, and I see women in blue, red, green, purple, and yellow kayaks coming up on us. They are polite, each one, as they pass us by. I know who they are the way I knew in the barracks. I nod my head that certain way and grin. The last one, in the blue kayak, begins her polite nod but changes it into a real smile. She recognizes me. As each one passes, their reflection lingers behind them. Now the last reflection pulls forward, out of my sight.

"Oh, my god. You are still looking."

"Yes, my love. Always."

"You know, you probably gave them nightmares the way there's not much left of you but your teeth."

"My mother had good teeth right to the end." That's all the words I have left.

I watch the water. The cobalt blue in the shadows I figured out, but these mirror glints of teal I never got on a pot right. The canoe slows and turns in an eddy, and now I see what is to come. I recognize where we are even before the lightning-scarred cypress slides into view. Her spring leaves make a green mist along the branches. She's lost some over the years. The canoe finds the path behind the tree, the place where a bit of the river hides behind itself. My gal puts down her paddle and lays her face into my lap. I don't know what I believe, but she believes in a heaven where loved ones wait. She has brought me home. She's giving me over to my pilot. I guess this is what I believe—that gestures of love are never lost.

I feel so many things. The annoyance of the great blue we've flushed is in my throat, the beat of her wings in my lungs. Arrowhead stalks stretch up my spine and bloom their white flowers into my breasts. I list toward the edge. A turtle swims away from us, the flip of her turtle feet a tickle along my ribs, and an alligator splashes off the sunny bank. My love's hand pulls me back, and I slip flatter into the boat until only the sky is above me. I see the alligator's old relative, the crocodile, thirty feet long and hungry, blinking its transparent eyelids and swimming in the ancient ocean that existed here above us all. The manatees are gone from this river, I know this, but I feel one resting between my hips. I feel it all. I feel the scarf unwrapped from around my neck. The heart of me goes with it, and we're slipped into the pitcher and now we fill with water and tumble down into the grasses and rich muck. Dragonfly nymphs with translucent bodies swim into us and snap their jaws.

In a chamber of my heart, plum purple grief pours out of my gal. It adds hue to the last circle of blood that swirls through my cells. It adds love, love, and love into the mix of the world.

Something essential has changed. Brown algae cover the rippling, underwater greens of eel and ribbon grass, coontail and pond weed. Sunlight can't reach the leaves. The steady, deep upwelling of water continues, but it's no longer enough. The surface world thickens the river with rain that passes though opulent lawns, sewage tanks, cattle pastures and the extravagant green of golf courses.

Happy Birthday to Me
2008

The plastic rattle of the wind chimes is always my first warning. I lift my elbows off the counter, tug the I-Phone ear buds out and down into my bra, and reach for the Windex in case the bitch from the new management team has come to spy. The door opens wider, and the outside air ruffles the plush of dangling alligators. It seems colder than when I clocked in this morning. Bad weather makes the tourists surly. The intruder moves into view, and she's a customer. I stop cleaning the counter. They always want to talk.

"Merry Christmas. Or should I say Christmas Eve Eve?" Tinseled triangles of green with flashing lights hang from her ears. They match the broach on her sweatshirt.

"Cute earrings." The sarcasm doesn't leak into my voice and the customer comes closer, still smiling. She's really happy. I should smile back at her. The latest required-reading, full-of-crap employee manual says I should. In thirty years here I've seen a lot of manuals.

"Do you have frogs?"

I should walk her over there. I should hand her one or two. I work on the smile. I nod in the direction of the display and feel the edges of my mouth stretch.

She touches all the frogs. Frogs fishing, book-holding frog teachers in pink bonnets, a molded circlet of lily pads each supporting a frog, each frog acting out a different emotion—the whole display pretty much creeps me the fuck out, especially the jump-for-joy frog. She has a wide open mouth with human teeth inside. I have nightmares where my grandfather, father, and I, all of us, in the night, gig frog after frog. My father gets the jump-for-joy frog right through her green and red plaid dress. The customer picks up a frog eating a fly. The rock it sits on has "ENJOY" scrawled across it.

I put the ear buds back in and place the screen discretely on the counter. I'm watching *The View* episode from yesterday. Whoopee isn't as funny as she used to be. The cold is still friggin' ridiculous, so I tap and flick until I figure out how to change the screen over to a weather forecast. On the radar image, up near Lake City, a line of red and yellow storms makes a diagonal slice over the peninsula. The text says squall line and dipping jet stream and Polar Express cold front. "Unusually dangerous downburst winds" and "precipitous drop in temperature" notices flash in red. If I look under the "Silver Springs, Florida" t-shirt, the one with baby orangutans hugging, and past the shelf in the window lined with zero-calorie, electrolyte-enhanced bottles of water, I can see to the outside. One of the potted palms tilts sideways against the glass. We've never had orangutans here.

The rest of the woman's family tumbles in the door and circles around her before spreading through the store. A little boy rushes to the Indian stuff. I see him palm a medallion into his pocket—beads on simulated leather. He plucks at the strands on a dream catcher and breaks one. He fake shoots a plastic rifle. He taps too hard on the glass protecting a real, found in the river, ancient flute. I ignore him. I ignore all of them and flip back to *The View*. Barbara drops names about her New Year's Eve special, and that new black girl they have on giggles about the fine handsomeness of their next guest. She should know that handsome isn't worth much.

"Do you have any more of these love bird frogs? This one has a chip."

Her earrings blink into the glass of the counter top. She puts the metal statue beside my screen. I tap it silent. I look up and see the two frogs cuddling on a porch swing. Their ankles cross in a coy way. The girl frog has oversized human eyelashes and red-painted lips. She's a foot tall.

"My mother-in-law will love this. She collects frogs."

My ex mother-in-law collected owls. I guess she still does. I guess women have to collect something so their families will know what to buy them for gifts. At my first his-family Thanksgiving, they kept at me to choose so I picked dragonflies. The stores here have monkeys, owls, turtles, flamingos, and bears—stuffed, statued, and on t-shirts—but no dragonflies. Still, his family found plenty of dragonfly shit. At least my Christmas Eve birthday, with its one-for-two-occasion gifts, limited things. Well, that's over. Tomorrow, for the first time in ten years, they can't add to the collection of refrigerator magnets, garish stained glass, and hand-painted light switch covers stored in my closet. Maybe, tomorrow, in celebration, I'll throw them out.

"See, here, on the base." The woman scrapes her fingernail over the place the veneer has chipped and makes it bigger.

"I'll see what we have in the back."

I scoop up my phone and the frogs and retreat to the storage room. Stacks of boxes, all stamped Made in China, line the walls. In the corner, on the third shelf down, a row of love bird frogs stare into each other's eyes. I don't have to go right back. She'll think I'm searching. I find the plastic case of markers and select a matching color to blot into the chip. The next customer will never notice. I pick up another frog pair and peel the China label off the bottom. The wind chimes sound as more customers arrive. The cash register is unguarded. I have to get back out there. I sit down on a wooden pallet, my knees bent to my chest, the frogs at my side. I'm crying. I light a cigarette.

The back door opens and lets in piped music telling people to hark the herald angels and outside air that chills my ankles. I slip the cigarette under my shoe and look up. A frizz of blond hair shakes in front of my face.

"Do you like it?" Betty Kay lifts her head and hands me a coffee from the concession she runs. She pats her hair. "The package calls it 'Blonded by the Light.' I thought I'd brighten things up for the holidays."

"It's something, that's for sure. Remember when we saved up for our first Miss Clairols? 'Champagne Dreams'—that was yours, wasn't it?" I take the lid off the cup and blow into it.

"Shut up. We were twelve. We didn't know not to leave it on that long. Besides, Miss 'Ginger Light,' you didn't look much better."

"Scrambled Eggs and Orange Juice." We say it in unison. It took the rest of the school year for us to lose those nicknames.

"Are you crying again? Jesus, you have to stop this. I'm telling you, you should take the same pills as me. Best thing I ever did."

"I thought you hated not being horny all the time. And that it made you put on weight. And I get to feel sad. The divorce papers went out yesterday, and remember, my father just died.

I'm a total orphan now." I take a sip, and the coffee heat stings my lips.

"But your Dad left ya'll years ago. He only came back because he knew you'd let him live in your people's lonely ass patch of pine flats that your grandfather left you instead of him. You got sucked into taking care of him."

"Hey, he paid me damn good to do that."

"I'm not saying it didn't work out for you, especially since you'd just walked out on Mr. Piece-of-Crap, but why do you still stay out in that old single wide? Get a place in town. And I'm not fat anymore, if you haven't noticed." Betty Kay puts a hand on a hip and strikes a pose. "I'm back down to my flirting weight. And you, your pants hang half off you. You don't have to worry about packing on a few pounds. Really, you should try some medication. I'm having the time of my life."

"I'll get better after the holidays. It always works that way."

"Get real. Miss Mary Sunshine, you're not. Well, in elementary school, I remember you as sort of bouncy and cheerful. But that went away. And look at me, if I wasn't taking that stuff, would I have sold my leaky house the minute the boys finally moved out? Would I have my sweet condo that's so teen-antsy they don't even think about moving back in? And really, I don't mind waking up without an itch in my hoo haw like I've had every day since I turned sixteen."

"Fourteen. Remember Wayne? First boy in our class to get a mustache."

"Aw, Wayne." Betty Kay sits beside me on the pallet and bumps shoulders with me. "And besides Wayne, we both had the hots for that nasty deejay. Dr. Cool, isn't that what he called himself?"

"Doctor of Chill, I think. God, he played 'Three Dog Night' every third track. I don't know why I let him."

"Let him what?" Betty Kay pays attention from time to time. She didn't back then when I hitched a ride to Gainesville and got it taken care of at one of those feminist clinics. Right now she's back to trying out hair styles—behind the ears, pulled into a bun, up, but with loose tendrils around her face.

"Nothing." I try the coffee again. Lukewarm is almost as bad as too hot. I drink it anyway. I wish I hadn't put out my cigarette. "That competitive suck-up over at the other shop told me my ex has marriage plans."

"To who? Do we know her? My guess is that slut from two grades behind us."

"Remember the guy who was a senior when we were freshman, and he tried to feel you up in the back of the science lab?"

"Yeah."

"His daughter."

"Oh, man, how did we get to here? Well, she's in for a surprise. Your ex has only got his looks for a year more, two at the most. Remember his dad? He was the oldest looking old man I've ever seen. And you, you're not doing much of anything to look good these days." Betty Kay points at the grown-out leg hairs showing above my ankles. "But still, those men out there trailing after their wives and packs of kids, they stare at you. You've got one of those long waists and straight, almost blond hair that swings when you walk. It makes men think things."

"Oh, great. Skanky, married men want me. And last time I got my hair trimmed the big gay offered me something called 'grey solution.' I didn't tip him much."

"Well, we need to celebrate getting rid of your ex just in time. Only, not these next few days. That's what I came to tell you. I'm cutting my shift short and leaving this afternoon for Vegas. I found last minute, way cheap tickets online. Vegas for Christmas—can you imagine anything better?"

"But today's my birthday eve."

"I know. I'm sorry. But, remember, this year's my first time with no kids. And you and Theresa have your thing you do every year. And in three days I'll come home with a fabulous present for you. Although, you seem to be all fabulous already."

She's seen my wires. She pulls the phone out of my pants.

"Wow, what did this set you back? And you have to buy a contract too, right? Did your Dad have a stash out there in a gopher tortoise burrow?"

I mumble something about life insurance and zip the phone into its shockproof, water-proof case with the interior rubber guardrails. The ad called it "the world traveler" case. I don't know where I think I'm going, but click, click, online shopping is easy. I won't tell Betty Kay about the fifty-four inch flatscreen that arrived yesterday. I paid extra to get it delivered quick, so Theresa and I can watch it tomorrow while we eat some vegetarian thing she brings over. Something crashes in the next room.

"What's out there? An army?"

"A customer wants this frog thing." I don't move. I just can't.

"Okay, I'll take care of it."

I hear her chipper, retail voice asking where they're from, apologizing for the unusual weather like somehow we're at fault, selling them more ugly stuff. I should have told her about the little shoplifter. Betty Kay can shake a kid down just by pretending to give him a big hug. "Aren't you just the cutest thing," she says while retrieving items out of their pockets.

"Bye, bye. Have a safe drive home. You'll be the star on Christmas morning with those frogs."

Betty Kay comes back and sits beside me.

"I have to go. We've got to watch our break times the way they're looking to fire people. And you better get out there. Let me haul you up. Hey, that's a nice watch. Are those diamonds?"

"Nah, zirconia." They're diamonds. I twist my wrist away.

Betty Kay knows her jewels, but she's in a hurry and I get away with it. I take another frog couple off the shelf to restock the display and go back out onto the sales floor. Just in time, because the bitch has snuck in. She's tiny, but bristles herself big like a cat.

"Just restocking while I had a chance." I hold out the frogs as proof. I go over to the display and fill the empty spot and take my time tidying and rubbing at the dust on the shelf.

"Why isn't the Christmas music on in here?"

She's come up right behind me. I turn and stare down at her. Her skin is perfect. This is my first younger-than-I-am boss. I flick the dust cloth between us, and she backs up.

"You know about that glitch in the wires. I've submitted a repair request." A couple of the old maintenance guys used to date my mother. They come and pull out wires for me every December. They fix them in January. My mother dated around a lot after my father left. Then she settled down with this one rich, married guy.

The bitch can't pinpoint anything I'm doing wrong, but I'm making her mad. This is my special gift as a member of the "service industry." Other clerks have tried to copy me, but fail. If I had more energy, I'd bend down, keep my butt pointed at her face, and pick imaginary lint up off the carpet. But I don't care enough these days. Nothing feels fun anymore. Although I get a flicker of satisfaction whenever I use my dead father's credit card. I go behind the counter, straighten the point-of-sale keychain display, and neaten the collar on my shirt. I look over at my boss. She's thinking hard about how to order me around. I smile at her.

"Are you here to give me my break? I read the new employee manual like you said, and we're supposed to get fifteen minute breaks every four hours. Or I could go ahead and take lunch now.

Whatever works for you?" She's sputtering. Now I'm smiling for real.

"So lunch, then." I grab my new leather coat from under the counter and leave through the storage area. The door opens onto a wall of cold, grey light. I close it and rummage through the overstock shelves to find the sweatshirts I should have already put on display and the flamingo-decorated tube socks that never sell. It doesn't take long to pull off my shoes and jacket, put on the extra layers, retie my laces, and zip the jacket all the way up over the hitchhiking alligator holding a "Take me to Silver Springs" sign. I open the door again.

"Sleigh bells ring. Are you listening?" The rest of the carol fades into crackles and snaps. The sound system goes wonky in cold weather. I hear thumping from the speaker under the building's eve and picture the dweeb in the control room smacking the machinery. He likes his eggnog. At least I can still feel happy when things screw up around this place.

Foil-wrapped paper poinsettias cluster around tinseled palm trees. What must be Mainland China's entire supply of white twinkle lights wrap around wire outlines of candles, reindeer, lollipops, and flamingos. Someone has already flipped the switch, and what with the overcast, they make a nice glow. Tourists hunch their shoulders against the cold. We'd have probably sold out of sweatshirts if I'd bothered to put them out. I pause under the "Spirit of the Swamp" sculpture or arch or whatever they call it. You can't tell if the puffy things are cypress branches or clouds. I could do better. I rub along a side and wonder, again, how to work the metal so it curves like this. Sometimes I still make things, but my public peak as an artist was set design for the senior class production of *Jesus Christ, Superstar*.

I veer off toward Betty Kay's concession for more coffee and pass the weird bird enclosure with its South American this, African that, and the Southeast Asian something else. The birds huddle in a corner with all their fancy headwork flattened the best each of them can manage. Betty Kay's place has a line, but she sees me. By the time I circle around the crowd and come up to the counter from the side, she has my cup ready and hands it over, never taking her eyes off the customer she's serving. Betty Kay taps her watch. She's leaving any minute. I head over to the animal exhibits to firm up my birthday plan with Theresa.

She's standing in front of the parrots. Their cages dangle from hooks at the entranceway to the exhibit. They look like go-go dancers. They're pissed off. Even I can tell that. Theresa, sensibly, wears sweatpants. She has a bright red bird on her arm.

"Hold on, let me put her in the cage." She whispers to the bird and runs a knuckle along its face. It rubs back. "I can't believe we have them out here in this weather. I said no, but the new management said the temperature falls 'within parameters.' Sure, if you're not in the wind."

Theresa stands back from the cages. A gust of the Weather Channel's Polar Express rocks them on their hooks.

"Screw them. I'm shutting this exhibit down. Here, take this bird while I lift the cage off the hook."

She opens another cage and puts a blue parrot on my arm. Its yellow crest rises in alarm, and the head twists sideways so that one eye points my way. Loose birds make me nervous.

"I don't think this parrot likes me."

"Macaw. And it doesn't like anyone. Just stay calm. It probably won't bite."

Animals first, then people—that's the way of it for Theresa, even if you've stayed friends ever since ninth grade when Betty Kay and I got in a little over our heads at a horse show. The college boys were down from Gainesville, and maybe we had led them to believe we were older than we really were, but still, they weren't listening. Theresa had a weekend job in the barn and found us all there. She backed them off. She had that manure shovel, but I think her look more than anything made them scurry away. She's got that look again as she pulls the cages down.

"I wish I had your attitude." I hold my arm as far away from my body as I can, but the bird weighs more than you'd think. I don't like animals much.

"Oh, honey. You do fine with that just-this-side-of-surly thing you do. I'm a patsy. They know they can get me to stay late or come in if the critters need something. But no way I'll let them get hurt." Theresa has the other two birds on her shoulders. The purple one bites along the curve of her ear. Three children, stair-stepped siblings it looks like, run past me to crowd around her legs.

"Are you taking them away? Can we see them?"

"You know, they grew up a long ways from here where the weather stays warm all year. I need to take them inside. But do you want to pet their wings first?" They ignore me even though my bird is bright blue and bigger. Theresa kneels and teaches the children how to use gentle touches. Theresa's kindness with children can make me hurt. She stands, and the children follow in her wake. My bird stretches its neck to pinch my neck skin in its beak. All I do is hiss and maybe say goddamnit a little bit loud, but Theresa, the two birds, and the children turn and stare at me. My bird adds an extra twist to its bite. I hate it, but I do not shake it off onto the ground and kick it. I even fake smile at the children. They move in closer to Theresa. She distracts the kids with bird facts, and our troupe moves on.

We leave the children behind at the employee gate, and after Theresa puts her birds in their cages, she chucks mine under the chin.

"Are you being a bad boy to my friend? Here, let's put you closest to the heat lamp."

"So you're rewarding him for biting me? Am I bleeding? And did you know that Betty Kay isn't going to be here for my birthday? She's probably out in the parking lot headed for Vegas right now. It'll just be us this year."

"About that."

"No. No 'about that.' I really need you this year. Of course I'm sorry that your girlfriend's parents still think you're a roommate, even after eight years, how stupid is that, but it works for us. She goes off for a family holiday without you and we celebrate my birthday instead of Jesus'. I mean I was actually born on Christmas Eve, and he was really born in March or something."

"She came out to them."

"Why the hell did she do that?"

"We're going to have a baby."

I can't stop thinking and doing bad things. Right now, even though I know I shouldn't, all I care about is how Theresa will never have time for me again. And she can tell. I've seen Theresa look at a horse that just tried to kick her the way she's looking at me.

"I have to go check on the otter." She turns her back on me.

"I know. I'm a selfish jerk these days. Just give me time to adjust." I follow close behind Theresa and trip into her as she stops and turns around. She puts a hand on my arm and shakes it a little.

"We're talking longer than just 'these days.' You have to get onboard with all this. You have five seconds to say something supportive."

"You're right." I put my hand over hers. "Okay, how about this. First off, you'll have to get one of those 'baby onboard' signs for your car window. And then we'll have to stop teasing about how you cradle-robbed to get a young girlfriend. I mean, I'm working on a joke about cradles, but I haven't figured it out yet. And, ohmyfuckinggod." I step back and point at her. "You have to spend every single damn holiday with her parents and that brother of hers, the one that sells timeshares, or Amway, whatever."

"Shaklee." Theresa almost smiles.

"Say it." I tap her chest with my finger.

"You're a little right. This whole 'acceptance' thing has a few drawbacks."

"I knew it. You would so rather kick back in my living room and watch the new flatscreen while we sip imported brews."

"Flatscreen? When did you upgrade? Does it have HDTV? I looked into it, but you have to have this whole cable package that costs. The baby is still just a glimmer in some sperm bank's dry ice, but we already consider every expense. Did my cousin give you a good discount over at Circuit City?"

"I ordered online. It was a better deal." Theresa's cousin would know my father was dead. "Hey, do you need some sperm money? I'll donate to the cause. I get to be an aunt, right?" I'll use the last of the stolen credit card's limit for someone else. How's that for not being self-centered?

Theresa looks at me as if the otter in the glass cage beside us had started talking.

"Did your dad have a policy or something?"

"Oh, he had a little bit for me to inherit. Hey, have you figured out how to free this otter yet?"

We both turn to stare through the glass. Past our reflections, the otter floats on its back in the concrete pool. A carrot balances on its belly, between its paws. It takes an occasional bite. It doesn't care. Nothing tastes good. The unhappiness coming through the glass almost puts me on my knees.

"I'm close. I found out its history, and I'm pretty sure it could still make it in the wild. But they'll just snatch another one out of a river somewhere. Is it right to set something free

and not worry about the consequences? I'll feel so guilty when I
see that next otter in this cage. Damn, it all keeps me from doing
anything. I have to think about it some more."

Theresa lays her hand flat out on the glass, and we don't
say anything for awhile. An odd chirp comes from under my
clothes. Theresa looks around for a lost bird while I fish out my
new phone. I thought I changed my ringtone to what they call
"old fashioned phone." We look at the screen together. I have
a text message from my ex husband. I've never received a text
message, ever, from anyone. "PU frt porch." Theresa and I don't
have a clue. One of the staff interrupts us.

"Ma'am? We're ready for the next reptile show. Which snake
should I use?"

She's so young and pierced, and her hair is short with red
tipped spikes.

"The indigo. But cut the show short. I don't want her chilled.
And look at this." Theresa holds the screen up to the girl's face.
"What does this say?"

"Pick up something from the front porch."

"Thanks. And you know you have to take out the face
jewelry. Sorry, orders."

"Yes, ma'am." She almost bows before she leaves. They all
adore Theresa. She turns the phone over in her palm a few times
before she hands it back to me. She doesn't say anything. She
wouldn't, she's not nosy like Betty Kay. We go back to staring at
the otter. Theresa takes a breath. Maybe she wants an explanation
about my sudden material wealth. I need to figure out a cover
story.

"Your ex knows how to text?"

"No, but I'll bet his new young thing does. She must have
moved in and wants to de-wife the house. The divorce papers
finally came through. I'm forty-nine tomorrow. Officially, almost
old. And officially alone."

"That's good, isn't it?"

"But I'm sort of like Betty Kay with her one man after another. Just because mine last ten years or so at a time doesn't make it any better. Worse, maybe. The misery stretches out for longer."

We both sigh, and the glass fogs over the otter. Theresa puts her hand on my shoulder.

"Come with me. I have to check the terrariums."

"Yes, ma'am." I smirk into the reflection.

"Shut up. When did we become ma'ams?"

The display areas are kept dark so the terrariums glow out of the walls. Most of the rectangles of glass have snakes behind them, but I always stop at the frogs. Today the giant toad has buried itself in wood chips, and only her eye ridges show. The next window should have peepers. When they get going with their calls, all the maybe millions of them at once, I can hear it inside the store. Only one thumb-sized orange back crouches on the branches. The plaque says they mate in winter.

My dad kept aquariums. One day I came home from making a papier-mâché manger scene in fourth grade art class, "the best one" the teacher whispered in my ear, and both the fresh and salt water tanks had disappeared. That's how we knew he was really gone. Mother moved a couple of chairs into the empty spaces and pretty soon we got used to the new arrangement. But I still remember how my father let me arrange the insides. It turned out best if from close-up you saw a whole story—a mermaid protecting her treasure chest from the faceless diver in his helmet or a pirate shipwreck with a shark coming out of it. But then I'd build the mounds of pink and green gravel so that from far away they flowed together like one of those abstract paintings where the shapes of the colors make you feel things. My mother held on to the house until I grew up. Then she lost it to the bank. She

never would take money from that married man. Then she died.
Emphysema.

"Hey. Wake up. Come back here and help me."

I follow Theresa to behind the wall. She takes out a rat snake
and lets it crawl under her shirt while she pours more shavings
into its tank. I spread them over the bottom, and while I'm
there, rearrange the rocks and branches so they are pleasingly
asymmetrical. That's what my high school art teacher called my
creations. My father owes me. I might have gone to the tech
school for graphic arts or even straight-out art school if he'd
stayed. Instead, I've worked here since summers in high school.
This place owes me.

The diamonds on my watch glimmer and say I'm way past
my half hour lunch. So what? They can whisper about us being
dead weight all they want, but there's no way they'd fire any of
us second and third generation workers. My grandfather used to
catch alligators for them.

"Theresa, I've got to get back. Tell your gal hi from me."

"Sure. I'm actually leaving to go pick her up right now."

I haven't eaten anything. Or had a cigarette. There's no
time to go to our "designated employee smoking area." The
Pick-a-Pearl store manager waves at me as I go by. I ignore
her. According to management bitch, her store brings in more
income than mine. But they gave her the stuff-your-own-animal
machine, so what do they expect. Otherwise we have pretty
much the same crap—except for the frogs. I have more frogs.
Past the pizza restaurant is an alley to the restrooms. I go back
there and light up. Something has trickled out from under the
wall and stained the concrete. I move to the other side and stand
behind the ancient diorama cases they have stored up on brick
blocks. The tiny ladies in fifties pedal pushers and the men in
palm tree shirts and the blond children in sundresses with peter
pan collars stare at me from their placement around edge of the

head springs. An Indian and an alligator wrestle in an arena. A potter leans over a wheel. Kids swim on a beach. Behind them, glass-bottomed boats sit on faded spring water. This is what it looked like when my father first worked here, before the big fire in 1955. He saved a lot of people's lives. They left casseroles on the trailer steps when they heard he was back in town and sick.

I'm way overdue to get back. I'll say I had to help with the animals and mention how the manual encourages "cross-departmental cooperation." I come out from behind the old displays, and the bitch fills the entrance to the alley. How can someone little block so much light? I drop the cigarette and kick it under the case. I don't think she's seen.

"There you are."

Her nose sniffs the air like a hound's. She can smell the cigarette smoke. She smiles and looks for my hands. I keep one behind me to get her hopes up. She steps closer. Wind, cold all the way through, rushes past her and fills the back of the alley. I reveal my hidden hand and spread the fingers wide to run it through my hair. I smile back at her, but I'm worried. I can't come up with a story about why I'm in the alley. I need to get by her, get out into the open. Her eyes have dropped to scan the floor for butts.

"Sorry, I'm a little late." I point at the bathroom door. "It was the pizza. It must have been off. You might want to let them know." My shoulder brushes against the wall as I try to move past.

Instead of giving me room, the bitch squats. Smoke wafts up from under the display. She stares up at me for a moment before she tilts her head to look underneath. She waddles forward and even puts her hands on the concrete to lean lower. I try to imagine next week at the staff New Year's party where I'm telling this story, describing how from this angle her cowlick looks like a hairy asshole, and maybe charming, at least for the night, that

new hire over in maintenance with my foul mouth and disdain
for authority. Her feet go still, and her rear end bobs in place.
Her hair brushes along the concrete as she reaches under the
case. She has the still smoldering butt in her fingers as she rises.
She straightens her knees without a groan or stagger, and I think
I hate her for that more than for what she's about to do.

"This is a wood display. You could have set the whole place
on fire. Did you know we burnt down in the fifties?"

"Actually my father, who died recently, helped pull people
out of flames."

"Yes, the management knows that. And we've made
allowances. But this incident takes it out of my hands. I'm sorry,
but I simply have no recourse."

She doesn't look sorry. And how can she prove that the butt
is mine? Are they going test it like in a crime show? The bitch
wraps it in a Kleenex. She might.

"I have no choice, the rules are clear." She takes a deep,
excited breath. "We no longer need your services." The bitch
says something about a two week severance that she isn't required
to offer under these circumstances but in consideration of my
family's long service and something else about staying put, my
locker, a security escort.

All I feel is relief. Each morning it takes everything I have to
get out of the house. Tomorrow I'll wake up or not, and it'll be
my birthday and no one will celebrate with me, and I won't have
to smile at anyone or pretend I'm having any feelings at all. In
some awful way, my life is now perfect. She's gone. It wasn't her
blocking the light. The sky has gone solid grey.

One of the boat captain's sing-song spiels ripples into
the alley. All my life I've heard this hum of information. An
occasional phrase gets magnified by the water and kicked up
into the shops—"the glory of underwater geysers," "from the
bowels of the earth." No one believes me when I say I've never

taken the tour. My mother used to sneak me in the park if I was too sick for school and she had to work. She'd leave me a thermos and some toys, and I'd sit on an out-of-the-way bench that overlooked the water and see the boats go by filled with kids. Sometimes I'd try to make herons out of pink, green, and orange Play-Doh, but their necks collapsed every time. Making the "I Dream of Jeannie" magic bottle worked better. I'd use a stick to draw the designs, and all the while, listen to those tall black men, the boat captains, tell stories about Indian maidens, old Negro aunties, and lost, drowned loves.

Someone rushes into the alley and I brace, but only the khakied white kid who runs the jeep ride lopes by. These days the management puts "naturalist" on their name tags, and has them say "eco shit this" and "eco crap that" every other sentence. Once I heard them lecture a tourist group about the "dangerous overuse of fertilizers" and how it harms the river while they were standing on the big lawn here—the lawn they keep bright green and thick with truckloads of fertilizers. He pauses at the bathroom door and stares at me. Has he heard I've been fired? I ignore him and he goes on in. They're all so earnest. I hear a pipe rattle, and a fresh spurt of liquid leaks out from under the wall. It stinks. Security will come for me soon. I can't stay here, in this closed-up space.

I leave the alley. No one comes after me or yells or points or grabs, but still I slip into the historical showcase room. No one much comes here, and the lighting is bad. Tarzan yodels from a video screen. I circle around a mish mash of mammoth bones, ads for waterproof Band-Aids, and movie posters. A carved miniature steamboat and Seminole doll with her striped skirt flared wide line the back wall along with a turtle fossil, shell ax, and a faded, falling apart book of poetry. Our storeroom has a few more of these molding on a shelf. I read one of the poems. That woman must have been on acid the way she describes the underwater colors. Or maybe things have changed that much. I don't think back to being a kid much, but sometimes I remember the "jeweled greens" and "blues brighter than any sky" the poet writes about. I rest my elbows on a glass case and stare through the scratches and reflections. A diving bell, saber-tooth cat skull, and underwater camera sit in folds of dusty velvet. Maybe I should take something with me—a little severance package of my own choosing.

The loudspeakers click and groan, and *Deck the Halls* pounds down from the ceiling. Before the end of the first "Fa la la la," I'm back out on the sidewalks. The boat guide's microphoned voice spreads over the lawns. I walk down to the dock and sit on a bench to watch the boat circle the spring head. Everyone onboard bends to look through the bottom except the captain. The glass bottom boat captains don't mix with us store people much. They're like the rock stars of the place. But even their stories have changed. Instead of bridal chambers, he's telling them about the five hundred and fifty gallons of water that burst out, right there, from deep in the aquifer every day and how the water below them could be from rain a hundred years ago or last week. I hear talk of pollution, algae, and nitrites. But still, they tell stories. He starts a new one.

"Ten thousand years ago we'd be on a sea, not of water, but of grass. Imagine that in all directions, for hundreds and hundred of miles, mammoths and ancient horses and saber-toothed cats roam on grassy plains. All of you are a tribe, one of the First People of Florida. You've traveled for days, and your gourds and leather skins of water have gone empty. Unlike now, fresh water is hard to find. And then you, maybe you young man, come close to right where we are now and you smell water. Not that there was a river here or even a lake. But see down below us, at that deep hole, ten thousand years ago that existed like it does now. Only this was just a crack in the dry earth and at the bottom of the crack, sweet water bubbled up from underground. You and your family stand around the edge, thirsty, and I'll bet some smart one of you, maybe you young lady, figured out the first bucket and how to lower it. And now here we are back at the landing and the present day. Please stay seated until we dock and open the gates. Don't forget, just up the walk we have plenty of places to quench your thirst here at Silver Springs. I'll bet, for today, they're even serving up some hot chocolate. And thank you for taking the famous Silver Spring's glass bottom boat tour."

People clap. I look over my shoulder and see security oafs search along in front of the stores. They're the regular football player type hires, but I don't know these particular two. I move off the bench and stand behind an information plaque. The collective sound of tourist comes up behind me, and I mingle with the crowd leaving the boat. I follow a family that veers off from the herd to walk along the river. I can't stop myself from acting the part of a spy on a mission. I must not be taken. Every espionage movie works the same—act casual, keep your head turned. Point out over the river so your back stays to the pursuers. Linger close to the family and act like one of them.

The father frowns at me. He's wary of the way I lean too close to his children. The gig is almost up. Find cover. Walls surround the park to keep the tourists in and the river and forest out, but at the edge of the lawn I find a gap between fence and water. I squeeze through a line of azalea bushes and hide behind a messy, still-wild patch with brush and unkempt palm trees. I watch through the branches. The oafs move down the line of shops opening doors and darting in and rushing out. They're ignoring the river, but my movies tell me they'll eventually come this way. They disappear into the Dip n Dots store. This is the time to move.

A breathy whisper of a song comes through the bushes. I crouch back down and look. The family's three or so year old has followed me past the fence to the river. She's singing something about under the sea. She goes to the edge of the spring and squats in that effortless way kids do with her knees up around her ears. She tilts her body over until her song makes ripples in the surface of the water. Little kids and poodles are alligator bait—that's what my grandfather used to say and then he'd dangle me off the side of the rowboat and say to kick. I'd scream and laugh at the same time. My grandfather would never hurt me. I knew that. The kid's forehead touches the surface. Underneath her is deep water, right off.

I reach through the bushes and put a hand on her shoulder. She doesn't startle. Nothing bad must ever have happened to her. For a second, fiercely, I want to ruin that somehow. But I turn her away from the water.

"Go away from here. Go back to your family." I cuff her on the butt, not hard.

She smiles at me and keeps singing that Disney song, but she's using mostly nonsense words. I hear shouting. I don't understand what they're saying, but I recognize the half-pissed, half-scared voice that parents use. The girl laughs in their direction and totters off with the wind flipping her barretted braids behind her. I pull back behind the brush but keep watch as her parents kneel at her side and pat her all over. They don't swat her, not once. They're foreigners for sure. The oafs have run half way down to them, but see the reunion and turn around.

They pass me. When they get to the far side of the bridge, I'll run. I lift up to look just as a wind slams through the park and smacks me in a full-body tackle out into the open. The oafs see me and puff up all over and yell. Their feet echo against the bridge. They hit the path and the thud of their weight shakes through the ground and into my lungs. My legs kick through the dyed red cypress mulch around the azalea bushes and push me up off my knees into a full-out race down the promenade.

Hoop after hoop of Christmas lights glitter over me. At my feet, the luminaries blur into waving lines at the edge of my vision. I pass the docked boats all named for Indian warriors—Chief Osceola, Micanopy, Yaahalochee, Neamatha and Yoholo. I can't stop myself from running. These barely out of adolescence, over-muscled boys, not much different than Betty Kay's kids, have morphed into something life-threatening. I'm sure that if they touch me something bad will happen.

Beyond the neon-lit butterflies and lilies, behind the carousel, I stop. Rhinoceros, elephants, and swans circle by. On top of them, the children's hands grip the poles and past them, through the rises and falls, I see the security guys. I slip behind the petting zoo. A billy goat shakes its bell, trots over to where I'm crouched, and presses its forehead against the fence to beg for food. More goats follow. They'll give me away. I keep moving. Children scream from inside Playland, but I hear men yell behind me. I run full out again. I follow the jeep trail along the chain linked boundary of the park, past where the concrete ends, to where the path narrows and roots hump in from the sides. The fence traps me. In movies they climb fences like these. I throw myself as high as I can and grab. The wire hurts my fingers, my toes can't find a hold, and I drop against the bottom of the fence. It gives way. I roll and the edges scrape over me and I'm out. The fence snaps back into place. I'm in the wild of the river.

Past oaks, bays, tripping through cypress knees, I stay upright. I run around the hollowed out remains of the old trees. I hide behind the trunks of the ones that have grown back on top of them. The men's voices, the music, the sounds of tourists fade. I run through the thickets of sprawling aster bushes with their ragged purple flowers. I run until all I can hear is the wind. I run until I have to stop. Shit, shit, shit, the cold is colder than before when it was already cold. The wind sneaks off the river and through the trees. I tuck the sweatshirt into my pants and stretch the tube socks up until the pink threads of the flamingos snap. The jacket zips all the way up through the collar. Trees tangle close all around me, but past them, past their tops, the clouds look green. And thick. And something moves around inside them. A quick, yellow-tinged dusk rushes toward me.

I hear the wallop of water on water from the river. I hear the thrum of water on wood. Drops—fat, cold, strong—hit the ground around me and make the dry oak leaves jump like crickets. I squat under the still green leaves of a bay tree, but the wind twists the branches and water dumps over me. My teeth shake, and each drop feels warm on my skin for a second after it hits me.

Wind, like hands on my butt, shoves me against the trunk of a tree. I hold on, but bark splits off in my fingers, and I'm blown on to the next tree and to another. I can't hardly see fuck all, but I can tell only a few trees are left between me and the river. I dig my feet into the mud and dead leaves, but the wind throws me, head tilted back, onto a trunk too wide to reach around. In the flash of the storm, I see my arms splayed over a lightening-split cypress tree as big as in Grandfather's old stories. The world shakes, and the sky explodes again. Light flares through the tree's three branches—thick, blunted like a swollen hand, far above me. I close my eyes and their shape burns behind my lids. Thunder blankets my skin and blurs sound. I'm yelling shit, shit, shit over and over again. My chest, belly, thighs press against bark. The wind drops, and I fall back from the tree and stagger down into an old fire pit. Soot smears over my hands and knees. I hear the rumble just before a straight along the ground wind slams me over and into a roll. Charred pieces of wood tumble and lift in the air, and beer cans and bottles race past and fling into the river. I don't know which way is which, not until the wind pauses and leaves my head and shoulders hanging over the edge.

Lightning turns everything into white and shadow, and the river churns under my face. White caps skim the surface along with leaves and broken parts of trees. My hair falls past me, and the ends swirl into currents. The world goes dark again. My shoulders and breasts weigh me forward until the sand and tree roots shiver under my belly. Water slaps into my face. My arm reaches over the bank and claws into the sand and I'm, for the moment, braced.

If I do nothing, my arm will weaken or the wind will get stronger or the river will wash away the edge, and I will fall. The water will hurt from the cold, just at first. I imagine the oblivion, the quiet and warmth under the water, deep inside the river. One of Nancy Reagan's old "just say no" television commercials comforts me. The dead drug addict sinks, arms and legs spread, under the water with light shafting though the silence. It always made Theresa and Betty Kay nervous when I pointed out how it made me want to do more drugs, not less. In my head, my father always waits. My father always said I was his. Now, I'll go to him. It seems right. I wait. My arm shakes.

I remember manatees here on this river, before the dam. I'm in my grandfather's old rowboat he fixed up with a motor. I've brought my coloring book and am adding a burnt orange baby bear to one of the pictures when my grandfather interrupts. He tells me to look for where the water goes flat. I point. He shows me how to pat the water, and a baby manatee puts its nose into my palm. The whiskers tickle. My grandfather becomes a shadow over me, over the manatee, out over the water. His shadow arm lifts and from behind me the harpoon goes into the baby's back. Sea pork he called it that night, and my father whaled on me until I ate what was on my plate. My mother kept her head down. My grandfather said nothing. Like always. The meat tasted salty, but that might have been from the mix of tears and snot.

The rain comes faster and thicker now, and I feel the slipping of earth. I wait. The sand under my hand collapses, and my palm sinks into clay and roots. I tilt forward and most of me is suspended. I'm floating in gravity. The river touches my nose. It will be over soon.

Goddamnit all to hell. Something slices into my palm. The pain stabs along a nerve over my elbow and stings into my armpit. My other arm flails until it finds a root, wraps around it, and I pull my arm out of the hole in the bank. Clay sucks against it, lets go, and my body lifts up and back onto firm ground. Lightning snaps, and I see my palm stuck through with an arrowhead. The stone gleams blue. I yank it out, and rain-diluted blood wraps around my thumb and wrist. Thunder rolls out over the sky, but under it, I hear the lower tone of more wind beating between the trees, coming closer. I jam the arrowhead in my bra and lie flat.

Lightning shows tree tops bent like rubber. The shredding of wood sounds all around. A branch kicks into my ribs, and I curl and turn face down. I rise to my knees, cradle my hurt hand into my chest, and hold to the earth the best I can to crawl through the rain. It waterfalls over my eyes, into my ears. I might as well be under the water. My hand feels a change. Instead of sand and grass, it sinks into a rot of leaves and roots. I keep moving, and the flared pleats of the big tree's trunk press along my shoulders. Water and wind stop hammering on my scalp, and I fist water away from my eyes. My head is protected somehow. I can open my eyes, but it doesn't make a difference. The world is dark. I twist myself sideways, wood splinters, and my pants pull down my hips to my knees. I shove until the space splits open enough, and I'm inside the tree. All of me fits except my feet. The last of the water pours off my face. I kick my pants the rest of the way off. Water seeps up through the roots and mud underneath me. Wind slams against the tree, and the sound of wood stretching echoes. Something scurries above me. I cover my head with my hands. Spider webs wrap around my fingers.

My sweatshirt bunches into the small of my back like an ice pack against my kidneys. Cold burns the skin around my eyes, along the back of my hands, and into my spine where my shirt has pulled up. It hurts more than the gouge in my palm. I worry about my belly the most. It aches deep through my liver and beyond. I've never felt this before—maybe my organs have frozen. I dig my uninjured hand into the earth, through what feels like a pile of chicken bones, and reach into a pocket of warm. I go deeper and something shifts under my fingers. A heart beats in my palm. I touch along thick thighs, the knobbly back, the eye ridges. The frog found shelter in the mud. I put it to the side. I scoop mud over my legs, and they feel warmer. This will work better with no clothes.

I shrug my jacket down over my shoulders. It sticks half-way, and each time I move, it binds tighter around my arms. I shake an elbow and bend it into the air. The jacket drops closer to my wrist, but my arm wedges into the trunk. I can't move. I imagine being stuck like this forever. In the dark, the tree sides move closer, and my breath catches more than it releases. My heart hits against my chest, and my ears fill from the inside with a pulse louder than the storm outside. I hit my head against wood to make it stop. My fists curl, thump into the ground, and my hand stabs at me again.

The pain stops everything, like on television when they charge the heart, and for a second my mind quiets. The storm, the river, and tree with me and the spiders and the frog and everything else protected by it make a picture in my mind. In the center of it, a little girl is painted in bright colors. She is happy. The bones around me aren't the remains of Kentucky Fried that got brought out here to set the mood for a night of drinking and sex. Instead, in my story picture, they belong to the mastodon,

wolf, and panther that walk beside the girl, all of them colored
in sun-lit shades of brown and beige.

I try again. I'm not sure of time anymore, and it seems only
yesterday that I had sex in the front seat of a Camaro, trapped
between the dashboard and the seat. I squeeze my shoulders
together, like I did then, and my elbow drops free. My shirt
grabs to my back, and I remember the bucket seats. My panties
roll into themselves and make a rope around my thighs, and I
remember the gearshift. Damn, if only he'd been that hard. My
laugh sticks in my chest, but my muscles relax and the clothes let
go their grip. Who knew that bad, quaaluded sex with someone
whose face I can't seem to recall was going to, thirty some years
later, help keep me from screaming?

My shirt and panties pull the rest of the way off. I unhook my
bra and wrap it around and around my hurt hand and tighten
the tie with my teeth. The arrowhead fits between the layers. I
dig around me until I sit deeper, and my kidneys shelter in sand
and clay and the long feathered ends of roots. Something hits my
feet, and I pull them as inside as I can and sit like a person doing
yoga. A hard, curved thing tumbles in along with them. I hold
it in my hands and feel the curve of a broken pot on one palm
and the mud packed inside it with the other. I shift my hands
and the mud crumbles and leaves a twist of fabric across my
palm. I wrap it around my neck like a scarf. I bring up handfuls
of the clay and spread them over my belly and out along the
insides of my thighs. My hands pat through the loose earth,
bones, rotten bark, and roots until I find the frog. It fits into the
triangle of earth between my thighs and cunt, and I cover it with
mud and press the curved piece of pot over it for protection. I
build towers of clay on my shoulders and spread them down my
arms. Rotting leaves stick up and around me. I don't know if
this is enough. I don't know how cold the night will get. My feet
push the clothes into the opening to block it. My hands cross

over my heart. The shivering has stopped. I half hum, half sing about walking in a winter wonderland, about rocking around the Christmas tree, about silent, holy nights. Ten thousand years ago they say it was dry here. There was no river, no cold weather. Best I can, I imagine the yeasty smell of sun-baked earth. I'm going to sleep now. I've done what I can to live.

There is light. Pearl slats of it come through the gaps in the trunk above me. I've slept with my head tilted against the shaggy insides of the tree, and every neck muscle is locked tight. I raise an arm to help lift my head, mud breaks off my shoulders, and cold air feels like sandpaper against where my skin is scrubbed raw. I kick the clothes out through the opening to stretch my legs into the world, and each of the hundred small twists of tendon hurts and hurts. I never liked the stupid story about the Little Mermaid and the way walking on her new feet felt like knifes cutting into her soles. I hump over the protected frog and scooch until enough of me moves outside to dip my shoulders down and through.

The sun glares too bright to see anything. The ground shakes underneath me as if it was floating on water. I hold still, blink, and the world forms again. It has changed. The bank is mostly washed away, and I and the tree fill the peninsula of dry land left. I'm not sure about standing, but I stretch out on my belly so that my thighs pull long and my knees straighten. The fabric, yellowed and ripped up, falls over my face. It feels like silk.

The river reaches over the edges, to my fingertips, and a low fog covers it. White steams off the surface and away into the sunlight. The blurred oranges of maple leaves come into focus. The fog lifts enough that I see ibis dig through the flooded woods on the far shore. Beside them, above them, a woodstork swings its vulture head from side to side. White lilies gleam in the shadows around them. The sun doesn't have a bit of warm in it. I rub my arms over and over, but they keep feeling like bread dough. The park has dry clothes and heat. And water. I'm thirsty all the way through my body, as if I'd been partying most of the night, and all I can think of is that long line of bottled water we sell in the store.

"You're a dumb fuck sometimes, you know." I'm talking out loud to myself, but really, the cold has made me stupid. Water is everywhere. I pull my hand to my mouth and suck on it. Some of the bank sifts into the river as I lean and cup handfuls of water into my mouth. The water tastes warm. I drink until my belly pouches. I splash it up my arms and over my chest, but it doesn't help. My skin stings in the cold.

I turn to warm my backside in the ground. While I pull one knee and then the other to my chest, I see a hawk glide through a sky the glassy blue that happens for only a few days each winter when the humidity clears. My back warms enough to feel the rocks and sticks hurting it. So what that the world is beautiful this morning? Enough of this wonder of nature crap. It almost killed me. I have to get warm. I need to stand.

I sit up first. The river left stuff behind when it dug underneath and then overflowed the bank. Vines twist around a dead fish, and the sunlight makes rainbows along its skin. Something glints, and I reach through the slime of the weeds and untangle an old hip flask—pitted etched silver, crushed on one side. I remember my treasures still in the tree trunk. My father and grandfather always went out looking after a storm. They'd find things and sell them to collectors. Fossils can bring in good money. I squint and look around me.

Bones. So many friggin' bones. Around me, under me, mats of grasses and long swollen roots are thrown over the debris, but I recognize things in the mess. I put the flask down. I think tossed away Sonny's pork ribs, drowned cows, feral pigs even while I'm reaching for the human skull. The lower jaw is gone, but the eye sockets are unbroken. To the side is another skull, smaller. It sits at the top of another bone, a thigh bone I'm pretty sure—not a child's, but small, a teenager's? Everywhere, all sorts of bones. I could lie here and my bones would join these. I wouldn't feel cold anymore. It would be peaceful. Except that I really want a cigarette. And my mind isn't peaceful. It rearranges the bones. It shows me how to wire them through with steel to make the necks of tall white birds and says to knit others into the shape of an owl. I'd use glass for the eyes. I hold what looks like a pelvis in my hand and see a raccoon's face, its body made of brushed copper. I reach for the small skull that will become an owl head and stop. Am I a ghoul? This was a child. Cold sinks past my skin and into my own bones.

Coffee, a smoke, a warm building. That's what I should think about. I couldn't have run very far yesterday. I untangle my clothes from each other, but everything except the jacket is too wet to put on. I push to standing and teeter over the river. The mist has dissolved and I see myself in the water—naked except for my shoes, collapsed flamingo tube socks, and jacket. It will have to do. I don't have much more strength. A breeze comes off the water and chills from the first edge of ankle that shows above my shoes, over my knees, through the hair between my thighs, and makes my belly prickle and my nipples stretch until they ache. I raise my hands, and the clay dried into the hair under my arms pulls and cracks. My feet stay in place, but in the river, I see my body dip and sway. My reflection is of a young girl, almost a woman, with black hair swinging. We're dancing. Or maybe fainting. A kingfisher trills over the water, a great blue complains from somewhere high up behind me, and I hear the phone from my childhood ring, the beige one with crayon marks that sat on the kitchen counter. A mockingbird sings along with it twice before I think to reach into the coat's pocket. I open waterproof snaps and unzip and touch and hold it to my ear.

"Happy birthday, sweetie. Do you know how early it is here? Good thing I stayed up all night, isn't it? I just played the slots in honor of your day, and won fifty dollars. That can only mean that you're going to have a fabulous year. Oh, here, say hi to Devon. He's kept me company all night."

I hear the echo of a male voice saying "Happy birthday, friend of Betty Kay." I make a sound. I'm not sure what sound.

"Well, there's a big laugh. I'm glad you're in such a good mood. Now, we're off to have one of those Las Vegas big butt buffet breakfasts. With mimosas, of course. See you soon, birthday girl. Gotta go."

I have a phone. It has bars. Meathead, that's what my father called me. I could have called for help. I can right now. But the phone goes back in my pocket without me having to think about it. I don't want anyone to find this place. Maybe, later, I'll send a testimonial in to the phone case company. Wet squishes through my shoes as I move closer to the tree. I reach in and feel, but the frog is lost back into the mud. I find the pottery and in the sunlight, the surface shows swirls of orange and purple in patches. It looks too modern to be worth much, but I lay my shirt flat and put the broken piece into it, add the arrowhead that's come loose from my bra bandage, and twist the shirt. I wrap it around my waist along with my pants. I put the flask inside the tree so I can find it again. The silver might bring in some bucks. The sunlight finally has heat, and I face my chest and thighs into it and warm enough to start shivering again. I loop the silk twice around my neck. I'm ready. I step through the bones, careful not to break them, and clutch the old cypress tree as I slide around it toward firmer ground.

The landscape has changed. Cedar limbs split off their trunks in jagged pieces that expose raw bright wood. Their old closet smell spreads everywhere. Whole oak trees have fallen and opened wide spaces to the sunlight. I walk past the tilted up underneath of one. It makes a circle of roots and dirt taller than my head. Palm fronds lie over everything, and I fall against hidden cypress knees. I'm dizzy. My hand hurts. Nothing is familiar. I trip to my knees, and a breeze dumps water off the trees and onto my naked, stuck in the air, butt. This is ridiculous. I'm ridiculous. All I have to do is keep track of the river, and I'll get home. I push to standing using the final wall of an old cypress stump, and, through the trees, carried on the cold air, I hear a faint, cheesy, speeded-up version of *Jingle Bell Rock*.

Just like I thought, the fence comes into sight. I find the opening, trot back along the trail, and step onto the first paved path. I brace for people to see me, for tourists to scream, but no one appears. I remember that the park closes on Christmas Eve. Even the animals stay in their stalls and cages this morning. Security will be huddled in their office. I could go there. I don't.

The macaw rolls his eyes, but doesn't bite as I share his heat lamp with him. My skin has feeling again. I go to find Theresa's locker. She uses her birthday as the combination, and she'll have extra clothes. I'll try to sneak out. I pass by the displays. The otter is a curled, tucked tight ball inside the hollowed-out cypress log they've put out on the concrete floor of the cage. She lifts her face to mine and stares, expecting nothing. I lean my forehead against the glass. I could be out of here and back in my grandfather's trailer watching the big screen in less than half an hour. I can see the dry cigarettes on the dashboard of my car.

The otter keeps staring at me. She sniffs, and her whiskers circle around her nose. She's not sad this morning. She's not anything. If I leave now, I can get my job back. My baby boss doesn't know about my mother and the old man that's still on the board of directors. They kept it real secret, but I'm pretty sure he loved her till the day she died. I might even be able to get the bitch fired. The otter turns her face away.

I smack my head against the glass a few times, but I can't stop myself from going back behind the enclosure and finding the door. I open it and make what I think might be come hither sounds to an otter. She ignores me. I see a cooler, open it, and pull out a fish. It stinks. The otter comes out from inside the log. She wipes her face with a paw. I step away and watch her follow me in her butt-bouncing way. I and the fish lead her through the halls, the boardwalks, and past the head-dressed birds. Wild ibis mingle with them, and as we pass they rise and fly low toward the water. The otter stops and her neck stretches into the air. We follow the ibis. We cross the bridge, and she puts her head through railing. She won't jump, even when I kick at her a little. She's making me mad, but maybe she knows best and the drop is too far. I dangle the fish again, and we walk together to the spring. I show her the gap in the fence and sit at the edge of the water. She takes the fish and bites into the spine. A wave of peepers calling for sex sings out from the trees.

I'm going to sell the family land. The way my grandfather took care of it, burning the high pines every few years, letting all those flowers bloom in the meadows between them, some eco shit organization will want to buy it. They'll put up signs about long-leaf pine forests and the role of fire and won't allow hunting. It would really piss my father off, but I think my grandfather would like his land kept the old way. And I'll let this place give me that severance package. I don't need to stay here. I'll have money for awhile. I'll figure it out. The otter hasn't left yet.

"Hey, this is your chance, stupid animal. Go."

The otter snorts, wipes her chin, and her butt humps into the air one more time. She belly slides into the water and disappears until she pops up over the central, deep spring, the one that existed here eons ago, the one that these days spews out less

water each year. Her back shines in the sunlight, and she's gone.
My phone rings.

"Hey, birthday girl. How's it going? Are watching that big
TV already?"

"Theresa, you know, it's always right to set something free.
No matter what happens later."

"What?"

"Hold on, I think I have another call."

I figure out the call waiting and say hello.

"Excuse me, sir. I must speak to you of the credit card."

My life of free-spending ends now. That's alright. I'm ready.

"Sure, about that. The card belongs to my father, and he
died." There's no point in lying. They'll give me a payment plan,
my credit will stay in the dumps for years, whatever. I'll pay
everything off eventually. They're not going to put me in jail or
anything.

"The limit has been reached. Do you wish to increase?"

I fall back on the perfect green grass and laugh. Over my
head, upside down, I see security guys coming down the hill. I
switch back to Theresa.

"I've got to go. Say hi to your baby mama."

I half-consider running, but they grab me under the arms.
The pot falls out of my clothes and slips back into the water. The
men lift me up until I'm on tiptoe, and they trot me over the
lawn, one looking at, the other looking away from, my naked
parts. The clothes tied around my waist drop, catch over my hips,
and the arrowhead pricks through the material and into where
my thigh folds. I reach for it, but the men take the movement
for an attempted escape and pin my arms tighter. My pants, my
shirt, the arrowhead unwind from around my body and fall to
the ground. I hear laughing, my own laughing, and see the men's
faces. They think I'm crazy, but it doesn't matter. I'll come back

to the river. They rush me toward the buildings, and the scarf turns into a silk dust that sparkles on my bare skin.

A couple of illegal space heaters makes the office toasty warm. A blanket wraps around my shoulders. Coffee is put between my hands. I ask, but both of them are non-smoking health freaks. Phone calls get made. The guards have on white boy hip hop, and it mixes with the loudspeaker's violin instrumental of *I Saw Three Ships Come Sailing In*. I'm not going to tell anyone about the bones. They'll rope it off, and scientists will come and cops, and the bones, labeled and dated, will end up in a glass case somewhere dusty.

My grandfather's boat is still in the shed, and we live in capitalist America. Even on Christmas Eve the art supply store might stay open. I'll load up on clay, carving tools, paper, pens, charcoal, and find the tree from the river. I won't carve the bones. They don't belong to me, even the animal ones. But they'll show me what to make. Wood can be shaped into tail bones that become rattlesnake rattles that sound in the wind. Shoulder blade shapes can become the wings of herons. Clay chest bones are dragonfly bodies, and I'll make yards of wings from a lattice of spider silk. Some seem best carved out of the silver of old cedar wood and others from oak trees. Goddamnit if I don't take the land money and go to some sculpture school and learn how to put glass and beaten copper together to make my owl. I'll find a grey and shiny metal for the heron. I'll do things that I can't even imagine yet. The bones and I will sit with each other again and again. Even after I put them back in the river, I'll sit with them. Even if nothing is done and algae slimes all the colors from the river, the bones will exist always and forever. Happy birthday to me.

Lakes of fresh water collect into underground caverns. The water floats in rocky layers, soundless, above the well of ocean that underlies. On the surface, above, the dry soil is sand mixed with the fossils of ancient shells from yet another ocean that once covered the land. The drinkable water waits the long wait for the whole earth to change again. The climate becomes humid and wet. Rocks shift. Pressure builds.

Ten Thousand Years Ago

He smells of old meat. Sloth, I think. When my sister and I were young, before we were given names, our family went a season of drought with no meat except for one sloth and her babies. Taller than anything I'd ever seen before, or since, it reared over our heads and waved black claws as long as deer antlers. It was easy to kill, the babies easier. I thought they had disappeared, but these people here must have found one, because I can smell the spoiled fat. These people who live so far from the sea, they pack together, and they stink—of the sticky pine in their fires, the sour bark drink they make, the rock dust that floats from their chert quarry, and the sloth. Most of them crowd behind the man sitting almost knee-to-knee with me. His people, and mine behind me, keep silent. Only the trading line drawn through the sand separates us.

The man stretches his arm over the pile of chert rocks at his side and knocks a fist against the topmost one. This is his offer. The gesture pushes the meat smell into my throat, and my stomach turns on itself. I hold my breath until my eyes water. From his position behind me, my brother presses a concerned hand into my back. I tighten my muscles against him in warning. We must not look weak. The man juts his chin at the stingray spines, dried fish, and the basket woven tight with sea grasses, tighter than they've ever seen. I tilt the basket to show how it holds even small berries. The salt smell of marsh rises out of the weave, and I'm able to breathe again. The man's expression has not changed. I let a handful of small shells trickle through my fingers, and their colors flicker in the light. They're too thin for tools, but usually everyone likes a few shiny things. This man is not impressed.

I search into his face. Rock dust has mixed with sweat and crumbled into the cracks around his eyes and mouth. The last sun of the day shines against the grease smearing his lips. It makes my skin sting with all-over sweat and disgust. I lower my head to disguise the spasms in my throat and concentrate on his hands. His whole life they've beat rocks into arrowheads, scrapers and knives. Cuts, fresh and scarred, layer in ridges over his knuckles and in the soft space near his thumb. These people have chert rock colored the blue of a cloudy sky. It flakes evenly, leaves sharp edges, and is the best in a season's walk. With it we will make easy trades and not be hungry the whole route back to the sea.

The man's hands separate and move out of my sight. My throat relaxes, so I raise my head. One of his young men, his son from the shapes of their noses and way they understand each other even in silence, has moved closer to the rocks offered in trade. He removes one. They think I offer too little. My sudden illness puts this trade in danger.

My family's morning meal of stewed beaver sits uncertain in my stomach, but I settle my mind and stare past the man. My mother always told us to look around, beyond the trading line. She would say that the trade is never with just one person. Behind this man, the faces strain and not enough of them are young. Their lake shrinks. When we arrived, we walked through mud that stank like spoiled bird eggs to reach open water and still had to swirl away the green skin over its surface before we could dip our gourds. Some of us wanted to go deeper to find sweeter water, but my aunt said a dry weather lake meant alligators crowded close. The smell of running bowels separates itself out of the general stink, and I know these people have had sickness. I scoop away the useless shells and open my palm toward the leather bag my brother holds.

He moves to my side and drops the bag at the edge of the trading line. The weight of it kicks up a circle of dust. My brother unwinds the cord with large movements, as if each length of palm fiber reveals a mystery. He makes a show of anything. My sister was a different kind of trader. She had a careful manner that made people feel respected. My brother reaches into the bag and pulls out both of the big shells from the ocean. I hide my thoughts, but I save them for later. He has made a mistake. He reveals too much too soon.

Holding the shells high, one in each hand, he rotates them. One has a thickness strengthened by rows of horizontal ridges that make it useful in many ways. The man nods his acceptance. My brother brings his other hand forward and lifts his arm even higher. This shell will complete the trade. Heavy, larger than two men's hands, it spirals into a sharp, but strong point. The setting sun spreads light that shines like the oil that weeps out of pine trees. It soaks into the rose gleam of the shell's open lip. This is a weapon. The young man standing over the rock pile twitches a shoulder to keep his hand from reaching. He earns a glare from his father.

My last meal rises too high in my throat to ignore. I grab my brother's shoulder and try to make my need for support look like a smooth switch of negotiators. My brother automatically braces under my weight, but he lets his face show everything—confusion, unease, and now eagerness as he sits in my place to finish the trade. I stare at him in warning.

I walk upright and slowly until I'm hidden by the smoke of my family's evening fires. They pretend to pay no attention to the trade, but every adult hand holds something that can be used as a weapon. A rock crushes acorn meat into a milky pulp, a hickory limb supports my aunt, a woman who doesn't need support, and a bone blade peels long strips of willow bark. We protect our pack of young, unnamed children by sending them for firewood. We keep a careful balance. In order to trade, we appear harmless, but people must never think us easy to take from. My feet stumble over a shell hammer hidden under a bush, and hands reach out to catch me. Ignoring everyone's worry, I lurch to the edge of the woods and retch as quietly as I can. For a while, I don't care about anything but the shaking of my gut and the wash of heat pouring out of me. I gag and spit until there's nothing left. I hold my ribs, stagger to the nearest log, and sit down.

"Take this." Our oldest man stands over me. He holds out a portion of broth from the fire. One sniff and I know we're still eating the last of the beaver. I cover my mouth.

"Try it, my young trader. I've taken all the meat out and added herbs. It should calm your stomach."

He lays the turtle shell in my hand and sits beside me. His knees sound like twigs breaking. He has become older this season. I nod in thanks, but I can't drink yet. My fingers trace the repeating pattern of ridges on the underside of the bowl, and the heat spreads into the small bones of my hands.

"We're all tired of the beaver." He cups his hand over my knee. "But when you're young, especially in our family, it excites to kill them. I remember. You feel like one of the brave beast hunters from the old stories when you spear something as big as three of you put together. How do you think the trade goes?"

The winds have shifted for the evening and moved the smoke away. We can see through to the trading line, and together, we watch my brother. My mother and sister were the best at this, and I've tried to copy them, but my brother, he has a different way. Right now, he's acting even younger and more inexperienced than is true to make the other man look good to his people. The man smears the line between them. My brother copies him. The trade is complete. I try the broth. It smells of mint and has salt from the last of our mangrove leaves. It falls into my stomach and settles easily.

"Old man, my stomach thanks you."

He pats my arm in his soft way. "I thought it might. This broth always helped your mother and her mother when they had life inside."

My hands understand what he means before my mind does. They drop the broth, and the liquid splatters, running over the top of the dirt in a tangle of small streams before soaking into the ground. After many fast and uneven heartbeats, his words make sense to me. I look up from the stained earth between my feet.

"Life?"

"You're tired, yes? Clumsy? Do you make water more? These are signs. Soon your belly will grow." He reaches for the overturned bowl and scoops up sand. He pours some over my hands. He's saying something about the coast and how we'll arrive there, where I can rest with the people who live on the dunes, when the time comes.

I stop listening to him. The full dark has arrived, and fires light half a face, a shoulder, the bend of a knee. I twist my hands, letting the sand scrub them clean as I watch my brother move in and out of view.

"Did you watch? I was clever with those shells, wasn't I?" His voice is too loud. He flits from fire to fire, and our family pets him with congratulatory taps and rubs. "Remember how my mother and sister used to look for how their eyes moved? I just did like they used to, maybe even better."

My aunt pauses in feeding him one of her baked roots and looks to see if I've heard.

"And did you see that man's face? He looked like one of those stones he spends all day chipping." With his jaw stuck forward and his lips pulled back, my brother copies the look of the man.

"It was unnecessary to trade both shells." My voice stays low, but every one turns to me. My brother's face, still imitating the trader's, goes slack at my tone. "You should have noticed the son. He would have made his father trade for just the one. Did you see how many people they are? Did you notice how little water is here? The young ones will have to split away soon and find other fresh water. They will need weapons for that. You did not attend well enough and have hurt our family."

My brother's face reddens. I know I speak too hard. My mother would have corrected him alone, like she did for me. I try to think of words that will ease him, but all the strength of my mind has left. In front of me, a fire has settled into steady flames that glow blue at their base. Orange snakes around one of the logs. The children run out of the woods, dripping branches and dead palmetto fronds from their arms. My brother yells at them to feed the fires.

His voice, their voices, fade until I'm in a memory of another fire. This fire billows high, and my sister and I hold onto my mother. She's not screaming anymore. Her hair is thick with sweat that stains the skin laid out underneath her. Her hand lays loosely in my smaller one. She no longer hurts me with her grip. I wish she did. The silence sounds worse than the screaming, worse even than the low grunting that followed. The blood from between her legs pools around us and flushes a deeper and deeper red in the flames. We were trading with the river people when the pains began. Two of their women kneel between my mother's spread legs. Blood and firelight splatter up their arms. Hope rises as my mother crushes my hand with new strength, and muscles ripple down her belly. The women lean in, blocking the light. By the time they lean back, my mother's fingers have dropped out of mine. My sister moans. When I raise my head to look, one woman cradles a lump of flesh in her hands. Small arms dangle from the sides. The fingers hang open and unmoving. The women leave, and firelight pours over my mother.

The fire changes to the one only two seasons ago that washed a red light over my sister's dead face. She is dead the same as my mother, dead with her child, dead in the same ruin of cold, black blood that spread past the layers of moss I had packed inside her. I'm crying, crying then and crying now, as a piece of wood shifts in the fire and throws light and embers over my face. They burn like small spider bites over my cheeks, and I fall backwards off my seat.

Flat on the dirt, my feet splayed into the air, I wonder what's wrong with my balance. The children catch sight of my feet swaying and point and screech with laughter as they race toward me. They clamber over my body and grab my feet and play the cat game by howling and pretending to bite me. They don't notice that I'm crying. The old man diverts them with a story.

"Did you know that my mother's mother's mother's brother was bitten by a cat? That it had curved, yellow tusks—tusks so long that they cut alongside his thighs as the teeth closed over his foot?"

They do know, but they leave me to gather around him. He puts his arms around the littlest of them. I've noticed that the very old of us aren't as careful with their hearts around the children. If we make good trades and find clean water, only half of these will die. It helps with that sadness to keep them unnamed and not think of them as anything but a pack until they're older. But I remember how it felt when an adult showed concern. I lay back face up on the ground and let his voice, the words, soothe me.

"Yes, he'd wandered away from our family. He knew not to, but the grapes smelled ripe and purple and he followed them deeper into the thicket, pulling them off the vines in handfuls and eating them right away. Sun-warmed and fat, they burst in his mouth. He ate and ate, not saving any to share, until he stumbled into a clearing."

"And saw the cat!" "Have I ever had grapes?" "He was bad, wasn't he, not sharing?" "I wandered away once." "You did not, you just hid behind a tree until you got scared and started crying." "Did he have a spear or any throwing rocks? If I had a spear, no cat would get me." The children's voices interrupt each other until our old man claps his hands twice.

"He had a knife, perhaps one of the very ones I keep safe for our people. We lived as hunters then so he was quick to raise the knife, but the cat leaped and knocked him to the ground. She bit into his foot and dragged him across the clearing. My ancestor brother screamed so loud that his family heard and ran to him. They reached the clearing and stopped. And the cat stopped.

She lifted her head, pulling our brother's leg into the air. He screamed again and again. No one moved until one of his family, a woman not unlike our trader here, stepped forward—just one step. Do you know what she did? Did she threaten him with a spear?"

"No!" The children yell it out in their group way.

"Well, did she get on her knees and beg for his life?" The old man lifts his thin arms into the air and acts out a mocking version of begging. The children copy him by scuffling in the dirt and pleading with each other for knives and necklace shells and persimmon cakes and otter skins. As their laughter quiets, the old man asks again.

"So, did he die? Did the cat drag him off and eat him? What happened?"

"The ancestor woman offered a trade." The oldest of the still unnamed children jumps to his feet. His voice sounds as solemn as his age can manage.

At this, I wipe the tears out of my ears and sit up. The danger is to hope for the young, but suddenly I want this particular boy to live.

"Yeah, Wolf. You tell him." The children, no matter what, always give each other names.

"Yes, she did." The old man and I meet eyes before he continues. "She made a First Offer. Right in that moment we became traders. She stood out in the open, unprotected, and promised that our family would never again hunt the cats. But the cat only glared and ground her teeth farther into the brother's foot. She dragged her catch closer to the brush, and our ancestor woman knew she had to offer more. She could tell the cat didn't have survival hunger because her brother still lived. And she knew something else. She knew from the stories of her uncles that the big cats were disappearing."

"Where did they go?" "I wish I could see one." "Have you ever seen one?" The youngest crawls and growls and annoys the others with pounces. Someone sits on her.

"No one knows where they went, but yes, I did see her once. I had just been named."

Years ago, the old man told this story to my sister and to me and to the girl older than us who fell out of a tree and the broken bone in her leg split through her skin, to the boy whose bowels changed to brown water, to the other boy whose teeth hurt until yellow blood leaked out of his mouth and he died screaming. Only my sister and I lived to have names. And now, of my pack, only I survive. I pull a child under my arm. She startles at my touch, but we both relax into the familiar story. The old man's voice strengthens as he remembers his youth.

"One afternoon I climbed onto the curved limb of an acorn tree. The family had eaten our fill of a giant turtle, and I balanced half-asleep as I stared out over the sea of grasses. But when the prairie moved and parted in a rolling wave, I woke up. A pack of horses ran right at me, and then, like a flock of shorebirds, they turned all at once away from a clump of scrub trees. That's when the cat leapt high out of the tree shadows and onto a colt. I could hear the smack of its chest as it hit. They dropped into the grass, and I held my breath as the cat's head rose into view. The sunlight outlined her tusks in yellow and, behind them, her eyes met mine. In my whole long life, I've never been so scared. Do you know why?"

All the heads shook, even though the older ones knew the answer.

"Because of that young woman's final offer—the one that made the cat release our ancestor brother. Our woman took another step forward into the clearing and promised that if ever a cat needed one of us, we would be hers. The cat turned her head this way and that and twisted the foot in her mouth. Then she let go. She stood over his body and roared. Her mouth opened wider than the tallest of you is tall and through it blew the smell of fire on the prairies, of rich muck at a river's edge, of fallen pine needles trampled under her paws, and finally, faintly, of the tang of seawater. The whole world watched in the breath that rushed over our family, and within it the exchange was made. We promised. We had made our first trade. From then and ever since, we've wandered as traders even as other peoples found or fought for places with sweet water and never left. And we, some of us, still carry that trade on our bodies. Who here has the mark of the cat?"

Two little ones proudly raise a foot into the air, showing off the bent-under edges and crabbed toes.

"Well, let me tell you. All of us have the mark of the cat, whether we show it or not. You, girl, you should know. What will feed your family the best? Hunting food? Stealing it? What?"

"Trade, old brother." The girl who speaks is my aunt's child, and her face forms a hazy reflection of my sister's.

"That's right. Do you know why?"

"Stealing is stupid. People you steal from won't let you play around them anymore." All the children stare at a small girl sitting at the edge of their circle. She lowers her head. The boy called Wolf takes over.

"I know we say that if you trade for the meat, then the hunter hunts for you and that if you hunt yourself, all you have is the meat and some of it goes bad and it takes a lot of time, but, old man, I want to hunt."

The boy grabs a branch from by the fire and pokes it into the other children. They turn away from him, but he doesn't stop. He never does. Perhaps we should let him leave. One of the children holds her side and cries. Wolf laughs. From the other side of the fire, my aunt and her adult sons stare at him until he drops the stick. They lean together and talk. This time of year, the hunters set long, thin fires that race across the grasses and push the animals toward them. We'll follow the smoke. We'll trade the boy off. We won't call it a trade, but that's what we do when someone doesn't fit. The boy drops the branch. The old man finishes his story.

"And our ancient sister, she made a good trade. Except for me, none of your mothers' or even their mothers' has seen a cat. None of us since that day our old brother lived has ever had to make good on the Promise. Although, when the big storms fly over the world and the winds twist and the clouds lower to the ground, when the sky glows the green of light through a murky pond and our ears fill with a sound louder than that of bison running—listen carefully. If you hear a wind that rumbles through your bones, it will not always be the wind. Someday the last cat will roar—lonely and hungry and remembering our Promise."

The youngest children gasp and look into the dark. The older two grab at them from behind, and they tumble into a squealing mass. The mention of mothers started me crying again. Tonight, I have no say over my emotions.

"Your foot smells so bad it would never get eaten."

"Yours smells like beaver guts."

I laugh and can't stop even while I'm still crying, and the children are all elbows and knees as they throw themselves over me. I tickle them away, but grab one of the "mark of the cat" feet as it flies by. I rub along its length, pull it back and forth, dig my thumbs deep into the skin. In a way, the twisting of our feet makes it easier to travel, because it hurts to stand still and feels better when we walk fast. It helps if we stretch the bottoms from the time of birth, before our soles harden. I let the children rub on my own marked foot. Everyone quiets as they concentrate, and I have time again to think.

How did life come inside me? Some say the moonlight. Others say washing too often, not washing enough, orgasms, holding another woman's newborn. It could be sex with men or eating foods that look like a woman's inner lips. On the coast they boil oysters, and the forest people make a stew of fungus. I've done all of these things. But that's of no matter now. What matters is to end it. Some say to jump back and forth over a dead snake until you collapse or to eat any red berries. I've heard of women who put ginseng root up their inside place. I remember the family who used a plant with spotted flowers. All of it seems like no more than the morning chatter of birds except for the plant, which I saw with my own eyes. If I'd traded smarter, I would have some of it now.

Not long after my sister died, we shared a water hole with a family on their way to setting up a hunting camp. So many of them traveled together, but everyone looked healthy, including the babies. That's when I held one. A woman saw me watching and plopped hers into my arms. It smelled like a fresh pelt from a wolf cub. When it whimpered, the woman leaned on my arm and tapped a finger on the baby's cheek. She murmured a word over and over in their soft language that rippled like river water. The baby had a name. These people named their children, even this baby too young to have survived a single illness.

Later that night, after we made a quick trade of shark's teeth for meat, I used a mix of gestures and common words to ask about their children's good health. They led me to a woman whose fire smelled of the plants hung over it to dry. She put her hand, with its swollen knuckles, over mine, and looked into my eyes until the sadness inside me rose to the surface. I shook her off and repeated my questions. In answer, she pointed at one of the plants hanging over the fire. She said it helped old women end having children and gave young women longer between each child. In hungry times, women stopped their growing until the rains came again.

She let me touch the plant. It smelled like mint, but sharper, and the leaves had the shape of a short, plump grass. She described the blooms and said the bush grew low to the ground at the edge of fire, where the prairies and hammocks meet. I tried to trade, but she refused. She said they needed it. That, even dried, it lasted only a few seasons.

I should have traded harder. I should have offered anything, even our ancestors' knives or at least my mother's pin that I now carry. Both come from the bone tusks of giant animals no one living has ever seen. Our ancient people scratched the shapes of the animals into the sides of the animal's own bones. In this way, our old people say, both the carver and the animal are known to us forever. If the plant woman's people valued the ancients like mine, they would have forced her to trade.

My old man hands me a refilled bowl, and I avoid his eyes. He keeps the old knives and names each child with them. His face, with its kindness, would harden against me if he knew my thoughts. He says the knives hold our past. I don't know what I believe, except that too many women die.

Around us, the quarry people mingle with my family. They have brought their bark drink, and we offer them the rest of our beaver kill. They speak in words that grind against the teeth like the sand that layers into everything we eat, but we understand enough for what we'll share tonight. This is the reward of a good trade. We don't have to hurry away before they regret their decisions. Tomorrow, we'll rest in place. Tomorrow, I'll look for the plant. But not here. The tread of too many people and scattering of stone flakes has made the ground bare. I saw a line of trees in the far distance as we arrived, leafy trees, not the tall pines. That means water. I'll go in the morning.

When I was young, I thought that the wind had feelings. This morning, it swirls the feathered tops of the grasses, and the sun glints against them like sparks in a fire. They brush against me, smearing the morning wet over my thighs as I follow an animal trail. My footsteps mingle with two-toed prints that make sharp cuts in the earth. The hogs don't usually attack, but the wind blows my scent behind me. They wouldn't notice until I came too close. My mother's voice, the memory of it, reminds me to check the ties on my knife and secure her bone pin where it fastens the waist belt with its supplies. I pull the water gourd tighter against my leg in case I have to run. I listen into the wind.

I know that the wind is not alive, but last night as I settled the young girl I'd been holding, I told her that, in a way, it was. I bunched the thin pelt of a deer around her face as protection from the ash of the smoky night fires, the ones that keep the mosquitoes away, and told about the wind. It gathers, I said. It gathers the smells and feelings and sounds that it passes over. It lets us sense the scatter of a herd, know that wolves hunt nearby, and feel the cold fingers in the air that comes before a storm. The smells of our fires and our cooking and our bodies are gathered as well, warning animals not to come near and keeping little ones safe with their family. When her eyes closed, I tucked the skin tight under her shoulders and left to assemble my supplies for the morning. No one argued with me. My family used to, but they've given up. After my sister died, I wandered on my own. Sometimes I think I might have died if they hadn't let me.

Today the wind smells of nothing but grass, as if it waits for the day to wake up and bring it news. I walk until the trail narrows to nothing. Even up on my toes I can't find the smudge of green on the horizon that points me to water. I drop to my hands and knees and look through the grasses until I find a rabbit's tunnel to follow. I try to stand, but stop halfway up, dizzy, and tilted to the side. I push against my knees and quiet a groan as my breasts, sore and too large, squeeze between my arms. After a few steady breaths my head clears, and I track the hint of a trail until it widens. Now I can stretch my legs into a run.

The sun lifts higher and warms the earth. The grasses rustle as they dry, and the wind lessens. It still contains only anticipation. I stop to listen, but all sounds are distant. When I float in the ocean and my ears swell, this is how the world sounds now. No flocks rise out of the grasses, and the low tremor of moving animals doesn't push up my legs from the soil. Even the usual snorts and squeaks of small, hidden creatures diminish. Except for the hiss of locust startled by my passage and the smack of my feet against the earth, the world holds its breath. A solitary bird flashes black and white over my head as it flies back toward where my family waits. I turn to watch and almost follow. It has two tails and wings bent into sharp edges.

I take a sip of water while I'm stopped. It hits bottom and rises again, spewing out of my mouth along with all the broth left from last night. Now, I've added something for the wind to share. I'm uncomfortable inside my body. Maybe I should turn back. My sister's face appears in my mind. She is dying and our eyes meet as she grips my hand. I looked away. I remember this now. I never let go of her hand, but I looked away. I didn't watch her eyes dull the way my mother's did. I failed her. Maybe I will die out here, but it will be from a snake bite or because I can't eat or drink enough. I will not die sweating in a pool of blood, scaring my brother, and leaving nightmares behind in the minds of children. I roll off the edge of my foot and push forward in my quick, hopping way.

I feel it first as a ripple under my feet. A small animal comes at me, shaking the grasses low. It'll smell me soon and veer, but I ready my knife anyway. The spotted fox springs out of the grasses and passes so close that the froth spraying from its mouth flings over my calves. It rolls one yellow eye in my direction, but takes no other notice of me. I turn in time to see the last jerk of a bushed tail. The grasses still and silence returns. The fox was scared, but not of me. Maybe it had a sickness. I put away my knife.

I take another sip of water and wait. Nothing happens, either in my belly or out in the prairie. I continue, but walk softly until I reach a clearing of rosemary bushes on a small rise. I stop and stretch as high as I can. The tree line is close. I listen and smell and look all round before I move again, but sense nothing but the thick, sweet scent released as I pass through the bushes. I'm eager to reach the trees. The woman said to mash the blossom and leaves in water and drink it. I'll arrive soon. I'll find the plant.

The prairie always ends as if someone made a line and told the trees to grow along it. With one stride, I leave the grasses and enter a thin gathering of oak. I smell the water hole somewhere close. The trees shadow and enclose me, and something inside eases. The prairie can make a person lose all sense of herself. We found a man once who had wandered for days. He was dried out and hungry, and his eyes darted everywhere, all the time, jerking his head in twitches. We fed him for a night, but in the morning he had left. And I'm doing it now—looking behind me and to the side, over and over.

I make myself backtrack. The plant lives at the edges. I circle the outside of the forest island until I find a patch of deeper green spreading into the grasses. I bend close and separate the twists of brown and yellow stalks away from the low plants and see the pink flowers. I squeeze the leaves. The smell is as I remember, and I rock over my knees in relief until my head spins and I sit flat on the ground. Spreading my legs around the plants, I hunch forward with my knife and cut one at the roots. I cut two more and leave the rest.

Holding the plants to my chest, I lie back until my head cradles into the earth. Buzzing things scurry from the sudden assault. The tuft of a young palmetto scratches my arm, and bent stalks press into my ribs. Ignoring them, I stare into the sun and let its high heat soak into me. The wind shakes the fronds, and light scatters over my eyes. From my hands, the cold smell of the plant spreads over my body. I lift one of them and bite off a branchlet of spiked leaves. An oily taste rolls around my mouth. The nausea rises, and I throw myself to sitting and pant and dig my fingers into the dirt until it passes. I swallow.

I can't risk wasting anything, and later in the day my belly settles. And it will help to mix it all with water. Securing the plants into my belt, I lean forward onto all fours and stand. I need to get to the water hole. This all might work. I can think into the future again. I'll make the best trades I've ever done on our way back to the sea. I'll finish teaching my brother. And I won't travel again. Next season, I'll remain at the coast and become a stay-put person.

Many animals have made trails to the water hole, but the water sits too far away to drink. I lean over and stare down the steep layers of rock cliffs, their edges ferned and moist, until I see the glints of reflected light that mean water. Inside my pouch, I find the long, corded rope split into three ends. I knot each end into a hole along the rim of my gourd. The people that taught me the stability of three and who made this rope so thin that it seems it should break but never does—they live on a dune near the sea. They make things that no one has ever made before. That's what they do. Their people, who live below, where the river coils into the sea, feed them and supply them, and then trade off their creations to our family.

The last time we visited, I went to the dune and sat with an old woman and young man and the little girl who helps them. They live in shelters topped with fronds woven tight enough to keep out the rain. Wind-clipped trees surround them, but still the sea blows enough to scatter mosquitoes. We sat and shared the paste of berries I'd brought from inland, and it stained our lips and tongues blue as we sucked on the sweetness. All that day, I watched them form baskets from plaits of sea grasses they sewed tight with strips of yucca. Last time we traded for open containers of vine and palmettos stems but these could hold berries, perhaps even seeds. The dune people always looked to make better things. Now, they talked of trying to make baskets hold water.

I asked if they could smear mud on the sides. They looked at me, and then talked back and forth and over each other. Their loud voices cut through the salt wind. There, on the coast, you can gather or fish most all the food needed. They don't lie in wait of animals, and nothing stalks them in return. I can speak their language, but always use my people's hushed carefulness. That day, I listened to them shout at each other. What type of mud? How long to dry? Inside and smooth it with a leaf or piece of skin or a mussel shell, or clumped outside for sturdiness? If they could get it summer sun dry maybe it would hold water, like the mud that cracks at the side of creeks when the tides empty. They turned to me and asked about the mud on streams and water holes in the plains. I told them about the stickiness of the red ones to the north and the silky gray of some river muds. The old one said that no matter how dry, all mud would eventually accept water. The day thrilled more than any trade, and at the end of it they gave me this rope and gourd with three holes. I recoiled at the idea of a gift, but they presented it as an exchange for my knowledge and ideas. To them, ideas exist as real as an arrowhead or whelk ladle. I still yearn to speak as they did.

The gourd fills. Hand over hand, I pull it up without spilling and drink and fill it again and leave the water hole before other animals arrive thirsty and desperate that the water is out of reach. Back at the edge of the prairie is an acorn tree with a low enough limb to reach. I climb to a branch wide enough to sit on. Through the leaves, a long wedge of prairie stays visible. I can stay here until my stomach is calm, and then prepare the plant. I find a spot where ferns soften the branch under my bottom, lean into the trunk, and close my eyes.

A slap of wind wakes me from a dream of seawater rising over a curve of beach, pushing into dunes, collapsing them. Trees fall off the edges and drown in the waves. I return to a half-sleep and imagine living where each day, at low tide, the day's food is an easy walk over exposed mud and sand. On the way back to the sea, I will collect many clays, and they will let me stay. I will gather food for them, and they will teach me. The wind pushes against me again, and this time I notice the long, soft shadows of late in the day. I reach under my belt and unwrap the fold of leather. The plants are not a dream. I take a deep breath to test the calmness of my stomach. The wind strengthens and whistles out of the prairie, cooling the sleep sweat lying thick over my belly and pooling into the folds of my groin. A gust howls through the branches.

I take a shell from my waist belt and brace it between my breasts. The flowers and their leaves fit into its hollow. I scoop a handful of water over them, press with the thick end of my knife, and mix. I lap the pulp into my mouth. The plant coats my throat with a taste like cold air. If anything, it calms my stomach. I mix plant and water again and again, swallow after swallow, until nothing remains. I'll find more tomorrow, before I return. The night animals will arrive soon, and I should climb higher. Standing on the branch, holding onto the trunk, I listen for the stirrings of early night, but the sounds stay muted the way they did during the day. The wind shakes into the trees. Above it, through it, comes a long wail that breaks at its peak. I look for a distant storm.

Dark spreads into the trees, but day lingers over the prairie. The wind hurries the afternoon clouds, pushing the last light in front of them and swirling yellows and reds over the earth's surface. A line in the grass follows a different path and different speed than the wind. I exist in one of the old man's stories. The last light of the day drops through the clouds and spears across my face, throwing a blur of stars and floating suns into my vision. My eyes clear, and the cat waits below me.

We stare at each other for all the seasons that have passed since the First Trade. I am my ancestor woman standing in the clearing, promising, and I am here, with the taste of the plant still in my throat. A picture story appears in my mind, not about our ancestors but about the ones that will come. It tells of my family waiting for me until they can't anymore and having to wrap our fire coals in sand and move on. My brother tries to stay and search but they won't let him. His trading is needed for their walk back to the sea. One morning they wake to find the old man dead. This next winter the little girl scared of the wind coughs to death. They don't trade Wolf away, but keep him and his name. My brother's charm stiffens into something he puts on only for show. He becomes skilled at making hard, uneven trades with desperate people and has Wolf hold a spear and stand guard at his side. My family prospers. By the ocean, I see a woman putting baskets made of only mud into a fire. I see another woman, on a river, hold clay between her palms and form the shapes of animals I've never seen. Sweet water, so much of it, rises out of the ground and pours over the land, over me. My mother's face looks at me with exasperation, my sister's with forgiveness.

The cat opens its mouth. I see past the curved tusks, the teeth, and the muscled tongue. Beyond, is only the dark. I can't hear past the beat of my heart, but I feel the whirlwind force of a scream as the cat leaps and I fall. We meet in a snarl of fur and teeth, skin and blood. I smell the scent of the whole world in our breaths.

About the Author

Sandra Gail Lambert's fiction and memoir have appeared in a variety of journals and anthologies including New Letters, The Weekly Rumpus, Arts & Letters and the North American Review. Excerpts of this, her debut novel, have won prizes from Big Fiction Magazine and the Saints and Sinners Short Fiction Contest. She lives with her partner in Gainesville, Florida, a home base for kayak trips to her beloved rivers and coastal marshes.

Author photo by Melanie Peter

FIC LAMBERT
Lambert, Sandra Gail.
The river's memory

DEC 0 8 2014